THE DUKE'S UNEXPECTED LOVE

The Strongs of Shadowcrest
Book One

Alexa Aston

© Copyright 2024 by Alexa Aston
Text by Alexa Aston
Cover by Dar Albert

Dragonblade Publishing, Inc. is an imprint of Kathryn Le Veque Novels, Inc.
P.O. Box 23
Moreno Valley, CA 92556
ceo@dragonbladepublishing.com

Produced in the United States of America

First Edition February 2024
Print Edition

Reproduction of any kind except where it pertains to short quotes in relation to advertising or promotion is strictly prohibited.

All Rights Reserved.

The characters and events portrayed in this book are fictitious. Any similarity to real persons, living or dead, is purely coincidental and not intended by the author.

ARE YOU SIGNED UP FOR DRAGONBLADE'S BLOG?

You'll get the latest news and information on exclusive giveaways, exclusive excerpts, coming releases, sales, free books, cover reveals and more.

Check out our complete list of authors, too!

No spam, no junk. That's a promise!

Sign Up Here

www.dragonbladepublishing.com

Dearest Reader;

Thank you for your support of a small press. At Dragonblade Publishing, we strive to bring you the highest quality Historical Romance from some of the best authors in the business. Without your support, there is no 'us', so we sincerely hope you adore these stories and find some new favorite authors along the way.

Happy Reading!

CEO, Dragonblade Publishing

Additional Dragonblade books by Author Alexa Aston

The Strongs of Shadowcrest Series
The Duke's Unexpected Love (Book 1)
The Perks of Loving a Viscount (Book 2)

Suddenly a Duke Series
Portrait of the Duke (Book 1)
Music for the Duke (Book 2)
Polishing the Duke (Book 3)
Designs on the Duke (Book 4)
Fashioning the Duke (Book 5)
Love Blooms with the Duke (Book 6)
Training the Duke (Book 7)
Investigating the Duke (Book 8)

Second Sons of London Series
Educated By The Earl (Book 1)
Debating With The Duke (Book 2)
Empowered By The Earl (Book 3)
Made for the Marquess (Book 4)
Dubious about the Duke (Book 5)
Valued by the Viscount (Book 6)
Meant for the Marquess (Book 7)

Dukes Done Wrong Series
Discouraging the Duke (Book 1)
Deflecting the Duke (Book 2)
Disrupting the Duke (Book 3)
Delighting the Duke (Book 4)

Destiny with a Duke (Book 5)

Dukes of Distinction Series
Duke of Renown (Book 1)
Duke of Charm (Book 2)
Duke of Disrepute (Book 3)
Duke of Arrogance (Book 4)
Duke of Honor (Book 5)
The Duke That I Want (Book 6)

The St. Clairs Series
Devoted to the Duke (Book 1)
Midnight with the Marquess (Book 2)
Embracing the Earl (Book 3)
Defending the Duke (Book 4)
Suddenly a St. Clair (Book 5)
Starlight Night (Novella)
The Twelve Days of Love (Novella)

Soldiers & Soulmates Series
To Heal an Earl (Book 1)
To Tame a Rogue (Book 2)
To Trust a Duke (Book 3)
To Save a Love (Book 4)
To Win a Widow (Book 5)
Yuletide at Gillingham (Novella)

King's Cousins Series
The Pawn (Book 1)
The Heir (Book 2)
The Bastard (Book 3)

Medieval Runaway Wives
Song of the Heart (Book 1)
A Promise of Tomorrow (Book 2)
Destined for Love (Book 3)

Knights of Honor Series
Word of Honor (Book 1)
Marked by Honor (Book 2)
Code of Honor (Book 3)
Journey to Honor (Book 4)
Heart of Honor (Book 5)
Bold in Honor (Book 6)
Love and Honor (Book 7)
Gift of Honor (Book 8)
Path to Honor (Book 9)
Return to Honor (Book 10)

The Lyon's Den Series
The Lyon's Lady Love

Pirates of Britannia Series
God of the Seas

De Wolfe Pack: The Series
Rise of de Wolfe

The de Wolfes of Esterley Castle
Diana
Derek
Thea

Also from Alexa Aston
The Bridge to Love (Novella)
One Magic Night

PROLOGUE

London—September 1792

JAMES STRONG FINISHED dressing and went to the schoolroom, where he took all his meals. Nanny was already there, fussy over the stupid twins.

It used to be James she fussed over. Not anymore. Instead, all her time and attention were devoted to his two half-sisters. Even worse, he had overheard the butler inform their housekeeper that his two cousins, also babies, were coming to live here next week since their father didn't want them.

He didn't even think of these girls or his stepmother as being part of his family. His family had been Mama. And his brother. They had been gone four years now, and he missed her every day. She had died giving birth to his little brother, what he had heard the servants referred to as the spare.

At eight years of age, James was the heir apparent to the Duke of Seaton. His father had wanted more boys, and his duchess had tried to give them to her husband. The problem was that she couldn't.

He only knew the stories from listening to their servants gossip. That there had been many attempts on the duchess' part to have another babe. How she had lost too many to count—both before and after James' birth—and how the last one had been what Cook called stillborn. From what he could understand, it meant that the babe had been born but never took a breath.

Having that babe had cost Mama her life.

He had sneaked into the parlor downstairs after Nanny had put him to bed, and gone to see Mama and the little boy who would have been his younger brother. Mama's appearance had frightened him, and James had hurried away, not wanting to remember her looking so awful. But the babe looked absolutely perfect, as if he were only sleeping. He'd had fair hair and lips that were shaped like a bow. Only when James had touched his brother's cheek and found it ice-cold did he realize the babe was truly dead. He had hurried upstairs to his bed, but he had told himself he would never forget the little boy who would have been both brother and friend to him.

His mother had been James' entire world. It troubled him because it was getting harder to remember what Mama looked like. She had been gone half his life now, and James could only see fleeting images of her in his mind. Still, he could recall the love she blanketed him with. Mama had read to him and played with him.

And then she was gone.

His father had remarried, seeking more sons from a new woman. James thought it was funny that the new duchess had given birth to two girls instead of a boy. She was going to have another baby in two months. Out of spite, he hoped it would also be a girl.

He sat at the table, where his breakfast awaited him, glancing at the two chairs in which Philippa and Georgina sat. Twins ran in the Strong family. His father was a twin to Uncle Adolphus, who had two sons, Theodore and Caleb. It was his uncle's twin daughters, Allegra and Lyric, who would be coming to live with them permanently soon, meaning James would get even less attention than he now did. His cousins had spent this first year of their life mostly in this house, and James knew his uncle didn't like girls. The new duchess seemed to love babies, though, and he had heard her say to their housekeeper that it was a good thing the twins would be left in her care from now on.

His half-sisters were a year old now, and though they favored each other, James could easily tell them apart. Mostly because they acted so distinctly from one another. Eating was a huge way in which the girls differed.

He looked as Georgie delicately picked up each morsel of food on the tray before her, holding it up and studying it from every angle before she thoughtfully put it into her mouth to chew. On the other hand, Pippa joyfully played with her food and then greedily downed each bite after doing so.

James wanted to like his half-sisters and secretly suspected he did, but he would never consider them family. Nor would he ever call the new duchess Mama, no matter how many times she asked him to do so.

He ate his porridge and ham, daydreaming as he did so. He would be leaving for school in a few days' time and was eager to go. His tutor, Mr. Timmons, had told him all about school. What his classes would be like. How he would live in a dormitory. When meals were served and what they consisted of. James couldn't wait to begin his new life.

Even if it did mean he would have to see Cousin Theodore.

Movement caught his eye, and he saw his father and the duchess enter the schoolroom. It irked James that they did so. He could never recall a time when his Papa had come to the nursery or visited at mealtime to see him, though Mama had visited him in both places frequently. This new wife must encourage the practice, though, and it made James dislike her even more than he already did.

"Good morning, my angels," the duchess declared. She glanced to him. "And good morning to you, as well, James."

Not wanting to be berated by his father for ignoring her, James inclined his head and neutrally said, "Good morning, Your Grace."

She frowned slightly but did not correct him. He had told her that he only had one mother and that she wasn't it. He had seen how his words stung by the pain reflected in her eyes, but James didn't care. He didn't need her. He didn't need anyone.

The duchess began talking to her daughters in a sing-song voice as the duke looked fondly upon the pair. His father had yet to acknowledge James' presence in the schoolroom, so he returned to his food, finishing the final bits of his porridge.

Then, surprising him, his father came and stood next to James.

Scrambling to his feet, he said, "Good morning, Papa. It is good to see you."

"Mr. Timmons tells me that you will be leaving for school early next week, James."

He nodded enthusiastically. "Yes, sir. I am eager to go and learn."

Going away to school meant not having to be around the twins and his stepmother. James also loved learning, and he couldn't wait to see what his classes might be like.

The only cloud on that horizon was cast by Cousin Theodore. Teddy, as Uncle Adolphus called his boy, was a year older than James and bullied his younger cousin unmercifully. Although they would attend the same school, he hoped he wouldn't see Teddy often and that he could make friends on his own with boys in his own class.

"Mr. Timmons thinks it might be good for you to go and see the office and warehouse, before you go," the duke continued.

He glowed with enthusiasm, glad his tutor had brought up the matter with Papa and thrilled that it might actually come to pass. James had never been to the place near the river where the office and warehouse were located. All he knew was that they received quite a bit of income from their ships, which traded around the world, and that Papa was loath to even mention the shipping line.

"Yes, Father, I would enjoy that very much. Mr. Timmons and I have been working quite a bit on geography lately. He went and retrieved manifests from the company offices, and we have been tracking various ships around the world. I have learned what cargo they deliver and pick up in exchange. Why, I've even learned—"

"That is all well and good, James," his father said, cutting him off. "You will go with your tutor then today and see the premises."

The duke's lips pursed in displeasure. "It is not a place you will frequent, however. The Strong family are not tradesmen. The shipping line is merely one avenue of revenue for us which my grandfather began. Why he placed our family name on it is a mystery. I warn you now, James—do not mention it to your schoolmates. We Strongs might profit from it, but it is not something to ever mention to anyone outside our family."

Papa paused. "You will also need to begin learning about Stonecrest and my other estates since you will one day be the Duke of Seaton."

Emboldened, James asked, "Will you teach me about Stonecrest and the tenants, Father? Or take me to these other estates? I have never visited any of them before."

The duke frowned deeply. "That is for others to do," he said dismissively. "I suppose the next time we are at Shadowcrest you can meet with the steward there. For now, go see Mr. Timmons. He is in the drawing room waiting for you."

He turned away from his son, and disappointment flooded James. He should have known better. His father never seemed to want to spend any time with him.

The duke ruffled Philippa's hair, smiling indulgently at her. He did the same to Georgina and then turned to his wife.

"Come. We have spent long enough here. You need to get off your feet."

The couple exited the room, and James looked to Nanny. "May I please be excused? I have finished my breakfast. Mr. Timmons and I are going to the waterfront today."

He refused to let his Father dampen the enthusiasm he felt regarding this special outing.

"Very well, my lord," Nanny said.

James raced down the stairs to the drawing room, where Mr. Timmons stood beside a large globe.

Hurrying toward the tutor, he said, "I hear we are taking a trip to the waterfront today."

"Yes, my lord. I discussed this with His Grace. I think it is important that you begin to understand more about your place in the world and the responsibilities you will hold one day when you claim your title."

The tutor spun the globe and then smiled. "Shall we go? His Grace suggested we walk to the offices in order to get our exercise. It is a long way, so we'd best get started."

James accompanied his tutor as they set out for an area of London they had never visited. He and Mr. Timmons walked the city every day when they were in town for the Season. His family arrived in town each spring and stayed through the summer, with his father and the duchess going to many social events. While James enjoyed spending time at Shadowcrest, the home ducal estate in Kent, he truly loved the hustle and bustle of the streets of London.

As they walked, Mr. Timmons pointed out various things to him. James had found he had an interest in architecture, and he and the tutor enjoyed studying various structures they passed.

"I believe when you leave for school next week that I will be returning to Shadowcrest, this time to assume the living," Mr. Timmons informed him.

"Father has agreed?"

His tutor nodded. "His Grace knows that I have been interested in the living there for a good while now. Assuming it will allow me to continue my studies independently, while also helping others in the neighborhood." Smiling, Mr. Timmons added, "I had to find something to do after you left for school."

"That means I will always get to see you when I come home on holiday."

"You will indeed, my lord. We will be able to continue our conversations on those occasions. In fact, you can share with me all that you have learned at school, and I will do the same with you. I will be free to pursue whatever I wish to learn in my post as vicar. As you, I am fond of architecture, but my true love is history and literature."

Mr. Timmons smiled mischievously. "Who knows? I may even try my hand at writing a novel."

"That would be wonderful, sir," declared James. "You are so smart and know so much. Write it—and I will be your first reader."

The tutor laughed. "That sounds like an excellent plan, Lord James."

James could smell the water the closer they came to the Thames. At one point, Mr. Timmons cautioned him, saying, "Stay close, my lord. Unfortunately, we are in an area of town where many despicable characters lurk. We wouldn't want anything happening to you, would we?"

He stuck close to Mr. Timmons' side, looking at his surroundings carefully and seeing the seediness surrounding them. People were dressed meanly and had a wariness about them he wasn't used to seeing. Some of them even gave him looks which frightened him.

They came upon a large building, and Mr. Timmons said, "This is the warehouse and offices for Strong Shipping. As you can see, it is close to the waterfront. The offices are on the top floor of the building. We shall visit them first."

As they entered the warehouse, his tutor added, "You will most likely not come here often, my lord. It is a peculiarity of the *ton*. They don't wish to have others think they dirty their hands in making money. That is why they look down at those in trade. You will own all this one day, of course, and that is why I wanted you to be able to see the operation and learn something about it. Perhaps you can visit once a year. I think it would be a good idea to make your presence known to the staff who manage things and the workers in the warehouse. After all, you are responsible for their livelihood, the same as you will be for the tenants at Shadowcrest and the other properties owned by the Duke of Seaton."

As they walked through the warehouse, James saw the vast stacks of crates, knowing what was contained in many of them because of his studies with Mr. Timmons. Everyone eyed him with curiosity, and he nodded in a friendly fashion to those whom they passed.

Mr. Timmons led them up a set of stairs, and they entered the shipping offices which bore his family's surname. He met a clerk who took them to the office of Mr. Stanley, who ushered them inside.

"Welcome, my lord, Mr. Timmons. It is good to finally meet you, Lord James."

"It is nice to meet you, Mr. Stanley. Thank you for running our family's business."

Mr. Stanley laughed heartily. "Don't let His Grace catch you mentioning business and the Strong name in the same sentence, my lord. His Grace may earn many pounds from the fleet of ships he owns and the cargo which is traded, but he would never acknowledge that to others in Polite Society."

James thought that ridiculous and said, "When I am the Duke of Seaton, I will be proud to be the owner of Strong Shipping, Mr. Stanley."

The manager roared with laughter. "You can do things your own way when you become a duke," he told James. "Dukes are a law unto themselves, the pinnacle of members of the *ton*. Come, let me show you around."

Mr. Stanley gave them a tour of the offices, and James met the rest of the staff. He asked numerous questions about what they did, surprising everyone.

"Perhaps you will be more hands on than the previous Dukes of Seaton have been," Mr. Stanley said appreciatively. "Shall we go downstairs to the warehouse now?"

They toured the entire warehouse, with Mr. Stanley telling them what goods had been brought in on recently arrived ships.

"The *Zephyr* came in only yesterday. We are still unloading it today. Would you like to walk to the harbor and see it?"

James replied with unbridled enthusiasm. "Yes, Mr. Stanley."

The trio went to the wharf, and for the first time, he saw a grand ship in person. A sense of pride filled him, knowing it was but one of the ships in the fleet owned by his family. He saw workers unloading the ship's cargo and became curious.

"Might we go on board?" he asked.

"I don't see why not," Mr. Stanley said, and the three of them boarded *Zephyr*.

For the next hour, James listened intently, learning about various parts of a ship and seeing where the cargo was stored. He also visited briefly with the captain of *Zephyr* and learned of the countries the ship had called at before making its way back to England, as well as talking with various crew members. What he learned was fascinating, making him even more determined to continue his visits to Strong Shipping.

Mr. Stanley escorted them back to the offices, and James asked if he might be put to work, helping the dockworkers who were bringing in crates to the warehouse, where a supervisor directed where the crates should go and be unpacked. He'd learned each crate was checked against a list to make certain everything was received.

"I am not certain His Grace would wish you to roll up your sleeves and do manual labor, my lord," cautioned Mr. Timmons.

"Oh, give the boy a chance to dirty his hands a bit," encouraged Mr. Stanley. "He's a boy. A little dirt won't hurt him." Smiling at James, the manager added, "It might be good for the little lord to see how hard his workers labor on behalf of the Strong family."

"I suppose," Mr. Timmons said reluctantly.

"I will leave you in the hands of our warehouse supervisor," Mr. Stanley declared. "But first, I would suggest you remove your coat and waistcoat, my lord. Your cravat, too. That way they won't be dirtied and your housekeeper won't admonish you or Mr. Timmons too much."

"Yes, sir!" cried James, ready to join the others.

He stripped off his coat and waistcoat, folding them neatly and giving them to Mr. Timmons to look after.

"I think I'll keep my cravat, though," he told the pair, removing and folding it before slipping it into his pocket. "I might need it to wipe away the sweat because it is hot in the warehouse." He then rolled up his sleeves, wanting to look like the other workers they had seen both in the warehouse and on the docks.

Mr. Stanley found that quite amusing. "I'll take Lord James downstairs, Mr. Timmons."

The manager left James in the care of the warehouse's supervisor, who put James straight to work, removing items from a crate and having him call each one out so it could be logged.

After two hours at that task, he asked if he could try something else, mopping his brow with the cravat and knowing Nanny would have a fit when she saw how dirty it—and James—had gotten. The thought of the servant up in arms had him grinning, though.

"You can take this list to the first mate on *Zephyr*," the supervisor said. "You remember your way to the ship?"

Nodding, he replied, "Yes. It's but two blocks from here."

"There and back, my lord. No stopping. And the first mate will also give you a list in return. Bring it safely back here."

"Aye-aye," James cried, imitating the sailors he had heard on board the ship earlier during his visit to it.

He left the warehouse and ran the entire way, feeling free and alive. Boarding *Zephyr*, he asked the first sailor he saw where the first mate was, and the sailor pointed to the hold. James descended the rope ladder and hurried toward the ship's second-in-command, whom he'd met earlier, waiting patiently until the man had finished giving orders to a group of sailors.

"I am to give this to you," he said proudly, presenting the list.

The first mate frowned at him a moment—and then smiled. "Why, I didn't recognize you at first, my lord."

James pushed back his hair, damp with sweat. "I have been helping in the warehouse. I am learning all about Strong Shipping today."

"Good for you, lad. I mean, my lord," the first mate corrected. He reached for some papers sitting atop a barrel. "These are to go back with you, my lord."

"Aye-aye!" James said, causing the first mate to howl with laughter.

He tucked the papers inside his shirt, climbing the rope ladder once more until he reached the ship's deck. He scampered down the wide gangplank and paused a moment, turning in circles and taking everything in.

This day had been the best of his life.

James moved away from the ship and turned down a street, walking two blocks, but not reaching his destination. Suddenly, things didn't look familiar at all, and he realized he must have made an incorrect turn and gone down the wrong street. He doubled back to get his bearings, but so many people and carts were in the streets, spinning him around, that it further confused him. He knew if he could simply make his way back to *Zephyr*, he could find his bearings again and return to the warehouse from his errand.

He fought the panic stirring within him as he moved toward what he hoped was the river. A rider on a horse whizzed by him, causing him to stumble and fall facedown into a mud puddle.

"Oh, no!" he cried, pushing himself to his feet, removing the sheaf of papers and finding them soaked and muddy. He would be in trouble now. He told himself he would accept whatever punishment would occur because of his carelessness, but that didn't stop the tears from stinging his eyes and pouring down his cheeks.

As he started up again, suddenly a strong hand gripped his shoulder, turning him.

A man with a patch over his eye and missing a few teeth narrowed his one eye, studying James as he wriggled, trying to free himself.

"You'll do."

Before James knew what was happening, the stranger grabbed hold of him, tossing James over his shoulder. Suddenly, the world was upside down as he bumped against the stranger's back.

"Put me down, I say," he shouted through his tears.

The man ignored him, striding down the street now at a rapid pace.

James began pummeling the stranger's back. "Let go!" he insisted. "My father will—"

"Will what?" the man demanded, stopping and slamming James to the ground.

The breath rushed from him, and he struggled to breathe. Before he could catch his breath, the man kicked James in the side so hard that he saw stars.

"You're a scrawny little thing," the man said. "No father would want a boy like you. Besides, we're desperate. We're about to pull away from shore and need a cabin boy and lookout. I was told to find one—and you're it."

Finally, air rushed into James' lungs, but before he could protest, the man picked him up again, this time by the waist, carrying James under his arm. He swung his fists helplessly, trying to kick but his side was so bruised from the blow the man had struck that it pained him to do so.

He watched as the ground beneath him changed into a gangplank and then a ship's deck. In horror, he realized he had been taken. He must tell this man who he was and get back to Mr. Timmons as quickly as possible.

The man took him below deck and dropped him on the ground, again knocking the breath from him.

"Stop," he managed to get out. "You can't take me like this."

The sailor grinned, and James saw the holes where teeth should have been. "I just did, boy."

Then he slammed his fist into James' face.

The pain was white hot. Warm blood gushed from his nose. He thought it might actually be broken. More blows rained down on him, and James curled into a tight ball, trying to protect himself as best as he could.

He didn't know how long the beating lasted, only that it finally ended after his head had been smashed to the ground. He blacked out and when he came to, the sailor loomed over him, his fist drawn back. James flinched, and the man laughed harshly, lifting him again and opening something, tossing James inside.

"This is the brig, boy. You'll stay here until we sail."

Almost broken, he said, "I am James. James—"

"You're Boy now. You'll have to earn back your name." The sailor cackled. "This is your home, Boy. Be glad you have one. And no more blubbering like you were when I found you. You bawl like a babe, and I'll beat you senseless. You understand?"

Tears blurring his vision, James nodded, terrified of being struck again.

"I didn't hear you," the man said.

"Aye-aye," he muttered.

"Ah, you're learning, Boy. That's good. Maybe we'll make a man of you after all."

The sailor left, and James lay on the dirty floor. It hurt to breathe, and he wondered if a rib or two had been broken. Once, Teddy had punched James hard in his side, his cousin saying he hoped he had broken one of James' ribs. His side had been sore for many days, but it hadn't hurt like it did now, the pain blinding with each shallow breath.

He closed his eyes, willing the nightmare to go away.

When he opened them, he knew time had passed. How he knew this, he wasn't certain, only that it had. Pushing himself upright, he winced, leaning his back against the wall.

It was then he saw someone sitting outside the cell he'd been locked in, a young man, with dark hair and a thin frame.

"Help me," he asked, his voice thin and scared.

"We've already sailed, Boy," the new sailor said. "I'm to watch over you. Help you. Your face is a mess. You'll have bruises for a long time to come, I'm afraid."

"He hit me over and over. In the nose." James reached up and touched his face, which was tender. He also felt the dried blood. "He kicked me, too. I think I broke a rib."

He winced as he touched the back of his head, where a large knot sat. He hurt everywhere, especially his head. His vision was blurry. His memory, too. He only knew someone had brought him here. Beat him viciously.

"I'll be back," the sailor said.

James closed his eyes again until the sailor returned. This time, he opened the cell door with a key.

"I've brought water to bathe your wounds," he said. "Strips of cloth to wind about your ribs."

"I'm so thirsty," he managed to say, even the few words spoken tiring him. "I want to go home," he added, his voice breaking because he could no longer remember where home was. His aching head seemed to have erased any memory of it.

The sailor gazed at him with sympathy. "This *is* home now, Boy."

"I'm James," he said stubbornly, the name rising from somewhere within him, and he clung to it.

"You will be one day. Just not today. Not for a while. Flimm has told the other sailors to call you Boy." The man shook his head. "He's a bad 'un, that Flimm. Most of the others are frightened of him. He's quick-tempered and even quicker with his fists." Smiling ruefully, he said, "Then again, you already know that, don't you?"

"I don't belong here." He knew that innately though he couldn't explain how or why.

"But you're here now. It's happened to many of us before you, Boy. Even me." He paused. "I'm Drake, by the way." He smiled. "A drake is a male duck who takes to water. I was also Boy once upon a time."

"Flimm took you, too?"

"Aye, he and another one. But it was all right. I'd lost both my parents. I was living on the streets. Stealing what I could to eat. Living on a great ship and being a part of the crew? It's like you've a whole family."

"Is your name really Drake?" he asked quietly.

"It is now. To be honest, I don't even remember what it was before they took me."

Determination filled him. "I'll never forget my name. I'm James."

Drake chuckled. "Well, let's get your face bathed and your ribs seen to, James. I have a feeling you won't be Boy for long."

He let Drake tend to him, thinking how he would make his way to the captain as soon as he could. He would tell the captain who he was, and they would have to turn the ship around and take him home.

Little did James know just how foolish that dream was.

CHAPTER ONE

London—August 1809

SOPHIE GRANT ROSE as her maid entered the bedchamber.

"Good morning, Mrs. Grant," Libby said, setting down the breakfast tray. "I hope you had a pleasant night's sleep."

"I did. I hope you did, as well."

Her maid helped Sophie dress, and then she sat in her favorite chair to drink her morning tea and eat her usual toast points. She liberally spread marmalade across the toast and bit into it, savoring that first bite, the citrus flooding her mouth.

Libby excused herself, and Sophie sipped her tea in solitude, reflecting on the upcoming business transactions for the day. Her husband owned one of the largest fleets in Great Britain.

And Sophie was a vital part of Neptune Shipping Lines.

She had come a long way from being the shy daughter of Viscount Galpin. She had not even wanted to partake in the Season when it came time to make her come-out because of her extreme shyness. When she worked up enough courage to tell her father her wishes, Papa laughed and told her she wouldn't be able to do so even if she wished. That he had lost too much money on bad investments and gambling debts and was barely hanging on to what they had.

He proceeded to tell her he had rented out their country estate because he was too poor now to keep it up. They would be taking rooms in London because he'd also had to rent their large townhouse. Much to Sophie's surprise, once they had settled in shabby rooms in a part of town she hadn't even known existed, her father told her she was to wed the following day. Nervously, she had waited in the parlor to meet her intended, a man called Josiah Grant.

When Grant had entered the room, Sophie had thought some mistake had been made because he looked old enough to be her grandfather. Her father had greeted Mr. Grant warmly, however, and after a few minutes, Papa had excused himself so that the two of them could speak alone for the first time.

Josiah had apologized to Sophie, telling her he knew he wasn't the groom she had anticipated and that he was assuming a large portion of her father's debt, when Lord Galpin should actually be bestowing Sophie's dowry in the marriage settlements. No dowry was left, however. Sophie knew she had no choice in the matter. Mr. Grant seemed kind, however, and she was ready to escape her father's household, wherever it was.

Little did she know the changes that would come to her upon becoming Mrs. Josiah Grant.

Sophie finished her tea and set the cup on the tray again, thinking of all she had learned since her marriage. While she had learned to run a household from her mother and had taken up that mantle at ten and four when Mama passed away, Sophie was granted entry into a much different world from the one she knew, thanks to her new husband. Mr. Grant wanted to teach her about his business. Since she had always had an affinity for numbers, they started there, with her examining several years' worth of ledgers for Neptune Shipping Lines. She took to bookkeeping with ease and assumed that position at the company.

That wasn't enough for her husband, though. He wished for her to learn all aspects of his business. Over the last several years, Sophie had learned about shipbuilding. The kinds of wood it took. What the sails were made of. How long it took to build a ship. She had been instrumental in hiring crews, as well as determining which cargo they would take on and the ports of call their ships would make. She had studied the best trade routes and the times of year which were optimal for voyages. She studied the London newspapers and figured out what goods were needed and which wants were wanted, dividing what their ships brought back into necessities and luxury goods.

Seven years later, Sophie knew as much about shipping as her husband, and he had promised she would run Neptune Shipping once he was gone. She had accompanied Josiah to a solicitor, where the details of his will were clearly spelled out, leaving everything to Sophie and her control upon his death. She went to the office with Josiah each day, assuming more and more tasks and responsibility as time went on.

Being a businesswoman and having to make decisions had brought her out of her shell. She was no longer the timid turtle who would vanish from view when someone looked at her. While she would never be totally comfortable in social settings, Sophie was quite at home in the business world. It had taken years, but those who did business with Neptune Shipping Lines now understood that Mrs. Grant would be present at every meeting, her seat at the table not only guaranteed—but her vote being the deciding factor.

She left her bedchamber, passing Millie in the hall, saying, "You may clean my bedchamber now. Please take my dishes to the kitchen, as well."

"Yes, Mrs. Grant," the maid said with a cheery smile.

That's what she enjoyed about living in Josiah's household. Their two maids always had a pleasant attitude and ready smile. At her father's establishments, servants were as timid as Sophie herself had once been, not wanting to upset or anger the volatile viscount. While Polite Society viewed her marriage to Josiah Grant as a definite tumble down the social ladder, she couldn't be happier. She had no fondness for the *ton* and had as little to do with its members as possible. Though a viscount's daughter, she and her husband were never invited to any events held during the Season. The few friends she'd had in girlhood had abandoned her once word of her marriage got out. Even if any had stayed by her side to begin with, they would have vanished once it became known that she went to the office each day and conducted business, both with Josiah and on her own.

She reached the foyer, and told the butler, who also served as her husband's valet, "Please let Mr. Grant know it is time to leave for the office."

"Yes, Mrs. Grant."

Two minutes later, Josiah arrived, looking a bit haggard. It worried her that his step had slowed in the last few months, and he did not seem to be the vital man he was when they wed. Then again, he was now past sixty, having recently celebrated his sixty-first birthday. It was time for him to slow down and take on less responsibility, but she did not quite know how to broach the subject.

"How are you this morning, my dear?" he asked, brushing his lips against her cheek.

"I am quite well, but you look tired, Josiah. Did you not sleep well again?"

He shrugged. "They say it is old age. That you don't need as much sleep as you once did." He frowned. "Frankly, I would give my right arm for a good night's sleep, but we shall talk of more interesting things." He gave her a sly smile. "Such as the new ship I think we should consider building."

"Oh, so you believe we need to add to our fleet?" she asked, a teasing smile on her own lips. "Escort me to our carriage, and we may discuss the matter."

On the way to the waterfront, where the office and warehouse of Neptune Shipping Lines were located, Josiah made his case for a new ship to be commissioned.

"Those are all solid reasons," Sophie agreed. "I will think upon it. Do you know when you wish for a decision to be made?"

He took her hand and squeezed it. "Whenever you think best, my dear. You know I trust your judgment implicitly."

When they first wed, Sophie had dreaded what would pass between them physically. She only had a vague idea of how a man and woman came together. Her new husband, though, informed her after their wedding breakfast that there would be no physical intimacy between them. He told her that he was too old and no longer interested in that kind of thing. He did say he hoped that a fondness might grow between them, however, and that he hoped she didn't mind if he used gestures of affection toward her if it did.

Josiah was easy to like, and they fell into a fast friendship. She didn't mind if he took her hand or kissed her cheek. It was all the affection she needed. Where once she had thought her largest goal in life was to wed a titled gentleman from Polite Society and become a mother, Sophie found she did not miss the idea of children because she was so busy with the company.

They exited the carriage and went to their separate offices. Five years ago, Josiah had given her his own large office, taking a smaller one next to it. He said that she was doing the bulk of the work and would need a larger space. Still, he was in and out of her office multiple times a day as they discussed matters of business.

She reviewed every item that was pressing and took care of it, giving instructions to Mr. Barnes, their secretary and the most trusted employee in the company.

After Mr. Barnes left, she took out parchment and created a list of the advantages and disadvantages of adding a new ship to their line. She played with trade routes, placing a new ship in different rotations, figuring what profit could be made by expanding after they paid for the building of the ship.

In the end, Sophie decided Josiah was right. Now would be an excellent time to make the addition. It would mean several visits to Greenwich, where Neptune vessels were built. Though not far from London, she decided she might make those journeys on her own and leave her husband behind to continue dealing with business at the office. Despite him brushing off her concerns, she was worried about his health. He was slower to move these days. His color did not look good to her. Perhaps it was time to call in Dr. Denney and let him examine Josiah and make a recommendation regarding the level of activity he should pursue or even changing his diet.

Deciding that to be a good course of action, she dashed off a note to the physician, asking him to call upon her at the office at his earliest convenience. She would discuss the matter with Dr. Denney before approaching Josiah.

Sophie took the note and gave it to her secretary, asking that a messenger deliver it immediately.

Returning to her office, she began reading over a new contract when Josiah entered the room.

"Am I interrupting you?" he asked.

"Never," she assured him. "Please, come and have a seat."

He took one in front of her desk, and she handed him the list she had composed of reasons why they should or should not add an additional ship to their fleet.

Sophie watched him peruse it, and he said, "Hmm. I see the good far outweighs the bad."

His gaze met hers, his eyes twinkling. "Does this mean I'll get my ship?" he asked playfully.

She burst out laughing. "You sound like a little boy wanting a new toy boat to sail along the Serpentine. While this is a much larger undertaking than that, I do believe the cost would be justified by the profit we could make. Yes, Josiah, you will have your new ship."

"Excellent. I knew you would agree with me. I will leave the details in your capable hands, but I have one request."

"What is that?" she asked, curious.

"I want it to be christened the *Sophie*."

Heat rose in her cheeks at the suggestion. "Why? Don't you think that is rather ... forward? Naming a ship after me? Why, you'll have the *ton* gossiping even more than they usually do. They will think I am the one who requested it myself."

Josiah clucked his tongue. "When have either of us ever worried about what Polite Society thought, my dear?"

"Never?" she countered.

He chuckled. "Exactly." Then he grew serious. "I mean it, Sophie. You have put your heart and soul into Neptune Shipping these past few years. I would like to honor you and name a vessel of beauty after you in tribute to all you have done. I want it to sail fast and have sleek lines—and be the envy of every shipping line in Great Britain. No, in all of Europe."

She was right in saying that tongues would wag with the ship being named after her, but Sophie decided that she did not care.

"If this pleases you, then I will accept this great honor," she told him.

He smiled indulgently at her. "I cannot wait to christen it. Why, we could even—"

Then an odd look passed over his face, and Josiah clutched at his chest, where his heart lay.

Panic filled Sophie as she sprang to her feet and rushed from behind the desk, her husband slumping in his chair, moaning softly.

"Mr. Barnes! Get in here!" she cried.

As the secretary raced into the room, she began loosening her husband's stiffly starched cravat, her fingers trembling.

"Summon Dr. Denney at once," she said, the order given calmly now as she got control of herself.

"I just arrived, Mrs. Grant," a voice from the open doorway said, and the physician rushed toward them, obviously seeing Josiah was in distress.

Grateful that he had answered her summons so promptly, she said, "He grabbed at his chest and then collapsed, Doctor."

She eased the cravat from his neck, and Dr. Denney ripped open Josiah's shirt. He placed his palm against the shipping magnate's heart.

Her husband groaned. Sophie's gaze met that of the physician's.

"It is his heart, I'm afraid. We must get him prone."

Mr. Barnes and the doctor eased Josiah from his chair and placed him on the ground. Sophie had already dropped to her knees, and she settled her husband's head in her lap.

"Fetch a blanket," she told Mr. Barnes, and the secretary ran from the room, returning with one which was in Josiah's office for the times he was chilled.

"It is what we term *angina pectoris*—chest pain," Dr. Denney said. "Most likely due to insufficient coronary circulation or inflammation surrounding his heart."

"What can you do for him?" Sophie asked quietly, feeling helpless as the physician merely shrugged, shaking his head.

She held her husband's hand and stroked his thinning hair with her free hand. He tried to speak, and she shushed him.

"No talking now. You need rest, Josiah. We shall work on getting you home so that you will be more comfortable."

He shook his head. "No . . . going home. This is . . . the end, Sophie."

"No!" she cried, tears swimming in her eyes. "I cannot lose you, Josiah. I need you."

"You . . . have all the tools . . . you need. To run this."

He glanced up at her, and Sophie saw the pain on his face, but his eyes held acceptance at his fate.

"You have been the best part of my life, Josiah," she said, tears now blinding her. "You changed everything about me. If not for you, I would never have gained confidence. Never found a purpose. I love you."

She meant the words, ones she had never spoken to him before. It wasn't a romantic love between sweethearts, but it was the love of deeply-rooted friendship. Josiah Grant had been her teacher. Her guide. Her confidant. Her companion.

"You are ready," he said, now wheezing. "You ... will see my legacy ... lives ... on ... ."

Sophie felt the life ebbing from him and knew she was helpless to stop things. She kept her gaze on him, smiling reassuringly, as he groaned again, his body stiffening. His face contorted, and she knew he was in agony.

"Go, my darling," she told him. "Don't hold on for my sake. I will be fine. You have prepared me well."

Her words seemed to calm him, and he gave her a final, weak smile. Josiah closed his eyes and grew still.

She looked down at the best man she had ever known, her throat thick with emotion, tears streaming down her cheeks. She glanced to Mr. Barnes and then Dr. Denney.

The physician said, "It is good that he went quickly, Mrs. Grant. Mr. Grant was always larger than life. If he would have recovered from this heart episode, he would have had to live a very quiet, highly restricted life. Something he would have chomped at the bit about. This way, he went out on his own terms."

"And he could go because he knew he could entrust everything to you, Mrs. Grant," Mr. Barnes pointed out. "You will continue managing Neptune Shipping Lines and do the excellent job you always have. Mr. Grant was right. He will live on through what is here—and what you will continue to create."

While Sophie knew both men spoke the truth, she had never felt more alone in her life.

Chapter Two

As they sailed along the Thames, Captain James Jones watched as London came into sight. Every time he had seen the great city, something tugged at him about it. Some familiarity, and yet he couldn't fathom why.

He had been all over the world, to ports far and wide. He often thought the sea was in his blood because it seemed such a part of him. Home wasn't any particular city or town. No, home was on the open waters, the only place he belonged.

"Ready to dock, Captain," First Mate Drake Andrews announced. "And thank God in His Heavens that we actually made it."

James nodded brusquely to his second-in-command and dear friend. He couldn't remember a time when Drake wasn't in his life. Drake was a dozen years older than James, but they had been close ever since James was a child. They never spoke of the origins of their friendship. He only saw fleeting images of it now and then after he awakened from a nightmare.

What he did know was that he had been abducted many years ago. Pressed into service. Not on a government naval vessel, but on a privateer. Closing his eyes, James could see Flimm, the evil sailor with a nasty temper. The man who had brought him aboard, beating him senseless, as he told James how worthless he was. Flimm had called him Boy—as had the entire crew—until James had been on half a dozen voyages and two years had passed.

By then, he himself had almost forgotten his given name. Drake was the one who reminded him of it. Drake had tended to James during those early days when every part of his body ached. When the knot on his head swelled and he vomited in a bucket over and over. After the nausea left, he found huge gaps in his memory. Drake told him sometimes head injuries caused memory loss and that it was probably better that he didn't recall his life before being brought aboard.

The years had passed. His friendship with Drake had grown. Once James had reclaimed his name, Drake told him he needed a surname.

James had drawn a blank.

So, he had done what Drake had years earlier when he, too, had been swept up and stolen from the streets to live a life at sea. Drake had chosen Andrews for a last name, after a captain he'd admired. James took the name Jones from a first mate who'd spent hours with him, teaching James to navigate by the stars.

The ship moved smoothly down the Thames, despite the damage done to her by weather, and he could see the bustling movement of people and wagons along the waterfront. Many times, the ships he sailed on stopped at Plymouth or Greenwich to unload their precious cargo. The first time he had come to London was a year ago. *Vesta* had lost her captain and first mate, the first due to illness, and the second time in a mutiny. James had been the one to step up and take control of the vessel, finishing its course, delivering goods, and receiving more in return. He'd guided the ship into London, where he'd gone to the Neptune Shipping Line offices to inform its owner of what had occurred.

Josiah Grant had thanked James profusely for his service to the company. When asked what reward he might like, James had said he wished to captain the vessel—and have Drake Andrews as his first mate.

The shipping magnate had nodded thoughtfully and turned to the woman who had sat in a nearby chair. He had thought her to be about his own age and wondered what her role was in the company, finally deciding she must be a trusted secretary to Mr. Grant. Though it would be unique for a woman to serve in that capacity, James was open-minded enough to know women were just as capable as men, having met—and bedded—many of them over his years of travel.

It surprised him when Mr. Grant had told him that Mrs. Grant had approved his request. He had thanked the woman, realizing that she was the much-younger wife of the elderly shipping owner. That she held such sway with her husband was highly unusual, but he had gotten what he came for and wouldn't question why Mrs. Grant had sided with him. Within a week, *Vesta* had set sail again, this time with James officially her captain and Drake serving as first mate.

"Docking now, Captain Jones," Drake called out.

They had reached their final destination after close to eighteen months at sea. He had a list of repairs which he wanted done before he took *Vesta* out again into open waters.

Turning to Drake, he said, "Go to the office and notify them that we have arrived. Since it is already close to seven o'clock, unloading can commence at dawn tomorrow morning. Request an appointment with Mr. Grant at ten o'clock if you would. Report back to me once you've done so."

"Aye-aye, Captain," Drake said, leaving the deck and hurrying down the gangplank which had just been laid.

While his friend was off on his errand, James gathered his crew.

"Thank you for your service on this voyage," he began. "We certainly saw the sights this time around. Two hurricanes. A lightning strike on the bow."

The men laughed heartily, and he knew many of them believed James himself had been the good luck which had allowed fortune to smile upon them and make it to safe harbors.

"But we traded all the goods we left with and brought home even more. We will commence unloading our cargo tomorrow morning at four bells. Workers from the warehouse should arrive on the docks then to assist in the removal of the goods. You will receive your wages once the ship has been emptied."

James glanced at his crew. "Until then, gentlemen, it is business as usual. I want the watch doubled, however, since we are in port. What good would it do to bring back items from half a world away, only to have them stolen in the night by thieves?"

"Will you be taking out *Vesta* again soon, Captain?" a sailor called.

"That will be up to Mr. Grant, the owner of the fleet," he replied, locating the voice. "I shall meet with him tomorrow morning and will know more after our time together. Are you sure you want to head out again with me, Thomas?"

The sailor grinned. "You're the best captain I've ever had. And that's not flattery. You just ask for hard work and treat your men right and fair."

"Then I thank you for your kind compliment, Thomas. I hope to maintain control of *Vesta*. If so, I want the needed repairs done to her and then will head out again as soon as possible. It's already late September and time to leave these seas for better weather in the southern hemisphere."

"I'll be the first to sign on as a crewman, Captain," Thomas promised.

James nodded respectfully to the sailor. "Cook should have something for you to eat now. Everyone get something in your belly and a good night's sleep. Except for those on the watch," he added, smiling. "If we work quickly tomorrow, I see you all with pay in your pocket, sitting with a woman in your lap and a mug of ale in your hand."

That brought rousing cheers from his crew as James called, "Dismissed!"

He returned to his quarters and recorded the information from today in his captain's log. Just as he finished, he heard a knock at the door and called, "Come."

Drake entered. "The dock workers will be on hand bright and early tomorrow morning, James."

His first mate only addressed him by name when they were in private.

"And the meeting with Josiah Grant?"

"His secretary, Samuel Barnes, assured me you could be seen by the owner, but it would have to wait until eleven o'clock tomorrow morning since another important meeting was scheduled tomorrow morning at nine. Mr. Barnes did say he would send a message to the Grant household to inform them of the meeting."

"Thank you, Drake." James sighed, leaning back in his chair, pillowing his hands behind his head. "What say you that we go and have ourselves a meal and a few pints on solid land? Get our sea legs ready for tomorrow's meeting?"

"You want me to go with you?" Drake asked, looking puzzled. "I know of no first mates who do so when a ship comes in to harbor. I should be here, supervising the unloading of the cargo."

"I want you on hand to discuss the damage *Vesta* suffered and back up my insistence to have it repaired as quickly as possible. The warehouse foreman will be on hand. We won't be gone that long. I can't see the meeting taking more than an hour. Then we'll both be back to make certain nothing goes amiss."

"All right," his friend agreed. "I'll go with you to this meeting." He grinned. "And I'll definitely accompany you now to fill our bellies."

"Good. I've already sent word to Cook that we will dine off ship." James stood and placed his hat upon his head. "And if we find time to spend an hour or two with a woman? Even better."

Both men laughed as they left the captain's quarters and descended the gangplank, which a member of the watch withdrew after they were safely ashore. He was glad to see his crew members taking their duties seriously and wouldn't need to worry about them protecting the precious cargo onboard while he was briefly away.

"Want to try The Falconer?" Drake asked, pointing to a building. "It's close."

"Why not?" he replied. "They'll all be the same."

They weaved their way around the pockets of people, pushing open the door to the tavern. The place was packed with sailors, raucous laughter coming in bursts from various parts of the room.

"Over there," Drake said, pointing in the corner to the lone empty table.

They took a seat, and a barmaid with ample breasts and swaying hips set down a round of drinks at the table next to them.

Turning, she asked, "What'll be?"

"Do you have food as well as ale?" James asked.

"We do. If you're hungry, I'd go with the fish chowder. I could bring a loaf of bread with it if you like."

"Then two of the chowders and bread, along with your largest tankards of ale," he told her. "And keep our whistles wet—if you know what I mean."

He gave her a suggestive smile, and she winked at him.

"I see you've already staked your claim for this evening," Drake joked. He glanced about the room. "I may have to look elsewhere. It seems you've taken the best available."

"She may not have me," he said, knowing that wouldn't be the case since in every port he'd been into since he was fifteen, women flocked to him.

"Ah, yes," Drake agreed. "Who would want a ship's captain, a strapping man several inches over six feet, with those broad shoulders and muscles from years working on vessels? One with sun-kissed blond hair and eyes a blue no man ever had?"

He laughed. "Don't worry. We'll find some willing wench for you to dip your wick in, my friend."

The barmaid appeared with a tray, setting down steaming bowls of the chowder and bread, along with the needed ale.

"Bread's fresh out of the oven," she said saucily, eyeing James up and down. "Don't fill up too much. I wouldn't want you to be unable to find my bed later."

He gave her a knowing smile. "And who says I wish to find your bed, lass?"

She leaned down, her nose almost touching his, her hand disappearing under the table. She found his cock, her fingers going around it, giving it a firm squeeze.

"You'll do," she said, raising up, giving him a satisfied smile.

"My friend will also need some company this evening after you close," he added.

She glanced to Drake, looking him up and down. "You're not half-bad yourself. I might just take on the both of you," she said pertly, turning and sashaying away.

"She's a bit forward," Drake said, tearing a hunk of bread from the loaf. Grinning, he added, "But I like her idea."

"I'm not one to share," James said, shutting down talk of the three of them together.

They dug into the fish chowder, finding it to their liking, and asking for second bowls of it, along with more of the bread and ale.

It was after they finished eating and were sipping their drinks in companionable silence that the old man approached them.

James figured him to be sixty or more, but when he arrived at their table, he decided his guess was off. The stranger was probably in his forties but looked much older due to hard years of drinking and poverty. His hair had thinned on top. His cheeks were sunken. His eyes were bloodshot and unfocused.

He was about to shoo away the man when their gazes met—and a chill ran through James.

"It's you," the man whispered in wonder, staring at him. "I knew you weren't dead. I knew it."

The old man began blubbering, collapsing in a heap on the floor. He gripped James' pants leg, burying his face against James' knee.

"What in damnation?" Drake demanded. "Get him off you."

He signaled the nameless barmaid, indicating to her to bring another round, even as he pointed to the man now clinging to his leg. She nodded in understanding and brought an empty tankard, setting it and a pitcher of ale on the table.

"Now, Charlie, this nice man has bought you a drink," she said, prying him away from James and pulling him to his feet.

"He's alive," Charlie said, wonder in his voice.

Hearing that name stirred something within James, but as always, any time he tried to remember anything about his life before the ship, it was as if a dark, heavy curtain descended, one which couldn't be lifted. He'd finally quit trying.

But could this old man shine a light on his past?

The barmaid leaned over to the next table, which had three men occupying it. She yanked the fourth, empty chair away and set it down, easing Charlie into it.

Picking up the pitcher, she smoothly poured liquid into each tankard and picked one up, passing it to Charlie. He slipped both hands around it and began guzzling, downing the entire contents.

She looked to James, who nodded, and she refilled it again before stepping away.

The stranger again drained the entire tankard and wiped his mouth with the back of his hand as he set the empty mug on the table.

Looking at James again, he said, "I knew you'd come back. You couldn't be dead." He shook his head. "He ruined me, of course. Told me to keep searching all the while berating me. Finally beating me. I even hired a Bow Street runner from my own pocket, but there was nary a trace of you. You'd simply upped and vanished."

Uneasiness stirred within him. "You're talking gibberish, old man."

Their gazes met. "Am I? Why, I could take you to Seaton right now, just to prove to him I was right—and he was wrong."

The name triggered something within James. An image of a tall man suddenly seemed burned into him. A man who was always moody and angry. Impatient.

A man who had startling blue eyes.

Just like his . . .

"Go on," he urged, glancing to Drake, who now leaned forward to catch the man's words.

"Could I have more, please?"

"No," James said firmly. "I want to know the truth, Charlie. Who are you? How do you know me?" He paused. "What's your name? And mine?"

Charlie hiccoughed. He began weeping again. "I never should have let you go. You were too young. But you were determined to . . ."

His head dropped to the table. He didn't move.

"He's passed out," Drake drily observed.

"I need to know what he knows," he said quietly. "I think I know him. Part of me . . . recognizes him." He shook his head. "He wasn't always like this."

"You think he knew you in your other life," his friend said. "We never talk about the before."

"No, we don't," James agreed. "I've tried over the years to think about it. I know Flimm beat me. Slammed my head so hard I saw stars." His gaze met Drake's. "You took care of me. You told me I might not ever remember . . . the before. Because of my injury."

James thrust his index finger against his temple. "But it's in here. I know it is. It just continually dances out of reach."

Drake nodded. "Then we better sober him up enough to talk to you. Jog your memory."

Pushing to his feet, his friend went to a man working behind the bar and had a few words. They nodded. A coin was exchanged. Drake received a pitcher and then returned to the table.

"There's a room at the top of the stairs. First on the left. We can have it for an hour. I've got the pitcher. You get him." He indicated Charlie.

He rose and lifted Charlie, tossing him over his shoulder. Following Drake up the stairs, they entered the room.

"Put him on the floor," his friend recommended. "The tavern's owner doesn't want wet sheets."

James unceremoniously dumped the unconscious Charlie, and Drake turned him so Charlie faced up. He tilted the pitcher, and water hit Charlie square in the face. He began sputtering and swearing, sitting up and pushing Drake away.

Taking the only chair in the room, James pulled it up and sat in it, leaning down and peering into Charlie's face.

"I'll ask again. We'll start with a simple question and go from there. What is your name?"

Looking miserable, he said, "Charlie. Charles. Charles Timmons."

James winced at the words. Images flooded him. Of a much younger Charles Timmons.

His tutor...

More and more came rushing back to him. A large house. Two little girls. A woman heavy with child. The man again, the one with the unusual cornflower blue eyes.

And walking with Mr. Timmons. Talking about history. Architecture. Horses. Going away to school.

He choked with emotion at the rush of so many memories, rising and pacing the small bedchamber, pushing his hands into his hair, feeling his head might explode.

Forcing himself to stop, he returned to his seat, where Charlie looked at him.

"You were my tutor."

"I was. A long time ago, my lord."

Drake startled. "Did he just say—"

"He did. I think . . . no, I know . . . my family was wealthy."

Anger suddenly seized him, and he grabbed Charles Timmons by his ragged shirtfront. "What happened to me?"

"You don't remember?" Timmons said, puzzled.

"No," he barked harshly. "I don't. I was taken. Beaten. I hurt my head. Everything was a jumble for a long time. Then the fog lifted. I was no longer confused. But I didn't remember much of anything."

He paused, a deep ache filling him.

"Start from the beginning, Mr. Timmons. And don't leave out anything."

The former tutor began talking rapidly, information pouring from him. When he finally stopped speaking, both James and Drake were in a daze.

"You are telling me that I am the Duke of Seaton's son?"

Timmons nodded. "And his heir. Your mother died giving birth to a stillborn son. His Grace remarried and had two daughters. Twins."

"Like him and Uncle . . . what was his name?"

"Adolphus. Yes, your father and Adolphus were twins. Adolphus had two boys and two girls who were also twins. They run in the Strong family."

Strong . . .

"That's my name. Strong," he repeated, trying it out. "James Strong."

"You didn't even know your own name?" Timmons asked, clearly puzzled.

"No. I didn't," he said, his eyes narrowing, rage again building within him. "So, I was lost on the docks."

"I never would have let you go to the ship. It was that warehouse supervisor who allowed you to leave the building. His Grace fired him. Or his secretary did." Timmons snorted. "A duke does not dirty his hands with a simple firing. I, too, was dismissed by the secretary. A black mark was against me. Thanks to His Grace, I could not find work."

Timmons began blubbering again. "I was to have the living at Shadowcrest. I wanted to study. Write. Serve others. And all I became was a broken man. A drunkard. I live on the streets. Steal what I can to sell. I've had no life. And look at you, my lord," he said accusingly. "You are the picture of health. Well dressed. You carry yourself with the same arrogance of your father."

James grabbed his former tutor by the shoulders, shaking him. "You don't know what I suffered!" he shouted. "You don't know the kind of life I was forced into. Everything was taken from me, even my memory. Yes, I am a captain now, but only after years and years of hard labor on ships, working my way up."

He released Timmons, pushing him away. "Where would my family be now?"

Frightened, the former tutor said, "I don't know. Possibly, the Seaton townhouse. Or they could have gone back to Shadowcrest. I have no idea if His Grace is even alive." His eyes grew large. "You would be the Duke of Seaton if he's gone. No, you wouldn't. The title would have gone to your uncle or cousin if Her Grace did not produce another boy after I was dismissed."

James looked to Drake, who stood resolute, and asked, "What would you have me do, Captain?" Then with a wry smile, he corrected, "My lord."

"Mr. Timmons will return to the ship with us," he stated. "I may or may not need him to accompany me to . . . my family's home. I want him sober."

"Is that even possible?" Drake asked, humor laced in his tone. "I think your Mr. Timmons is a drunk of the worst kind."

"I want him cleaned up. He's not to have a drop of alcohol. You and I will go see this Duke of Seaton and then attend our meeting with

Mr. Grant tomorrow morning."

"You mean your father," prompted Drake.

"Possibly my father," he amended, but in his heart, James knew that would become the truth.

He had waited so long to discover something—anything—about his past. Now, it had confronted him.

"Let's take Mr. Timmons back to *Vesta*. I want him sober and in decent clothing by tomorrow morning."

Drake sighed. "I know of one barmaid who will be disappointed."

James narrowed his eyes. "Are you, my friend?"

"Friend to a duke's son?" Drake said lightly. "I would say I most definitely am."

"Then quit harassing me."

Drake chuckled. "But it is ever so much fun, my lord."

He growled, scooping up Mr. Timmons and tossing him over his shoulder. The man protested as James moved down the staircase and then gave up his struggles.

They reached his ship, and the gangplank was lowered for them. No one on the watch questioned their captain bringing someone back with him. He carried Timmons to the brig and set him on the bench.

"Get food in him. Plenty of hot tea or coffee. Something for him to wear. And stay with him, Drake," James warned. "I don't want to come down here tomorrow and find him gone."

"I'll sleep outside his cell," his friend promised. "And play nursemaid to him before that." He gave James a sympathetic look, placing a hand on his shoulder. "Go and get some rest, my friend. And I mean that. To me, you will always be my friend and brother-in-arms. If it is true that you are who Timmons says you are, I will understand why you will no longer be able to offer your friendship to me."

He snorted. "If it is true that I am this Lord James, then I will decide who my friends are."

Drake shook his head. "That's not how it works, Captain."

"Then I will change the rules," he declared.

CHAPTER THREE

JAMES ROSE FROM his bunk, having gotten little sleep after the night's revelations. Every time he closed his eyes, new images flooded him. He could see the pictures in his mind, but he needed someone to help him make sense of them. Give them context. He did believe Charles Timmons was telling the truth and knew that he'd had a family before he had been stolen from them. How it had occurred was one of the questions he wished to have answered. He had mixed emotions about that family, however. There were still gaps—many gaps—in his memory.

He only hoped he could find the person who could fill them in.

He shaved and dressed, making his way down to the brig, where Drake sat against the wall.

His friend came to his feet and said, "You look as if you didn't get much sleep, Captain."

James was grateful Drake had not addressed him as *my lord* and said, "I was a bit restless."

He looked to the cell and saw a sleeping Charles Timmons and glanced back to Drake.

"How is he?"

Drake chuckled. "Well, I poured two pots of cooled tea down him. Fed him, too. Timmons mostly had sobered up by the time I let him close his eyes. While he was sleeping, I was able to shave him and trim his hair, since he was dead to the world."

Drake indicated a pair of folded clothes sitting in front of the bars. "When he awakens, I'll see he washes up and changes into these."

"Where did you find them?" he asked, having a feeling they were Drake's own clothes.

"They're mine," his friend confirmed. "They may not fit him perfectly, but they'll be better than the rags he wears now. Especially if you want him to go meeting a duke."

"I will see that you're compensated for the clothing, Drake." He swallowed. "I know I asked you to be with me when I met with Mr. Grant this morning, but I am also asking that you go with me as I try to find what is supposed to be my family."

Drake placed a hand on James' shoulder. "You know I am your fastest friend. I will be with you through this, through thick and thin, until the end. And if you're a duke's son? I will be happy for you, James. I always knew there was something special about you."

He chuckled. "You saw potential in a dirty child, half-beaten to death?"

"Even back then, you had a resiliency about you, James. You were also smart. Well-spoken. I should have guessed you were more than a typical street rat." Drake frowned. "I can't recall what you were wearing when Flimm brought you to *Zephyr*, though. All I remember is the mud covering you, thick in your hair. And the blood."

Drake gave him a rueful smile. "And the bruises once I got you cleaned up." He shook his head. "Flimm was a bloody bastard."

"And he got his just due," James said firmly, reflecting on how the hardened sailor had lost his life in a knife fight half a world away while on shore leave.

"You need to clean up a bit yourself," he said.

"You want me to leave Timmons?" Drake asked, surprised.

He shrugged. "The man isn't going anywhere. He's locked behind bars. I was merely being overzealous when I asked for you to guard him all night. Meet me in my quarters after you clean up, and we'll have something to fill our bellies before we start this most unusual day."

James went on deck and tapped a sailor to haul water to the brig.

"There's a man there who is sleeping now, Minnix. When he awakens, he will need to be bathed. It may have been a good while since that has occurred, so ignore his protests and scrub him from head to toe. Clothes have already been set out for him."

"Aye-aye, Captain," the sailor said, hurrying away to follow James' orders.

He went to the mess and told Cook, "Breakfast for two in my quarters at once," seeing Cook nod in confirmation.

Returning to his rooms, he ate with Drake. Once the men had eaten, he said, "I am going to supervise the beginning of the cargo being unloaded. It is almost six o'clock."

The words were barely out of his mouth when four bells sounded. "See? Right on time."

"I'll accompany you, Captain," Drake said. "We should let our guest sleep a little longer before we rouse him. If you need his word, a rested Timmons will make a better impression on the toffs who may be your relatives."

"Don't worry about that. I've already assigned Minnix to wash and dress the man when he does awaken. I want Mr. Timmons to get as much rest as possible and have his wits about him since he will be the one to lead us to this duke's residence."

As they made their way to the top of the ship, Drake asked, "So, you'll go to see your family after your meeting with Mr. Grant?"

"I think that would be best. I'm sure the rich laze about and wouldn't be awake before our meeting in the shipping office."

They arrived on deck, and James saw the gangplank had already been lowered. Activity aboard *Vesta* had started in full force, with crates being hoisted to the deck and carried down the gangplank. He spied Thomas at the end of the gangplank on the wharf, talking with a woman. Irritation filled him, thinking the lightskirt was on her way home and trying to earn a final bit of coin to end her evening. He didn't need a woman's presence to distract any of his men, nor the workers from the Neptune warehouse.

Charging down the gangplank, James roared, "We'll have none of that here, you lady-bird. Be off!"

The woman, whose back had been to him, turned. To his surprise, he recognized her.

"My apologies, Mrs. Grant. I was not . . . expecting you at such an early hour."

She smiled graciously, causing something to tug at his heart.

"Why, good morning, Captain Jones. Mr. Barnes sent word last night that your ship had come in. I am only sorry that I had already left for home and was not available to greet you and the *Vesta*'s crew personally."

Feeling a bit flustered, James said, "That's quite all right, Mrs. Grant. I wouldn't have expected you to do so—nor did I expect to see you at the docks right after four bells."

"Thomas and I were going over the lengthy manifest," she told him. "As you can tell, my warehouse workers are already busy helping your men unload the cargo."

She turned, indicating several wagons and teams of horses standing nearby, workers loading crates onto the first cart in line, which pulled out when it reached capacity.

"Based upon my experience, we should be able to finish unloading a majority of the goods you have brought home by day's end. I believe it will take another three hours tomorrow morning, though, before we'll have all the crates placed in the warehouse."

She glanced at the ship. "Thomas has also told me that *Vesta* received some damage due to running into foul weather. Might you walk me through that now? I would like to see it firsthand."

"Wouldn't that be more appropriate for Mr. Grant and his secretary to do, Mrs. Grant?"

She shook her head sadly. "My husband is no longer with us," she informed him. "He passed away six weeks ago."

Sympathy filled him. "Then I am very sorry for your loss, Mrs. Grant. Although I only met Mr. Grant the one time, he was a most kind gentleman."

James was curious as to what this woman's role now was in her dead husband's shipping line, but it was not his place to ask such an impertinent question.

"Would you mind taking me about the ship now, Captain Jones? I need to see the repairs that must be accomplished before *Vesta* can sail again."

"Of course, Mrs. Grant."

He offered his arm to her as they moved to mount the gangplank. She accepted, tucking her hand into the crook of his arm.

A woman's touch had never affected him as much as in this moment.

James was not a stranger to women. He had been with countless women of various nationalities around the globe, ranging from quite homely to incredibly beautiful ones. Mrs. Grant came out on the pretty side, with her golden-brown hair and warm, brown eyes, but somehow her light touch and proximity moved him in a way he had never experienced before.

They reached the top of the gangplank, and she released his arm, saying, "Thank you for steadying me on the way up, Captain Jones." She gazed around her. "Oh, there is nothing like being on a ship!"

He spent the next hour guiding her from place to place, showing her the damage which *Vesta* had suffered, and they discussed the necessary repairs. Much to his surprise, she understood exactly what needed to be done, even musing about the best way to do it, suggesting several ideas to him.

As they moved from spot to spot, she told him about a new ship which she had commissioned to be built in Greenwich.

"It was my husband's idea to add a new vessel to our fleet. We were speaking about doing that very thing when he passed away moments later." A determined look filled her face. "I will keep my promise to him and see this dream of his come to fruition."

Despite the tremendous age gap between the pair, James believed the Grants had had a good marriage. It surprised him that the thought filled him with envy, though.

He shook his head, tamping down the attraction he felt to this widow. He might be a ship's captain, a noble occupation, but she was far above his station.

Once more, he guided her down the gangplank, and when they reached the bottom, she said, "I hope you will keep our eleven o'clock appointment this morning, Captain. I wish to hear in detail about the journey *Vesta* has been on and discuss your future with Neptune Shipping Lines."

James couldn't help himself and asked, "Who is helping you to run the company, Mrs. Grant?"

She smiled, mischief glinting in her eyes. "Why, *I* am running my company, Captain Jones. Who else would do so?"

Despite the knowledge she had revealed about ships during their tour, James still found it difficult to believe that a woman could be in charge of a fleet of ships.

"I see you are having trouble accepting the fact that a mere slip of a woman is the head of a shipping empire."

He winced. "Was I that obvious?"

Mrs. Grant laughed merrily. "You actually appear more broad-minded than most men," she told him. "I have spent well over seven years coming to the Neptune offices on a daily basis. I have done everything from helping architects design our ships, to having a hand in hiring the ships' crews. I started out keeping the books for my husband's company, and my role has expanded throughout the years. If he were here, Mr. Grant would be the first to tell you, Captain, that I am just as capable—if not more so—of running this company which he entrusted to me than any man."

She smiled brightly at him. "We shall discuss more when you come to visit me at our office. Don't forget to bring your captain's log with you."

"I'll be bringing my first mate with me," he told her. "Drake Andrews. He is a valued crew member, as well as my good friend. I would like him present at our meeting."

She nodded thoughtfully. "That is a very wise move on your part," she observed. "While a captain may be in charge of his ship and the ultimate responsibility of her lies with him, his first mate knows all those grubby little details. It is good that you trust Mr. Andrews. I would be delighted to have him attend our meeting. For now, however, I need to go and prepare for the meeting preceding ours, as well as tend to the usual business of the day. Good day to you, Captain Jones."

James watched as Mrs. Grant walked along the dock. Though still early, the wharf had come to life. He saw, too, how others moved out of her way, opening a path for the direction she moved.

That meant she was known and had the respect of the people in this world, which told him a great deal about her.

She might be young—and a woman—but Mrs. Grant knew her stuff. She was running a business in a day and age when no woman was in such a place of power. Even if it had been a queen sitting upon Great Britain's throne now, he doubted she would have as much power and say as Mrs. Grant. A queen would have a legion of advisers, including her royal council, telling her what to do. It seemed as if Mrs. Grant depended only upon herself.

That intrigued him. *She* intrigued him.

But it could go no further than that. The pretty widow was his employer. Around her, he would keep his hands to himself. But his thoughts of what she looked like beneath that practical gown she wore?

He could fantasize all he wished about that.

James went to Thomas and asked how the unloading process was going.

"Running smoothly, Captain."

He returned to his quarters, knowing he should be preparing for the possibility of what he might say if he actually met members of his own family today. That meeting could be life-altering.

Instead, his thoughts turned to his upcoming meeting with the enigmatic Mrs. Grant.

Chapter Four

Sophie walked the few short blocks to Neptune Shipping Lines and entered the warehouse, which was buzzing with activity. She spoke to her manager for a few minutes, and he agreed that it would take all of today and a few hours early tomorrow morning for the unloading of *Vesta* to be completed. She had learned from experience not to rush the process. It took a good deal of time, for every crate would be opened and checked against the manifest during the transfer process. It was vital to log the contents of each crate before moving the goods to another part of the warehouse.

Satisfied that things were well in hand, she went upstairs to her office, where Mr. Barnes greeted her.

"Good morning, Mrs. Grant. I assume you have been at the docks?"

"Yes, Mr. Barnes. I asked Captain Jones to give me a tour of *Vesta* since the ship has suffered some damage."

"Was it serious?" the secretary asked. "Weather-related—or from pirates?"

"Weather, thank goodness."

Sophie described the two hurricanes *Vesta* had sailed through, as well as the unusual lightning strike it had suffered. She mentioned the patchwork of repairs which had been done in order to get the vessel and its cargo safely back to England.

"It is good you saw this firsthand, Mrs. Grant," Mr. Barnes said. "I assume you will work on a report and have word sent to Mr. Purdy in Greenwich?"

"Yes, my thoughts exactly." She smiled. "You often know my mind before I even do, Mr. Barnes. I don't know what I would do without you."

The secretary smiled, pleased at the compliment. "Once you have finished it, I can send your report by messenger or deliver it in person."

"Let me think on that," she said. "I will be in my office."

"Remember you have your meeting at nine o'clock this morning with—"

"I haven't forgotten. Please have tea prepared for when Mr. Blankenship arrives."

"I will, Mrs. Grant. And I have already stopped and picked up some of the sticky buns Mr. Blankenship favors. There are even enough for Captain Jones to have one if he so desires."

"Oh, the captain is bringing his first mate, a Mr. Andrews, to our meeting."

Mr. Barnes grew thoughtful. "Now, that is interesting. We have never had a captain include anyone else when he has met with you or Mr. Grant."

"I know," she said. "I find it rather refreshing. Don't you believe a first mate would know more about what was going on onboard a ship than its captain? I would think the crew would be slightly more relaxed in the first mate's company, which could lend itself to discovering some interesting information." Sophie paused. "Although I do believe not much gets past Captain Jones."

"I recall how Mr. Grant was impressed with the young man. Wasn't he the one who quelled the crew's mutiny?"

"Indeed, he was, Mr. Barnes. Captain Jones is quite impressive. I hope he is with Neptune Shipping for many years to come."

She realized her remarks regarding Captain Jones sounded too familiar and quickly said, "As I said, I will be in my office."

Sophie entered the large room where she spent a majority of her waking hours. She had had little social life before Josiah's death. Oh, he would take her to the theatre or opera on occasion, simply because he knew she loved the fine arts. As far as attending social events, however, they had no true friends. Their life revolved around Neptune Shipping—and each other.

She removed parchment from her drawer and spent the next hour writing a detailed account of the damage she had observed on *Vesta* and her recommendations for its repairs. Reading through it once, she believed she had covered everything thoroughly. Quickly, she penned an additional copy and set the pages aside.

Sophie leaned back in her chair, thinking about how long the repairs might take. Obviously, *Vesta* would have to be sailed to Greenwich. She wanted the shipyard that built all Neptune vessels to handle the extensive repairs. Captain Jones would need to be onboard, supervising a skeleton crew, in order to get the vessel to where it needed to be.

She was determined to be on that ship when it sailed.

The distance was short. It wouldn't take them much time at all to arrive. Sophie felt it important to walk through the ship with the head of the yard, who would be supervising the repairs. She told herself she was doing it because of the ship.

And not the man.

"Liar," she said softly to herself.

The physical attraction she felt toward Captain James Jones was overwhelming. It had taken her by surprise. While she recalled the man coming to their offices when *Vesta* last came into port, she had focused on Jones' account of the uprising and how he had dealt with it. More of her time had been spent perusing the manifests he had brought with him, evidence of how he had saved Neptune. Too many mutinies wound up with all its ship's cargo lost, along with the lives of various crew members. Captain Jones, by sheer force of will, had literally saved the day—and much of *Vesta's* profits.

It had been easy to grant him the captaincy of the ship when he had asked for it. If he hadn't have done so, she would have suggested it to Josiah herself. In Captain Jones, they had found a true leader, one who dominated physically and yet whose keen intelligence and talent understood how and why men behaved as they did.

Josiah had agreed with her in an instant, and her husband had told Jones that he would be granted the official role of captain for the length of one voyage of eighteen months. When *Vesta* returned to London, Jones was to meet with them again. They would evaluate how he had performed, based upon his captain's log and the precious cargo he brought back.

Her time spent with Captain Jones this morning, however, already told her that she would not hesitate to send him back out to sea with a Neptune vessel. In fact, once *Vesta* was repaired, she might even give him a choice of a larger one. Sophie then thought that he would be the perfect candidate for their latest ship being built. If things were timed perfectly, Captain Jones could make a final run with the repaired *Vesta*—and then assume responsibility for *Sophie*.

Sophie . . .

She was still most reluctant to name the ship after herself, especially with Josiah now gone. Who named a ship such a name? All the ships in their fleet were named for Roman gods and goddesses. Her name sprang from Sophia, which was Greek for wisdom. She didn't think she was particularly wise, and naming a vessel after herself seemed incredibly inappropriate, as well as egotistical. Yet she had promised Josiah she would agree to his suggestion. It would be something she would have to ponder. As of now, she still had more than a year before that decision would need to be made.

Her thoughts returned to the very handsome Captain Jones. As a widow, she had a bit more freedom in society than did a married woman or young woman who had never been wed. Not that she kept to Polite Society's rules. They had ostracized her long ago. She could only imagine what was said of her now. It was one thing to wed beneath her, though her husband had more wealth than a majority of gentlemen in the *ton*. It was another to accompany her husband to his office each day and dirty her hands in business.

But to actually be running a company?

She assumed most women would faint simply upon meeting her.

Sophie was already shunned by Polite Society. Not that they cared anything about her. But what she was thinking was something scandalous. Something that she never thought she would consider, much less participate in.

She wanted to have an affair with Captain James Jones.

The thought was laughable. Why, here she was, six and twenty, and she had never even been kissed. But the rugged seaman had caused all kinds of wicked thoughts to race through her since their time together this morning. Sophie knew she had no chance at marriage with anyone from any class. Gentlemen of the *ton* would be excluded as suitors. Men she did business with had come to look at her as an anomaly. Yes, they respected her knowledge and prowess in financial affairs, but they would never consider her marriage material, especially since Josiah's death had left her with a vast amount of wealth. That very wealth would intimidate every man whom she considered her equal.

And even if one of them did decide to break down the barriers between them and offer for her? She would be a fool to accept. If she did, she would be left penniless, thanks to British law, which upon marriage made everything belonging to a woman no longer hers. If Sophie wed, her new husband would be in control of Neptune Shipping Lines, and who knew what he might do with that vast wealth. He could sell the company. Run it into the ground. Turn it over to others who would not give it the love and care it deserved.

No, Sophie could never wed and see Josiah's dream placed in the hands of someone else. Her husband had entrusted his legacy and the shipping line to her. She would nurture it. Help it continue to grow and flourish. She intended to make Neptune the most well-known, respected, and largest shipping company in the world. It was certainly a lofty goal, but one she believed over the coming decades she would accomplish.

A husband could play no role in that scheme.

But a lover? Why not?

She had no friends, only a few servants who cared deeply about her, and Mr. Barnes, who was like family to her. With Josiah now gone, Sophie realized how narrow her world had grown. She was lonely. Terribly lonely. And while business affairs took up a huge part of her day, she still went home to no one. She had no companion to share amusing stories with. No one to sit at her table while she dined. Her life was spent in solitude.

That was why the idea of taking a lover was so appealing, especially for a limited time. If Captain Jones chose to continue his employment at Neptune, he would be an ideal candidate for the position. He would only be in port for a short while. Actually, he would be in England a bit longer than usual, thanks to the repairs to be made to *Vesta*. During his time at home, though, they could embark upon a love affair. Something told Sophie the very handsome captain knew his way around a woman. A man who looked like Captain Jones must certainly have a vast amount of experience in the bedchamber.

And she was eager to learn all she could from him.

The problem was how to go about it. She could understand a man trying to tempt a woman into coupling with him. Did women do the same? She had no idea. She also worried that he might think her request—and his acceptance—would hinge upon his continued employment. In no way would Sophie hold Captain Jones' response against him. Whether he agreed to bed her or not, he would still be offered command of one of Neptune's sailing vessels.

How to make him understand would be a delicate dance of words. She had no idea how to initiate such a conversation. Perhaps she should get to know him a bit better before she suggested changing the nature of their relationship. Not that they currently had a relationship.

"Oh, this is so frustrating," she said aloud, blowing out a breath.

She calmed herself. The idea had only come to her. She was usually deliberate in her thinking and never rushed into decisions. Perhaps she needed to warm to the idea of taking a lover and exploring physical intimacy. Just because Captain Jones was in port now did not mean something had to occur between them. It could even wait until the next time he sailed into British waters.

Yes, that might be best. Get to know him some while he was in port. Let the two of them become more comfortable with one another. Perhaps even have something of a friendship develop between them. Then she could ask him to help her discover whether or not she possessed a sensual nature. She had been a virgin this long. What would another year or two matter?

Then it occurred to her. A child might be a result of a love affair. The thought frightened—and thrilled—her. Surely, a man of the captain's years and experience would know how to prevent a child. But the idea of having a babe suddenly appealed to Sophie. She had given up on the idea of motherhood when Josiah had said there would be no physical intimacy between them. Helping him run Neptune Shipping had proved intoxicating, and it had consumed her during their years of marriage.

Yet why create and build a shipping empire if no one would be there to take up the reins decades from now?

The thought of having a child—even children—greatly appealed to her. Again, she would never marry because she would refuse to lose control of all which had been built. But for Josiah's company to live on, not just for the decades remaining to her, but for a hundred years or more to come?

That was exciting.

So, Sophie had two dilemmas now. One, how to ask Captain James Jones to become her lover. Two, how to get a child off him.

She giggled, something she rarely had done even as a child. Who would have thought she would have such a problem to solve?

A light tap sounded on her door, and she said, "Come."

Mr. Barnes appeared. "Mr. Blankenship has arrived, Mrs. Grant, along with his solicitor."

"Please escort them to the conference room, Mr. Barnes. I assume the refreshments await us there."

"Yes, ma'am."

"Please join us then."

Barnes usually sat in meetings with clients, taking notes for her to refer to later.

She rose and went to her meeting, her focus back on business again.

An hour later, she thanked the two men for their time and returned to her office, where she wrote a note to Mr. Purdy, who was building her new ship and would also be the one she entrusted *Vesta* to for her repairs. Once she completed it, she left her office and stopped at Mr. Barnes' desk.

"Here are the notes from the Blankenship meeting," he said, handing them to her.

"Thank you. I will review these this afternoon." She gave him her own letter and both copies of her report. "See this is posted to Mr. Purdy, along with one copy of the report of the repairs which *Vesta* will need. My note apprises him of this and asks for the earliest date for these repairs to occur. I will most likely accompany Captain Jones to Greenwich to discuss the repairs."

That might give her the opportunity to share her proposal with the handsome sea captain and possibly allow them to embark upon an affair.

"I'll see that it is sent to Mr. Purdy as soon as the meeting with Captain Jones concludes, Mrs. Grant."

The door opened, and her heart sped up as Captain Jones appeared in the doorway, along with a man a good ten years older and quite nice-looking himself.

"Captain Jones," she said. "I see you are punctual."

He smiled, causing warmth to flood her. "At sea, one must learn to be flexible, Mrs. Grant. On land? I find it much easier to be prompt." He paused, indicating his companion. "Might I introduce Mr. Drake Andrews, First Mate of *Vesta*?"

She offered her hand to the seaman, who grasped it firmly. "A pleasure to meet you, Mrs. Grant. Captain Jones shared that you recently lost your husband. My condolences."

"Thank you, Mr. Andrews. Won't you both join me in our conference room?" She looked to Mr. Barnes. "Please see that more tea is brought." To her guests, she said, "Mr. Barnes has provided sticky buns for us. I hope you'll enjoy them."

They adjourned to the conference room. With Mr. Andrews in tow, Sophie would be able to strictly stick to business.

But it wouldn't hurt to study Captain Jones during their meeting.

Chapter Five

Sophie poured out for both Captain Jones and Mr. Andrews and said, "Enjoy your refreshments while we get to know one another for a few minutes."

Turning to the first mate, she added, "Mr. Andrews, please tell me a bit about yourself."

The older man looked slightly startled at receiving attention. "Why, I have been with Neptune ships for many years, Mrs. Grant. I started as a cabin boy and have made my way up the ladder over the years until now I am First Mate on *Vesta*."

"So, you have spent your entire life at sea then," she commented.

"Aye-aye," he responded, looking sheepish. "Sorry, Mrs. Grant. Habit of a sailor."

"No apologies are necessary, Mr. Andrews. With you having served in so many varied positions, I wonder if you are interested in being a captain for our fleet someday."

Now thoroughly flummoxed, Andrews said, "Why, Mrs. Grant, I'm afraid I hadn't thought that far in advance."

"It would serve you well to have that as your goal, Mr. Andrews. While very few men are granted the opportunity to captain a sea vessel, surely it should be your ambition to do so. Too many times, people equate ambition with greed when they are nothing alike. You yourself know you have spent a majority of your life on the open waters. You have worked your way up from the lowest position aboard a ship to that of second in command. I think it would be your goal to one day attain a captaincy."

Andrews nodded thoughtfully. "I'll admit that I hadn't thought of myself in those terms, Mrs. Grant. I look at Captain Jones here, and it is obvious that he commands respect. He is one who always uses his authority wisely."

"Do not sell yourself short, sir. You are at this table today because of the man you are and the talents you have displayed. Captain Jones recognizes those skills and the experience which you possess. You are not in your position merely because you are his friend. You are an asset, both to him and Neptune Shipping Lines."

Andrews sat a bit taller. "I thank you kindly for the compliment, ma'am."

She turned to Mr. Barnes. "Would you please retrieve the copies of the report I created? The one which is to go to Mr. Purdy?"

"Yes, Mrs. Grant," the secretary said, exiting the conference room and quickly returning.

Sophie nodded, and Mr. Barnes handed a report to each gentleman.

"I would like you to read over this if you would. I would appreciate your opinion on it and ask if I need to add anything to it."

Both men turned their attention to the report she had written regarding the damage to *Vesta* and her recommendations on how to manage the repairs. While Sophie watched both for their reactions as they read, she had to admit that she spent more time gazing upon Captain Jones. His long, strong fingers held the report in one hand. She couldn't help but think of those fingers gliding along her body.

She turned her gaze away, hoping no one present noticed the color rising in her cheeks. Sophie breathed in and out slowly, trying to gain control of her emotions.

When she did, her gaze returned to Captain Jones. His brow was furrowed slightly as he read, and she couldn't help but look upon his sensual lips.

Quickly, she focused her attention on Mr. Andrews, who placed the final sheaf of paper on the table and nodded thoughtfully. His gaze met hers, and an understanding passed between them that no one would speak until the captain finished studying her recommendations.

He did so, his eyes meeting hers. "You did a remarkable job of capturing everything you saw onboard yesterday and what we discussed in regard to *Vesta's* repairs. In fact, you took things a step further, adding a few thoughts of your own, which we did not discuss."

"Do you approve of my additions?" she asked, interested in his opinion.

"Aye, Mrs. Grant, I most certainly do. You've quite a grasp regarding ships and how they are built. What makes them seaworthy."

She smiled, satisfied with his reply. "You have brought *Vesta* into port twice now, Captain Jones, with her limping along each time. I know the damage the first time was caused by the mutiny which occurred, while in this instance, the harm was weather-related. You are quite the commander in being able to pull off what you have, and I know that Mr. Andrews here has been a great part of your success."

Captain Jones nodded in agreement. "Mr. Andrews is most certainly my right-hand man, Mrs. Grant, in all ways. I believe, as you do, that he should be given command of his own ship in the near future."

"No," Andrews protested. "Not the near future. This was only my first voyage officially acting as your first mate, Captain. I would need to get another three or four of those voyages before I would consider that I had enough experience to lead a crew."

Sophie said, "You are wise in knowing that it takes experience to not only sail a ship, but to lead the men on it, Mr. Andrews. That alone puts you ahead of so many others who wish to hold a position of authority. I do not believe it would take three or four more trips to sea, however, before you are ready. If you remain teamed with Captain Jones, I think you would come along much faster and be prepared to assume your own command sooner, rather than later."

She cleared her throat. "Let me share an idea with you both. *Vesta* will need extensive repairs which cannot take place at the docks in London. She will need to be sailed to Greenwich, where our shipbuilder's yard is located. If you approve, I will forward this report to Mr. Purdy, the owner of the shipyard we work with. I would ask, Captain Jones, that you and First Mate Andrews maintain a skeleton crew to sail *Vesta* there. I myself would like to accompany you and discuss these extensive repairs with Mr. Purdy, along with the two of you."

She paused, gauging their reaction before continuing. While Andrews nodded eagerly, Captain Jones' face was unreadable.

"While we are there, I would also be checking on the progress of my new ship, which is being built for Neptune Shipping Lines. All Neptune ships have been constructed in the Purdys' yard. The current build should be completed within the next eighteen months or so."

Sophie placed her hands on the table, folding them. "What I propose, after seeing this new vessel, is for Captain Jones to take on the new ship. It will be the largest and most modern in our fleet. In turn, he would pass over command of *Vesta* to you, Mr. Andrews. Does the idea appeal to either of you?"

Both men contemplated her offer, and she added, "This way, once *Vesta* is ready to sail again, the two of you might take her on a shorter run, somewhere around twelve to fifteen months. By then, Mr. Andrews should be seasoned enough to take on command of *Vesta*. We would work hard at retaining whatever crew he might wish to keep with him to ensure his success as a captain for the Neptune line."

Looking to Jones, she said, "And you, Captain, would have your pick of any crew member from our fleet. We could also sign on any other seamen you wished to be a part of your crew. So, what say you?"

To her surprise, Captain Jones said, "I am not going to be able to commit at this time, Mrs. Grant."

"Of course," she said quickly. "I understand it is a lot of responsibility to take on. Why don't you sail *Vesta* to Greenwich for me and at least see the new ship, which is in its infancy of being built. We could even meet with its architect, and you could have full access to the plans and what the ship will look like upon completion. At this early stage, I am certain you could even make a few suggestions, which could then be incorporated into the build."

"I will go with you to Greenwich, Mrs. Grant," Jones confirmed. "*Vesta* is still under my command, and I wish to see her fully restored. I would also enjoy viewing the new vessel. I have never been in a shipyard and seen how a ship is built. It would be a wonderful experience and honor to do so."

She saw something in his eyes, and then felt as if he was holding back. "Would you be able to make your decision at that point regarding my offer, Captain?"

"I will be frank with you. I have some . . . family issues which need to be settled."

"Oh, I did not realize you had family, Captain Jones. Then again, I know very little about you. Perhaps we can get to know one another better during our time in Greenwich."

He nodded brusquely "That might be the case. For now, though, I must address these family . . . matters."

He was deliberately being vague, and Sophie began to wonder if his family included a wife and children. In her fantasy of coupling with Captain Jones, she had not thought of him as being wed.

"Is your family here in London? Or England?" she asked politely, curious as to what his answer would be.

"Sometimes, they are in London. Other times, they are in the country."

She tamped down the frustration at his reply, wondering why he would be so reluctant to take advantage of an incredible career opportunity.

"Are you certain you will be able to sail *Vesta* to Greenwich?" she asked pointedly. "I do not need you to accompany me, of course. You can tell from my report that I know my ships," she said, her tone firm and professional. "I was merely extending the offer as a courtesy to you, Captain, and for you to be able to see my new ship."

Her eyes flicked to the first mate. "You, Mr. Andrews, are still invited to come, of course. If Captain Jones finds himself tied up in family issues and cannot extricate himself, I am sure you would be more than capable of sailing *Vesta* the short distance to Greenwich for those repairs."

Andrews looked dumbfounded. He turned to his captain and friend.

Irritated, Sophie said, "You would not need Captain Jones' approval for this, Mr. Andrews. After all, I own *Vesta*. I believe you are perfectly capable to sail her while the captain attends to . . . personal matters."

"Thank you for your faith in me, Mrs. Grant," the first mate told her. "However, I would prefer to be under Captain Jones' command in this instance."

"Well, I may not be able to wait for it to be convenient to Captain Jones," she snapped. "I've a business to run, Mr. Andrews. That means getting my ships in shape and getting them back on the water."

"When would you need *Vesta* sailed to Greenwich?" Jones asked.

She looked to her secretary, realizing time was of the essence. "Mr. Barnes, would you be able to leave now and deliver my note and report to Mr. Purdy? It could be in his hands by day's end, and you could bring his reply to me tomorrow."

"Of course, Mrs. Grant. I will leave at once."

The secretary stood and went to Mr. Andrews, asking, "Might I have this copy to give to Mr. Purdy?"

The first mate handed it over, and Barnes hurried from the office.

"Mr. Barnes should return sometime tomorrow, so I will know more then. Perhaps we could meet again tomorrow, say late afternoon. Would you be able to tell me then if you could sail *Vesta* to Greenwich or not, Captain Jones? Or will your family concerns take precedence?"

"Hopefully, I should know more about my family commitments by then, Mrs. Grant. What time would you have us meet?"

Being even more curious about him now and his situation than before, Sophie decided a meeting away from the office might be productive and give her some of the answers she searched for.

"Come to my house for tea tomorrow, Captain. Four o'clock." She provided her address to him.

"I will see you then," Jones guaranteed, rising.

Mr. Andrews did the same.

As Sophie came to her feet, she said, "I know the unloading of *Vesta's* cargo will be completed sometime tomorrow morning, and you will be dismissing your crew. They should report to the warehouse for their pay after you do so."

She turned to Andrews. "Since you are so familiar with the crew, why don't you select a half-dozen trusted men to retain for the trip to Greenwich? You may compose your list and drop it off with Mr. Barnes when you come tomorrow to collect your own pay."

"I can do that, Mrs. Grant. Should I tell the men they are to remain in Greenwich and bring *Vesta* back once she's right again?"

"Based upon my experience, I believe it will take between ten days and two weeks to see *Vesta* restored. I will see that Mr. Barnes provides you with ample funds so that you and the crew members might return to London during that time. If you are pleased with their performance, the same skeleton crew can come to Greenwich again, at company expense, and bring her back to the London docks."

"Yes, Mrs. Grant," the first mate said.

Her gaze met that of Captain Jones'. "I hope you are able to settle your pressing affairs with your family. I will see you tomorrow afternoon for tea."

The men said their goodbyes and left the conference room, while Sophie took a seat again.

This complicated matters a bit. If Captain Jones did have a wife and children, her idea of suggesting an affair to him would not be appropriate. She didn't know much about him, but she believed him to be a man of integrity, one who would never be unfaithful to his wife. Then again, she had heard talk of sailors who had multiple wives scattered in ports around the world.

Sophie tabled any decision regarding Captain Jones and a love affair. She would meet with him tomorrow and hope that whatever family matters which troubled him would be cleared up by that time.

Only then, once she knew his status, would she embark upon a plan to bring him to her bed.

Chapter Six

James had been stunned by Mrs. Grant's offer to captain the new vessel being built for Neptune Shipping Lines. He wanted to leap at the opportunity and immediately agree to be at its helm as it made its maiden voyage from England, crossing the Atlantic, heading for exotic locales.

Yet the possibility that he had a family stood in the way. He had no idea about his father. If he even might still be alive. Last night, in the little sleep he had gotten, he had dreamed of his mother. Her image had come to him clearly for the first time in over two decades, and he felt her loss anew, the pain washing over him.

More was coming back to him as today progressed. He could picture two little girls and their mother, realizing they were the second family his father had started after he lost his wife. The girls had been possibly a year old or so, twins, and their mother had been quite pretty.

As he and Drake left the shipping offices, his friend said, "Well, that was something. Mrs. Grant is a force to be reckoned with. What was her husband like?"

James turned them toward a hansom cab, signaling it to stop, and gave the waterfront as their destination. The cab driver looked a bit leery, and James knew the wharf wasn't the safest of places.

"You may drop us a few blocks from the docks," he instructed the driver, who looked relieved upon hearing it.

As they settled into the cab, he told Drake, "I only met Mr. Grant once, after we brought *Vesta* in the last time. He was old, much older than I had expected. Probably in his early sixties."

"Poor Mrs. Grant. To be married to someone so ancient, and her being so pretty," Drake remarked.

"You think her pretty?" he asked.

"I most certainly do. Don't you?" his friend asked.

He'd thought her pretty this morning as he'd guided her about *Vesta*, showing her the ship. Upon meeting her again, though, she seemed more than pretty. Again, he knew that was the attraction he felt toward her which was coloring his view.

"I find it quite remarkable that a woman, especially one so young, has such a depth and breadth of knowledge regarding ships," James said.

"Her report on *Vesta* and the recommendations she made for repairs?" Drake shook his head. "I'd have been hard-pressed to come up with some of those solutions. The woman certainly knows ships."

"She was present when I met Mr. Grant that one time," he shared. "I thought her to be a secretary at first, before he consulted her. I see now that she was, even before her husband's death, the real power within the company. After our conversation this morning, I think Grant was allowing her to run the company in his stead as he grew older."

"Well, that is remarkable indeed," Drake praised. He paused. "What do you think of her offer to the both of us? Frankly, I had never thought beyond attaining the position of First Mate. Mrs. Grant definitely got me to thinking otherwise. Bloody hell, James. I am three years shy of forty. I still have many years left in me. Why not a captain?"

"You know as much as I do," James told his friend. "You taught me most everything I know. You have the tools to make for an excellent captain of *Vesta*. No more seasoning is required, Drake. You could take her out on her next voyage once she's in tip-top shape again."

"If I did so, what would you do until the new ship is completed?"

He shrugged. "Who's to say I want to even captain a new vessel?"

Drake snorted. "Don't give me that, James," he said, for once not calling him Captain. "To be captain of the premier vessel in the Neptune Line? One which would sail faster and carry more cargo than any other ship Neptune owns?"

"I wanted to tell Mrs. Grant I would do so," he admitted. "But I have the Sword of Damocles hanging above me. Until I know of my origins and discover what family I may have, my decisions regarding my future must wait."

"Then we are to collect Timmons and be on our way to the Duke of Seaton's?"

"Aye," James said, falling silent the remainder of the way.

His thoughts turned to the widow once more. The pretty widow who now appeared beautiful to him. She had knowledge far beyond that of other women and a graciousness about her that he found appealing.

And lips that begged to be kissed.

James had found it difficult at times to focus on what was being said because he constantly studied her mouth, thinking what it would be like to have his on hers. To kiss her deeply. To run his fingers along her bare skin. To push his hands into her dark hair, causing it to tumble from its pins.

That was certainly not how he should be thinking about his employer.

And yet he couldn't stop the desire which flowed through him . . .

The hansom cab slowed, and James shouted, "We can disembark here."

He paid the driver and then asked, "Would you wait for us here? My ship is only a few blocks from here. We will be going to Mayfair next."

The location simply came to him.

"I would pay you for your time as you wait and then more when we arrive at our destination if you agree."

The cabbie grinned. "Certainly, Captain. I'll be right here."

He gave the man an extra coin, and the driver tipped his hat to James.

"It will be a tight fit," he told Drake as they made their way to *Vesta*.

"Then leave me here," his first mate suggested. "We've been gone too long as is. While Samuel and the others are trustworthy, I would feel better staying behind and supervising the movement of the cargo. You don't need me to go with you to Mayfair, wherever that is."

"I've recalled taking walks with Mr. Timmons. I think I know this great city from years ago because we walked it so much. Mayfair... seems familiar to me. I think that is where Seaton's townhouse lies." He paused. "I am happy for your company there, but you would probably be better served staying behind."

"Just promise to tell me what passes between you and this duke," Drake said.

"I will."

When they reached the ship, James remained on the docks, checking in with Samuel and the warehouse agent, while Drake went to collect Charles Timmons.

When Timmons appeared, shock ran through James. This cleaned-up version was merely an older one of the tutor he now recalled. The shave and haircut had done wonders, along with new clothes. While they didn't fit Timmons perfectly, they were a vast improvement over what he had been wearing the previous evening.

The former tutor crossed the gangplank and said, "Hello, my lord. I can see you recognize me now."

"Yes, I do. Since we spoke last night, more has come back to me. I still have blanks which need to be filled in, however."

"And you are looking for answers within His Grace's household."

"You've said that before. His Grace."

"Yes, that is how a duke is addressed. His wife is Her Grace. All gentlemen of rank below that are simply my lord, down to a viscount."

He mused, "I suppose I knew that at one time."

"It will come back to you," Timmons promised. "And what doesn't? You can learn." A hopeful look crossed the tutor's face. "I know I not the most reliable of men now, my lord. My love of drink has almost killed me more times than I can say. But if I can keep away from it, I would be honored to be a part of your household again and teach you all you need to learn to exist in Polite Society."

"I will think on it, Timmons," he said. "No promises. I know not what awaits me in my father's household. That is, if this Duke of Seaton is my father."

The tutor gave him a knowing look. "Oh, he is, my lord. You will see the resemblance between you when you meet him."

"I have a hansom cab waiting. Come with me," he said, and Timmons fell into step with him. "Are we going to Mayfair? That name came to me, out of the blue."

"We are. It is where a majority of the *ton* make their home. His Grace has one of the grandest houses of all, on a beautiful square. The only other house on the square belonged to the Marquess of Edgethorne. It sits opposite your family's residence, with a private park in the middle, only accessible to the two families."

Another flash of memory hit him, running through the park, his mother chasing him. Sitting on a bench in the sunshine, her reading to him.

"Yes," he said quietly. "I seem to recall it."

"You spent many a day with Her Grace there, from what the servants said. You do recall your mother is no longer alive?'

"Yes." An emptiness filled him. "She died when I was a boy. Before you came to us."

"That is correct. And His Grace remarried. You had a stepmama and two half-sisters, Lady Georgina and Lady Philippa. But you called them Georgie and Pippa."

James nodded slowly. "I remember them. They were very young. And quite different in temperament if I recall correctly."

"Right again, my lord. It seems you have more memories locked inside you than you first thought. I have heard head injuries can be nasty things."

"Mine was," he said curtly. "I don't wish to talk anymore, Timmons."

The tutor fell silent as they reached the waiting hansom cab. James looked to his companion, and Timmons instructed the cabbie as to what square to go to in Mayfair.

"Right away," the driver said, taking them from the waterfront and the strong stench of fish.

As they drove through the crowded London streets, James felt more comfortable in his surroundings. His gut told him when they should turn and the direction they were heading. Names of various areas came back to him. He only hoped more memories regarding his family would be unlocked once they met him.

If they chose to meet him.

That was James' greatest fear. That he had been gone for so long, and they no longer thought him alive. He looked at it from their perspective, a stranger showing up at their door, claiming to be a long-lost family member. Would they accept him? Would Charles Timmons be able to convince them that James was this duke's son?

And if so—what would the next steps be?

He might be welcomed and taken into the bosom of the family. He might be acknowledged but asked not to come around, his presence no longer necessary. Or they might outright reject him, thinking he and Timmons schemed to have James declared the missing son who had miraculously been found after so long a time.

His gut churned, even as nerves poured through him. Half a dozen times, he almost told the cabbie to halt and turn around. But he would always live with the knowledge that he had family somewhere. He owed it to him—and them—to see his mission through.

The horses turned right into a beautiful square, a gated park in the center of it. On his right sat a stately home which was vaguely familiar to him. As the horses ran the length of it and made the curve, the other townhouse came into sight.

And oh, what a sight it was!

The residence took up the entire side. He'd never seen so grand a place in all his life. The stucco-fronted exterior had been painted cream, with beautiful arches and so many windows he couldn't begin to guess at the number of rooms contained within the four stories. His heart quickened as the blood rushed to his ears.

He did recognize it. This was his home. He had lived here once upon a time, so very long ago. Thick emotion clogged his throat, and James blinked away sudden tears.

The hansom cab came to a halt, and the driver called out, "Here we are, Captain!"

James swallowed and leaped from the cab, giving the driver a coin. "Thank you," he said.

For bringing me home . . .

"Shall I wait?" the driver asked.

"No," Timmons answered. "We may be here quite some time." His gaze met James', and the tutor gave him an encouraging smile.

The hansom cab vacated the square, but his feet seemed like great blocks of stone, keeping him fixed to the pavement.

"My lord?" Timmons asked, concern clearly written on his brow.

James stared at the entrance to the magnificent townhouse, which appeared as a palace to him. It was hard to believe he had once lived here. Been a part of a life so foreign to him that he held no true understanding of it. Yet if he truly were a member of the duke's family, then that family had been taken from him.

And he was determined to get them back.

Boldly, he marched to the front door, using the knocker to rap. Timmons joined him, standing slightly behind him and to the side. He took a breath and held it as the door swung open.

"Good after..." The footman froze, mid-sentence. His eyes widened as he looked at James, his jaw slack.

"I would like to see the Duke of Seaton. His Grace," he added, thinking of how Timmons always referred to Seaton.

Still, the footman merely gaped at him.

Sharp clicks sounded in the foyer as someone angrily crossed it, saying, "What is the matter with you, "Dursley? Why, you should nev—"

An older man appeared. One James recognized from many years ago. His features were familiar, but his dark hair had now turned iron-gray. Then from the recesses of his mind came a name.

"Powell? If possible, I would like to see His Grace."

The butler looked as if he had seen a ghost. "Lord James?" he said, his voice barely above a whisper. "Is it truly you?"

Timmons stepped up. "It is, Powell. We are here to see His Grace."

Tears formed in the butler's eyes. "Oh, my lord. We thought you long dead. Please. Come in."

The butler nudged the footman aside, opening the door wide, so that they were able to step into the grand foyer. James turned in a circle, seeing how lavishly it was furnished, with polished marble on the floor and paintings on the walls, along with furniture which was never sat upon against the walls. Straight in front of him was an enormous staircase.

Up those stairs might be where he found his family.

Looking to Powell, he asked, "How did you know who I was?"

Flustered, the butler took a moment to regain his composure before answering, saying, "Your eyes alone would tell the world that you are a Strong, my lord. Not all—but many of the Strongs bear the same cornflower blue eyes." Powell paused. "Beyond that? You favor His Grace quite a bit, though you are taller in stature and broader than he ever was."

"It is the physical labor I have performed all my life," he said.

The butler winced. "I will not ask where you have been, my lord. That is not for servants' ears."

James glanced about and saw beyond the original footman who had opened the door another footman, three maids, and what appeared to be the housekeeper had arrived in the foyer, all of them eyeing him in wonder.

"Mrs. Powell," he greeted, recalling that the butler's wife supervised the servants in the household.

She bobbed a curtsey. "Lord James. It is good to see you again."

"It is good to be here. I think. Might I see His Grace? Or has the family gone to the country since the Season is now over."

He knew what the Season was and even recalled coming to town each spring for it. Usually, his family departed for the country after it ended. Since it was late September, he assumed they had already returned to Shadowcrest. He suddenly knew the name of the estate, but he couldn't remember where it was located.

"Might we speak in His Grace's study, my lord?" Powell asked.

"Of course. Timmons?"

The tutor accompanied them to the room, one in which James knew he hadn't come too often. If at all.

Once the door was closed, the butler said, "His Grace suffered an attack of apoplexy three years ago, my lord. It was near the end of the Season, three Augusts ago. Since then, the family has remained in town, to be near the doctor. Dr. Nickels comes and looks in on His

Grace each morning."

"How is his health now?" asked James, familiar with how serious apoplexy could be.

A shadow darkened Powell's face. "His Grace is bedridden, my lord. Paralysis has set in on his left side. His speech is impaired. He speaks very little and even then, it is quite hard to understand him. Sutton has had the patience of Job as he has cared for your father."

The name Sutton meant nothing to him, and he assumed it to be a servant, most likely the duke's valet.

"There is no hope of recovery?" he asked.

"None, my lord. Still, Dr. Nickels calls each day. Her Grace sits with His Grace and reads to him." Powell hesitated.

"Go on. I should hear it all," he insisted.

"Your uncle took it upon himself to move here. He has brought all his children."

Theo . . .

The name of his tormentor came to him like a bolt of lightning.

"I knew of two. My cousins Theodore and Caleb. No, wait. There were others. Twins?"

"Yes, my lord. Miss Allegra and Miss Lyric. They were born on the same day as Lady Philippa and Lady Georgina. Do you recall them?"

"Barely," he admitted.

"Three of your four cousins, along with Mr. Strong, now live here." Powell blinked. "My goodness gracious. You have other sisters, too. Half-sisters born after the twins."

James' head was spinning. "Who?"

"Lady Mirella is a year younger than the twins. Lady Euphemia is the youngest of the girls and two years younger than Lady Mirella."

He couldn't help but feel a small sense of satisfaction, hearing that his father had sired four girls and no more sons. Then it struck him.

It meant that one day *he* would become the Duke of Seaton.

James grew dizzy at the thought and closed his eyes.

"I know it is quite a lot to take in, my lord," Powell apologized.

"No," he said, opening his eyes. "It is good for me to learn of these siblings. Half-siblings, that is. But I am able to see my father?"

"He has no visitors, other than Her Grace and Dr. Nickels."

"None of his daughters visit? What about Uncle Adolphus?"

The butler's eyes narrowed. "Mr. Strong *never* visits His Grace."

Powell's tone alone spoke volumes.

"I would like to see His Grace," he insisted.

The butler considered the request. "I believe it best if you spoke with Her Grace first. She could discuss His Grace's condition with you in greater detail. Then, I'm sure she would be happy for you to visit with him."

Powell looked to Timmons. "I think it best if you stay here, Mr. Timmons, while Lord James has a private audience with Her Grace."

"Might I go to the kitchen for something to eat?" Timmons asked. He looked to James. "I promise it is only for a bite to eat."

He understood that Timmons did not wish to be left alone in this room, with the decanters of liquor sitting on a sideboard near the window.

"Yes, please see that Mr. Timmons is taken care of while I talk with Her Grace."

"Very good, my lord. Mr. Timmons, do you recall where the kitchens are?"

"I do, Mr. Powell." The former tutor looked to James. "Summon me when you have need of me, my lord."

The three men left the study, and the butler led James up the wide staircase and down a long corridor filled with objets d'art and paintings on the wall. They entered a drawing room which was possibly as long as the deck of *Vesta*, and a memory came to him of being here, with the room filled with people.

"Make yourself at home, my lord. I will have Her Grace join you. Would you like me to send for tea?"

"Yes," he said, thinking it would give himself something to do with his hands, holding a teacup, because right now, he felt big and awkward and not someone who belonged within these walls.

Powell excused himself, and James wandered about the drawing room, examining the furniture and knickknacks and studying the paintings on the walls.

Then he sensed the air change and looked to his left, seeing a woman approaching him, disbelief in her eyes. She was a decade or so older than he was, with a trim figure and abundant blond hair the color of dark molasses. Their gazes met and she stopped in her tracks. James moved toward her, close enough that she reached out and took his hands in hers.

"James. It is you," she said, clearly amazed.

"I have returned from the dead," he quipped.

"Thank God you are here," she said, her hands tightening on his, distress on her lovely features.

"What is wrong, Your Grace?"

With vehemence in her eyes and tone, the duchess said, "Adolphus Strong is bleeding this family dry—and you are the only one who can stop him."

Chapter Seven

James heard the anger in her words and could even see it shimmering from her. While his gut told him that had never liked her, he realized the boy he had been had never given this woman a chance.

"Come and sit, Your Grace. You can tell me what you mean."

They went to a nearby settee, and he sat next to her, facing her.

"Oh, I am making such a mess of this, James." She smiled at him through watery eyes. Cocking her head, she studied him a moment. "I am very sorry that we did not get along all those years ago."

"I should be the one apologizing to you," he said. "I was a boy who had lost his mother and was angry at the world. It didn't help when my father brought home a new wife, who immediately became with child. Even though the twins were girls, I felt I was being pushed aside. Replaced in my father's heart."

He paused. "Not that I ever was in Seaton's heart. I don't recall much of what went on back then, but I do know you tried to be kind to me. That I was quite prickly and pushed you away."

She nodded. "You did. But I was young, too, barely eight and ten when I entered this household, merely a decade older than you. I was an only child and had no experience around other children. I desperately wanted you to like me. Even love me. And I wanted to love you. Seaton had told me that he needed me to be a mother to you." She smiled ruefully. "I am afraid I tried a bit too hard. In looking back, I should not have forced my affections upon you as I did."

The duchess hesitated a moment, and then she asked, "What happened to you, James? Where have you been all these years? Here you have returned after so long a time, and I am dumping my troubles upon you."

"We can save that story for a later discussion. I want to know what you meant when you said Uncle Adolphus is bleeding the family dry. I have only vague impressions of him."

She sighed. "I have no proof of anything. I must be frank about that. It is only instinct that is telling me he does so."

Twisting her hands in her lap, she said, "We came to town for the Season as we always do. It was the usual swirl of social events for several months. Leading up to it, I saw nothing out of place. Seaton was his usual self. And then he collapsed just as we were leaving for the last ball."

Tears swam in her eyes. Instinctively, James reached for her hand, which was cold to the touch. She looked at him gratefully before continuing.

"Doctor Nickels told us that Seaton had suffered an attack of apoplexy."

He had witnessed three different sailors struck by it. Two of those seamen died the same day. The other lay in a bunk, paralyzed, wasting away.

"He was never the same after that night. Seaton has been confined to his bed ever since. The left side of his body is frozen. Paralyzed, what Dr. Nickels calls it. His speech is impaired, James. He can speak, but it is very difficult to understand what he says. He used to resort to writing what he wished to communicate since his dominant hand was not affected by the episode. Lately, though, he has become too weak to even do that."

"Does he understand what goes on around him?"

The duchess nodded. "I believe he did up until a couple of months ago. He is going downhill rapidly, however."

"And you are saying that my uncle stepped in?" he asked, leading her to the heart of her accusation.

Her eyes narrowed. "Oh, he did more than step in. Adolphus has the tongue of a serpent. Lies pour from his lips. He says all the right things. That he wants to hold everything in trust for the dukedom. Take care of his dear brother's family by looking after the ducal properties and investments."

She pulled her hand from his and stood, beginning to pace the room.

"Adolphus immediately moved into this house, bringing with him all but one of his children. Seaton's secretary was dismissed, as was the steward at Shadowcrest. I don't worry as much about Shadowcrest, simply because he placed Caleb in charge there." She paused. "That is your cousin. Caleb is Adolphus' second son."

"What happened to me years ago colored my memory," James admitted. "It was only until this week that I began to recall things and sought to come here. I do remember Caleb, though. He was younger than I was. A sweet boy."

"Caleb is still the same. Adolphus ordered Caleb to leave university to take on the role of steward at Shadowcrest. For one so young, I believe he is doing as good as job as he can these past three years serving as Shadowcrest's steward."

A shadow crossed her face. "I wouldn't know firsthand, simply because I have remained here with Seaton and the girls. My girls are being held hostage by Adolphus. He has used them as leverage against me, so that I will do as he asks and not question him on his actions regarding this family and its wealth. He has also forbidden the girls from visiting their father, saying it would be too troubling for them to view Seaton as he now is. Frankly, I would be afraid to leave His Grace for fear I would return and find him dead." She paused. "And I would attribute his death to his brother."

Anger began to simmer within him. He recalled how Theo had bullied him and suspected the boy had done so at his father's urging.

"I assume Theo is serving as secretary for His Grace."

"Yes, he is. Adolphus replaced Seaton's secretary of many years with Theo, who is just as odious as his father. As a woman, I have no control over anything. I do know Adolphus and Theo meet with Mr. Rainn, the family solicitor, regularly. I don't trust the man, and I have *never* trusted Adolphus Strong. Theo, as well. They are far too much alike, both of them scheming, greedy men. I hear rumors of debts being run up by the both of them. Once, I overheard Adolphus railing that he should have been Seaton. Only six minutes separated his birth from his twin's. I believe that has eaten away at him all these years. With Seaton in such poor health now, Adolphus has taken over in all but title."

The duchess looked at him pleadingly. "You must bring a halt to this James. *You* are Seaton's heir. Adolphus—all of us, actually—assumed you died many years ago. When no trace was found of you, and I didn't birth any sons, Adolphus knew he would be the one to claim the title upon his brother's death. While he might not hold it for long, due to his age, he knows Theo would inherit all after him."

"None of what you say surprises me. Though my memory is spotty, I know I never much liked Uncle Adolphus or Cousin Theo. Caleb was another matter. I suppose he was too young for his father to get his hooks into him."

"Both men are vile," the duchess stated. "When Matty tried to stand up to Adolphus, he banished her to Shadowcrest."

Matty . . .

James frowned, an image of a kind-looking woman with dark hair and cornflower blue eyes coming to him.

"Matty," he repeated.

"Yes," Her Grace said. "Your aunt Mathilda. She always had a great fondness for you and truly mothered you after you lost your own mother. Matty never wed and was a part of this household until Adolphus grew tired of her challenging him and the changes he was making, both in this household and the business. I have wanted to visit her at Shadowcrest, but as I said, I am loath to leave His Grace and my girls. Even Adolphus' girls."

She startled. "You don't know about your other sisters. I gave birth to two more babes after you vanished."

"Yes, Powell told me of the new additions in my absence."

She returned to the settee, taking a seat, and said, "You are Seaton's heir apparent, James. You are the one who should be making these decisions, not Adolphus and Theo."

"I will do anything that you ask. What do you want from me, Your Grace?"

"First and foremost, I want Adolphus and Theo out of Seaton's household. Frankly, I do not mind if his girls stay. I have come to be a mother to them over the years. Your aunt passed away birthing a child fifteen years ago. You must meet with Mr. Rainn, as well, and though I do not wish to tell you what to do, I would find a new solicitor. I think Mr. Rainn has helped in draining funds from the family, especially those coming from Strong Shipping. Adolphus also replaced the head of the company, and I believe a good deal of the profits are going directly in your uncle's pockets, thanks to Mr. Barclay."

"Strong Shipping..."

His thoughts whirled as panic flooded him. More of that day coming back to him, hitting him full force.

"James? You've gone white as a ghost."

He looked at her. "More memories surfacing, Your Grace."

She patted his hand. "I asked you long ago to call me Mama, and I understand now why you were not able to do so. I do not want formality to stand between us, however. If you cannot call me Stepmama, would you consider addressing me as Dinah?"

"I do recall how much I loved my mother, and I would like to reserve that address for her alone. I am happy to call you Dinah, however." He smiled. "Especially since you aren't that much older than I am."

"I have been remiss. Much too casual in referring to you as James, my lord. I should be addressing you by your title. Do you recall that you are the Marquess of Alinwood?"

He shook his head slowly. "No, that doesn't sound familiar to me at all."

"The son of a duke is usually addressed when he is young by his first name. The servants would have called you Lord James upon occasion and mostly my lord in everyday speech. You were about to head off to school, though, and the tutors there would have called you by your title."

Shaking his head, he said, "This world all seems so foreign to me, Dinah. The fact that you keep referring to your husband as Seaton surprises me, especially since you have been wed to him for so long."

The duchess looked blankly at him. "I know of no woman in Polite Society who calls her husband by his given name. Among the *ton*, a wife always refers to her husband by his title. Then again, I have heard of infrequent occasions. Women who do use their husband's first name. Those are the rare love matches among the *ton*.

"You have much to learn, James. If you will allow it, I will guide you through your new role. For now, I am certain you wish to see your father."

Uneasiness filled him at the idea, but he knew he must see Papa in the flesh.

"Would it be convenient for us to go to him now?"

"Of course. I was reading to him when Powell came to tell me you were here. Frankly, I thought him mad." She smiled. "Oh, James, I am so glad that you have come home. You will sort out this whole mess, and I know you will—when you assume the title—lead this family with honor."

They stood and as they moved toward the drawing room doors, those very doors were flung open. The man who barreled through them had a familiar look about him, as did the younger version of him who followed.

"What is the meaning of this?" his uncle demanded, striding across the room to confront them.

Adolphus stopped and stared at James. Color flushed his face. "Imposter! Pretending to be my poor dead nephew."

Cousin Theo joined them, looking at James condescendingly. "You think you can profess to be my beloved cousin, showing up and trying to steal a title and this family's wealth? Get out!"

James knew who he was now. Generations of good breeding took over.

Holding his temper, he calmly said, "I was never a beloved cousin to you, Theo. You bullied me unmercifully throughout my childhood, egged on by your father."

Theo's jaw dropped.

He turned to his uncle. "As for you, Uncle Adolphus? You are—and never will be—the head of this family. The Duke of Seaton, *my* father, holds that role. And I, the Marquess of Alinwood, will succeed him upon his death."

His uncle, his face still flushed with rage, shook his fist. "I will not allow you to come in and tear this family asunder."

"No, that is what you have done, Uncle. And it shall cease at once."

Adolphus' eyes cut to Dinah. "I see Her Grace has poisoned you with her lies. I should have exiled *you* to Shadowcrest, along with that harpy Mathilda. Neither of you can be trusted."

"No one will be banished except you, Uncle," James said firmly. "You, as well, Theo. You are relieved of your duties as Seaton's secretary. Both of you are to pack your things and leave this house immediately."

"I won't do it!" Adolphus proclaimed. "You are not Alinwood. You are a fraud."

"How can you say that, you greedy fool?" Dinah demanded. "Why, Alinwood favors his father to the extreme, even down to the Strong eyes. I am certain he still bears the birthmark on his shoulder. Would seeing it be proof enough to you?"

James did have a mark on his left shoulder, simply another confirmation that he was a Strong.

Dinah turned to him. "Your father has the same crescent moon on his left shoulder. Show them, my lord. Show them now—so that they will leave this house forever."

He stripped away his captain's jacket, one he had brushed to a fine sheen. Not only for his meeting with Mrs. Grant but in anticipation of meeting his family once again. After removing it, he held it out to the duchess, and she accepted it. He slowly untied his cravat, his gaze locked upon his uncle. Pulling the cravat from his neck, he handed it to Dinah, as well.

Finally, he unbuttoned and untied his shirt, pulling it over his head, now bare to the waist as he balled the shirt into his hand.

Closing the gap between him and Adolphus Strong, he presented his shoulder.

"See, Uncle? You should have no question now as to whether or not I am James Strong, Marquess of Alinwood."

"They could have schemed about this together, Father," Theo protested. "They were alone when we reached the drawing room. For all we know, this imposter is the duchess' lover."

He shook his head. "You are grasping at straws, Theo. This golden goose you latched onto will lay no more of her eggs for you and your father. You are to leave the Duke of Seaton's residence, or you will be thrown out."

"I will bring in solicitors," Adolphus said. "And the courts. You will not get away with this."

"The girls will remain here," Dinah said firmly. "They will be under His Grace's protection."

Adolphus snorted. "What good are females anyway? *You* should know that, Your Grace," he said snidely, smiling as she flinched. "Come, Theodore."

"We are leaving, Father? How can you give into this rogue?"

"He is doing so because he knows it is a lost cause," James told his cousin. "Get out—and never darken this household again."

Theo glared at him, but James glared right back, winning the contest as his cousin turned away and took his father's arm.

"Come. We have no need of them, Father."

"I should have been the duke," Adolphus growled. "Six measly minutes separated. Six!"

"Your days of pretending to be Seaton are over," James said. "Neither you nor your son shall ever be the Duke of Seaton."

Adolphus scowled at him. "You will never make for a duke. I will tell Polite Society—"

"You will tell them nothing," the duchess said, glowering at her brother-in-law. "You have had an easy life for three years, Adolphus. Take your ill-gotten gains and be off. You no longer are the heir apparent to the dukedom. You have no power in Polite Society." She paused, looking to James. "Seeing my stepson here, I would venture he would not be pleased to hear you gossiping about him or this family."

"You are *threatening* me?" Adolphus growled.

James stepped in. "Her Grace is merely warning you to walk the straight and narrow path from now on, Uncle. If you don't? I shall be the one you face." He cracked his knuckles and flexed his fingers. "These hands have done things to men that you do not wish to ever know."

He watched as fear replaced the anger and pride in Adolphus Strong's face.

"Either walk away on your own, or I shall throw you out myself. And I wouldn't be above breaking bones to do so."

Theo, who was not physically imposing, clutched his father's elbow and pulled him from the drawing room.

"You were magnificent!" Dinah cried, as the door closed.

"I will look into matters with this untrustworthy solicitor. I will do the same at Strong Shipping. If I detect any unusual activity, I will replace Mr. Rainn and Mr. Barclay. For now, though, I believe it is time to visit my father."

Dinah led them from the drawing room and down the long corridor. She stopped at a door.

"This is not my father's rooms," James protested.

Disgust filled her face. "They have been these past three years. Adolphus insisted that his brother be moved to a smaller room. He said the more cozy atmosphere would be good for His Grace's recovery."

Understanding filled him. "And he took the rooms belonging to the duke."

"You see how things have been. I am grateful you are here to protect your father and your family now."

She opened the door, and James followed her inside.

Chapter Eight

James saw the bedchamber was a typical size. His eyes were drawn immediately to the man in the bed.

Slowly, he moved forward, noticing a servant sitting at the duke's bedside. James did not recognize the man, who looked to be thirty at the most.

His attention returned to his sleeping father, and pity filled him.

The mighty Duke of Seaton was but a shell of his former self. Or at least what James remembered of him. He had not spent much time in his father's company, but he did recall how tall and healthy the duke had once been, a larger than life figure.

The man lying in this bed was now a shadow of the memory James held. His hair had turned snow white, similar to his twin's hair, but that was where the resemblance ended. Seaton must weigh a good four stone less than when James had last seen his father. His face was lined, his broad chest now sunken.

His eyes cut to the servant, whom he assumed to be the duke's valet.

"I am Alinwood," he said for the first time, the title sounding odd coming from his lips. "I am His Grace's son."

The servant had risen and now bowed, but he did not wear the air of befuddlement the other staff members had when James had first entered the townhouse.

"I am Sutton, my lord. Valet to His Grace."

Dinah joined James and said, "Sutton has been invaluable to us, my lord. His uncle was His Grace's previous valet, but the job of caring for an invalid proved to be too much for him at his age. He was pensioned off and suggested his sister's boy for the position." She smiled gratefully. "That is how Sutton came to be with us."

James knew the youth and strength of this servant had been put to the test in caring for Seaton, and he said, "I am grateful for your service to my father, Sutton."

Genially, the valet said, "I'm happy to be of service to His Grace. He can be a bit prickly at times, but we get along well enough."

He recalled what a temper his father possessed and how servants had cowered, especially when the duke flew into a rage. It must be frustrating now to be bedridden and have his speech impaired.

"Sutton has been a saint," the duchess declared. "We could not have done without him." Looking to the valet, she added, "Why don't you give us a few minutes alone with His Grace?"

"Yes, Your Grace," Sutton said, leaving the room.

James pulled up a chair, offering it to Dinah, but she said, "No, you take it. This is his good side. He will want you to be close and on this side of him when he awakens. If you hold his right hand, he will be able to feel that. From what he has managed to tell us, touch on his left side is invisible to him."

Taking a seat, James hesitated a moment, wondering if he should take his father's hand while he still slept.

Dinah said, "Be patient when he speaks. As I mentioned, Seaton is quite hard to understand. Naturally, he becomes frustrated when he is unable to communicate his thoughts to us."

"I will keep that in mind," he said, placing his hand atop his father's.

James did not recall ever touching the duke previously. Seaton had not shown any physical signs of affection toward him. He could recall no hugs or kisses.

His touch caused the duke to stir. James only wished he could send some of his warmth into his father because the duke's hand was ice-cold.

Seaton's eyelids fluttered several times and then opened fully. He glanced down at their joined hands, and then his gaze moved to meet James'. He saw the eyes widen in disbelief.

"Ame? Ame?" the duke repeated urgently.

"Yes, Papa. It is James. I have come home."

A tear trickled down the duke's right cheek, and he said something which James did not understand. Those he didn't comprehend the words, he understood the emotion behind them because he, too, was feeling things he had never experienced before. So much had been locked within him, and as the minutes passed, more memories were flooding him.

Finally, his father ceased the gibberish and simply looked at his son. Then he asked, "Ere oo go?"

"I have been away at sea, Papa. Not of my own choice."

He decided to present a sterile version of his story because this old man did not need to be burdened further by more than what he already carried.

"When I was returning from *Zephyr* that day, a sailor caught me. Apparently, it was a common practice to take boys off the street and make them into cabin boys on a ship. I was brought to the ship against my will and locked in the brig until we had sailed from England."

More tears came streaming down the duke's cheek, and James noticed they were only from the right side. The left part of the duke's face was frozen in a garish expression, and James assumed this was part of the lasting results of the apoplexy attack.

"Why so long?" the duke managed to clearly say.

"I suffered a head injury, Papa. It caused my memory to be fuzzy. Also, I was frightened. Taken from all that I had known, with no one believing who I was. That first voyage was almost two years long. By its end, I had no recollection of my previous life as a Strong. I did what I had to do to survive in a new world."

James felt Dinah's hand on his shoulder, and she squeezed it in a show of support.

"I am sorry you are ill now, Papa," he continued. "But I am here. I will act on your behalf. Speak as you wish others to know. I understand Uncle Adolphus and Cousin Theo have taken control of the family and our finances.

"That stops now."

"Ood," the duke said, looking satisfied.

Dinah stepped to the other side of the bed and said, "They never visited him a single time. You will be pleased to know, Seaton, that James has tossed the pair from your house. I want James to meet with Mr. Rainn and hopefully, he will sever that business tie for good and find a new solicitor."

The duke nodded, his head at an odd angle.

"Eventually, I will need to go to Shadowcrest," the duchess told her husband. "James, as well. Caleb has been made steward there. He writes me monthly to let me know about the estate. So far, I believe all his transactions to be honest ones though it wouldn't hurt for James to examine those ledgers, as well. I also want James to go to Strong Shipping because Adolphus installed one of his own men as head of the company. My intuition tells me that he has been siphoning profits from the company these last three years."

She smoothed her husband's hair. "I hadn't wanted to trouble you with any of this, Seaton. Now that James is back, though, he will deal with any wrongdoing."

The duke mustered half a smile and bestowed it upon his wife. "Ood," he said. "Tired . . ."

James squeezed his father's fingers. "Rest, Papa."

He stepped away from the bed, and Dinah suggested they return to the drawing room. Sutton, who lingered outside the bedchamber door, returned to the duke's side.

On their way there, they encountered Powell.

"Have everything of both Mr. Strongs packed and delivered to whatever hole they crawled from before they arrived here."

The butler's lips twitched in amusement. "Certainly, my lord. Packing will commence immediately."

"I also need you to send two footmen with messages. One to Mr. Rainn's office. The other to Mr. Barclay at Strong Shipping. Both men are to come here at once. Not at their earliest convenience. Now," he said firmly.

Powell nodded, and James saw respect in the servant's eyes.

"At once, my lord."

Once in the drawing room, she praised him. "Thank you for taking charge of the situation, James. The sooner we remove anyone with a connection to Adolphus, the better."

"I hope the men I have summoned will be here within the hour. In the meantime? I believe I should meet the rest of my family."

His stepmother smiled. "I think that is a wonderful idea." She looked to the grandfather clock, which stood nearby. "The girls will be coming to tea here in the next few minutes. It will be the perfect opportunity to introduce them to you."

She rang and when a servant appeared, James saw it was the housekeeper again.

"I could not do without Mrs. Powell," Dinah informed him. "She is my jewel."

The housekeeper flushed at the compliment. "Shall I make up a room for you, Lord Alinwood?"

He had not thought about staying at the townhouse but decided it would be a good idea.

"Yes, Mrs. Powell. Please do so. I may not spend every night under this roof because I still have business matters to attend to, but it will be nice to have a place to come home to and a bedchamber to call my own."

"His lordship will be staying for tea with the girls, Mrs. Powell."

"I will make certain that Cook knows," the housekeeper said. She looked to James and said, "It is ever so good to have you home again, my lord."

"What do you think all the girls will make of me?" he asked.

"They will be very accepting," the duchess assured him. "You mentioned business affairs to settle?"

"Yes, I am the captain of a ship. Ironically, it belongs to one of our competitors. Neptune Shipping Lines."

Dinah's eyes widened. "Oh, have you met her? The woman who now runs a shipping empire? Mrs. Grant?"

"You know of her?" he asked, clearly confused as to why a duchess would know of Mrs. Grant.

"Mrs. Grant is the talk of the *ton*. Her father is Viscount Galpin. Rumor has it that between his gambling and poor investments, Lord Galpin literally sold his daughter in marriage to the owner of Neptune Shipping. That was scandalous enough, but Josiah Grant then took it upon himself to teach his new young wife all about his business. To think, a viscount's daughter going to an office every day. It is said she knows all aspects of the business, even more so than her husband ever did. And now she is a widow and has inherited the entire company and runs it herself? Tongues have wagged in regard to Mrs. Grant and her situation."

James had had no idea that Mrs. Grant came from the *ton*. Pity filled him at hearing she had been sacrificed to pay for her father's mistakes. Then again, she had come out quite wealthy, inheriting a huge shipping empire and now running it.

"I suppose she does not mix in Polite Society?" he asked.

"Never. Josiah Grant was a common man who worked his way up, investing wisely. The *ton* is fascinated and yet repelled at the same time by her."

"I have met her and can assure you that she is a lovely, gracious woman. One whom I admire very much. It would take someone quite special—male or female—to commit and learn all about a business at such a tender age. Having come from the *ton* and having had no experience in the business world, Mrs. Grant has accomplished things no man or woman could have done. She is intelligent. Beautiful. And most capable."

"It sounds that you admire her a great deal," Dinah mused.

"I most certainly do. And my allegiance for the immediate present must be to her. I cannot leave her in the lurch even if she owns a company which competes with our family's. I need to see to the repairs to *Vesta*. We came through two nasty storms, as well as suffering a lightning strike. We hobbled into port, though, and as captain I must see *Vesta* in tip-top shape, restored to her former glory, so that a new captain may take her helm."

"How long will you be away doing this?" she asked, clearly concerned by his upcoming absence.

"I am committing now to the family. But I must sail *Vesta* to Greenwich and stay a few days as the repairs begin. I will also need to return her to London once she is seaworthy again."

Worry creased her brow. "How long might that be, James? You have so many obligations here. Especially now that you have rid of us Adolphus and Theo."

"I will make things right before I leave for Greenwich," he promised. "I will stay there a couple of days and then come back to meet my obligations in London. I may have to leave one final time to sail *Vesta* back to the London docks."

James knew he actually didn't have to bring *Vesta* home himself, but he realized his life at sea had now ended. Responsibilities to his family and his father's holdings would keep him in London as he cleaned up the mess his uncle and cousin had created. He also knew he must get everything in good order because he was to be the new Duke of Seaton one day.

Selfishly, though, he wanted to sail the restored *Vesta* one last time before he gave up the sea.

"My first allegiance will always be to the Strong family," he told Dinah. "But I must finish my current commitments and close that chapter of my sea life."

"I understand," she said. "I know we are taking you away from something which you obviously love, James. For that, I am sorry."

"No, don't be, Dinah. For years, I longed to have a family and never thought it would be possible. And now that I have one? I will never give it up."

The door opened and in spilled half a dozen young ladies, chatting happily. As they moved across the room, he and Dinah came to their feet. The motion alerted the girls to the presence of a guest, and they all fell silent as they lined up in front of him.

"Girls, I would like to introduce you to Lord Alinwood. James has been found and is now home for good."

Five of the six looked thunderstruck, but one of them, long and lean, with dark brown hair and the Strong eyes, threw herself at him.

"James!" she cried, hugging him tightly.

He returned the embrace, and then she pulled away. "You gave me my name," she said, smiling brightly.

"Then you are Pippa," he surmised. "I tried to teach you to say Philippa, but you never could. All that came out was *Pippa*."

He glanced to the remaining five, his eyes resting on the one who most resembled Pippa. "You are Georgina. Georgie."

The young woman curtseyed to him. "I am, my lord."

"He's *family*, Georgie," Pippa said impatiently. "You don't have to curtsey." She glanced to him. "Does she?"

He laughed. "You haven't changed a bit, Pippa. You were always spontaneous and had a zest for life." Glancing to Georgina, he said,

"You were thoughtful and deliberate."

Georgina smiled. "Then I have not changed either. Pippa is the impulsive one. And a tomboy. When we are at Shadowcrest, she runs about in trousers."

"Well, they are comfortable," Pippa said. "And we haven't been to Shadowcrest in forever. I want to go, James. And you must come see it."

"We will, Pippa. Why don't you and Georgina introduce me to everyone else?"

Georgina took the hand of the only auburn-haired of the six and pulled her forward, saying, "This is your half-sister, Mirella. Pippa and I are ten and eight now, and we will make our come-out next year. Mirella will be ten and seven soon. I think we should all do our come-out Season together."

He had no idea what a come-out involved and merely nodded pleasantly as the girl curtseyed to him. "It is nice to meet you, Mirella. You have the Strong eyes, but I don't recall knowing anyone with red hair."

"It comes from my grandmother. Mama's mother," Mirella explained.

He couldn't remember meeting either of Dinah's parents, and said, "Who is my other sister? There'll be no halves. We are all Strongs—and we will always stand strong together."

Pippa caught the hand of the tallest of the bunch and brought her to him. "James, this is Euphemia, but no one calls her that. She is Effie to everyone. I don't even think I could spell Euphemia if I were pressed to do so."

Effie curtseyed. "It is nice to meet you, my lord. And if you are wondering, my blond hair came from His Grace's mother. But I do have the Strong eyes."

"Effie is a tomboy like I am," Pippa said proudly. I taught her to ride and fish, and she is constantly bringing home strays when we are in the country."

"I have never been around animals," he said. "I have spent my life at sea. Perhaps you can introduce me to some of these animals, Effie." He looked to Mirella. "Do you also have a fondness for animals?"

"I love to dance and sing, my lord. I play the pianoforte and also enjoy painting."

"I would never wear trousers," Effie told him. "I leave that to Mirella and Pippa. But you must say hello to your cousins, my lord."

The remaining two stood side by side and closely resembled one another. One was slightly taller than the other, but neither was as tall as his four siblings.

Both young women stepped toward him and curtseyed at the same time.

"I am Allegra," the taller one said, her hair sable-colored, which made her Strong eyes stand out. "This is Lyric, my twin."

Lyric's hair was a few shades lighter than Allegra's, more of a deep brown. She smiled shyly at him. "It is good to meet you, my lord."

"All of you must call me James," he insisted.

Dinah touched his sleeve. "While it is acceptable for your sisters to do so in private, my girls will refer to you as Alinwood when others are present. As for Allegra and Lyric, they should always call you Alinwood, my lord."

Her tone told him this was the first of many lessons he must learn in order to fit into his new world.

"I see."

"And one day, when you claim the dukedom, we will all refer to you as Seaton."

James didn't like that at all, but he would address that matter when the time came.

"Why were you at sea, James?" asked Mirella.

He decided to present a filtered version of events, purged of the horrors, just as he had done so with his father. These girls did not need to be exposed to the evil in the world.

"Ah, I see the teacart being rolled in. Shall we sit and chat over tea?"

As they all moved to seats, Pippa said quietly, "Tell as much as you can. It must be ugly, else you wouldn't have been gone for so long."

Once they all had tea and had placed refreshments on their plates, he told a version of his history that filled in a few blanks for them and yet left much unspoken. Pippa asked the most questions, her interest in geography obvious, but each of the girls took turns speaking up.

After tea had concluded, Dinah sent them all away, saying she had to speak to him in private. She did ask Lyric and Allegra to remain behind briefly.

"I need to tell you that your father and Theo have left the house," the duchess explained. "I requested that the two of you remain here under my watchful eye and the protection of His Grace and Lord Alinwood."

Lyric looked relieved, while Allegra said, "Thank you, Aunt Dinah. Then again, I suppose he didn't really want us, did he?"

Her words were telling, letting James know these two had been at the least, overlooked, and at the worst, neglected, by Adolphus Strong.

"You are wanted here," Dinah assured the twins.

"Aunt Dinah has always been like a mother to us," Lyric told James. "Mama died on Christmas Day many years ago. Having a baby killed her. Papa never seemed much interested in us. Allegra will tell you as much."

"You are Strongs," he said. "Cousins to me and my sisters. You will always be welcome in this household."

"Thank you, my lord," Lyric said. "But we don't expect you to help us make our come-out, do we, Allegra?"

"No," the other twin said firmly. "If we do so, Papa must pay for that. Not you."

He still didn't understand what the term meant and would ask

Dinah. He gave the young ladies a reassuring smile.

"Come to me if there is anything you need. Things can go on as they have before I arrived. Her Grace will watch over you and see you have everything that you need."

"Thank you, my lord," the twins echoed.

"You may go now," Dinah said, and Allegra and Lyric vacated the drawing room.

"My uncle has never been much of a father to them, has he?"

"No," the duchess said. "And they were barely walking when they lost their mother. I have tried my best over the years to shower them with affection because they received none at home." She sighed. "The only good thing about Adolphus moving his children here was that I have been able to spend more time with Lyric and Allegra."

"Unusual names."

"Their mother was quite talented. She played the pianoforte. Their names come from music."

A knock sounded, and Powell entered. "My lord, Mr. Rainn and Mr. Barclay have arrived. I placed one in the parlor and the other in the library. I thought it best to keep them apart—and waiting."

"You displayed good sense, Powell," James praised. "I shall visit with Mr. Rainn first."

As the butler led James to the parlor, he felt the weight of his entire family resting upon his shoulders.

Chapter Nine

Sophie paced the parlor, awaiting Captain Jones' arrival. Mr. Barnes had arrived earlier today with a letter from Mr. Purdy. The shipyard owner was happy to accommodate her request for repairs to *Vesta*, as she had anticipated, and said to bring the ship as soon as possible.

The door opened, and Millie rolled in the teacart.

"The raisin scones are piping hot," the maid informed Sophie. "And Cook did those little sandwiches you like, Mrs. Grant."

"Thank you, Millie."

The maid left, and Sophie heard the clock chiming in the foyer. At the same time, a knock sounded on the door, and she knew Captain Jones had arrived. She took a deep breath, expelling it slowly, wanting to appear calm when her guest entered the parlor.

Moments later, Millie entered the room again. "Captain Jones is here, Mrs. Grant."

"Please send him in."

She steeled herself as her guest sailed through the doors, causing her heart to hammer against her ribs. A rush spread through her as he made his way toward her. Rising, Sophie inclined her head, hoping he wouldn't offer his hand. She feared she might faint at his touch.

"Good afternoon, Mrs. Grant," he rumbled, his deep voice low.

"And the same to you, Captain. Won't you please have a seat?"

"I can go directly to the docks after we finish here, Mrs. Grant. I will let him and the others know when *Vesta* sails. Are you still interested in traveling to Greenwich aboard the ship?"

"Yes, Captain. Will you have time to see the new ship being built?"

He hesitated a moment. "Yes, Mrs. Grant. I would very much enjoy seeing the plans and the progress which has been made."

"Have you given any more consideration to the offer to become its captain?"

"No, ma'am. I have not."

His answer disappointed her. "Once you see the plans, I hope to sway you, Captain."

He didn't reply, merely biting into his scone. Captain Jones was a cautious one. Or perhaps a man interested in money. While Neptune Shipping paid their captains handsomely, this man was due more, thanks to his leadership in trying circumstances.

"Did you pick up your own pay yet?" she asked. "If you have, I wish to tell you that you will be receiving a bonus."

"A bonus? Whatever for? I sold all of what we took on the voyage, and I brought back what I was supposed to."

She shook her head. "My dear Captain, did it ever occur to you that not many men in your position could say the same? You have already quelled a mutiny and brought goods back from that voyage. This time out, you suffered natural disasters—and still accomplished your mission. I think a handsome bonus is in order. You should receive some kind of reward."

"Not for doing my job," he said flatly. "I did what Mr. Grant hired me to do. I will accept nothing extra, Mrs. Grant."

This was a proud man. She wouldn't press him further. He might be deserving of a reward, but she believed if she gave it to him, he would keep nothing for himself and merely distribute it to his crew members.

Setting down his saucer, he said, "If we have nothing further to discuss, Mrs. Grant, then I will be on my way."

He rose, and she did the same, flummoxed at his quick departure and not knowing how to broach the very delicate subject she wished to discuss with him.

"I will see you on *Vesta* the day after tomorrow," he told her. "We should leave no later than seven o'clock that morning."

"Then I shall be there at six," she said. "Thank you for coming to tea, Captain."

"Thank you for serving sugar and cream in it, Mrs. Grant," he said, the corners of his mouth turning up slightly.

"Perhaps we shall try two lumps the next time," she said pertly. "Good afternoon, Captain."

"Good afternoon, Mrs. Grant."

Sophie watched him leave and then took her seat again, thinking over the last half-hour.

He had seemed different. While he had appeared to be quite self-assured in their previous encounters, this afternoon he radiated confidence. She wondered if it had anything to do with his family. Her curiosity about them—and him—was overwhelming.

She hoped that she would get some answers from the enigmatic Captain Jones when they met again.

And more than answers, she wanted a kiss from him. Several kisses, which she was determined would lead to coupling with him. Something told her if she didn't do so soon with Captain Jones, the opportunity would be lost forever.

⸻

JAMES LEFT MRS. Grant's house and hailed a hansom cab to take him to Strong Shipping. Though Dinah had put Seaton's carriage at his disposal, he had not wanted to show up in it when he visited the pretty widow. He had not informed Mrs. Grant that he was a marquess, much less told her he would not be able to captain her new vessel. He should have done so. But if he had, it would have meant an end to their acquaintance.

And he wasn't ready to take that step just yet.

The last twenty-four hours had been full of revelations. Before he met with Mr. Rainn, the duke's solicitor, he had Powell send for Drake, asking his friend to bring four trusted sailors with him. His first mate had already done as Mrs. Grant asked and hired on half a dozen men to help sail *Vesta* to Greenwich for repairs.

James had spent half an hour with the solicitor, who grew increasingly anxious at the questions he was asked. Finally, Rainn admitted that Mr. Adolphus Grant had paid him a handsome sum to alter the Duke of Seaton's will. By claiming the title and becoming the new duke, Adolphus would have control of Strong Shipping, as well as all entailed and unentailed estates. Yet his greedy uncle had also made certain that the will stripped Dinah and her four daughters of all protection and funds owed to them in her marriage settlements. That would have forced the women onto the streets.

Threatening the solicitor with a long prison sentence for his complicity in the schemes, Rainn had agreed to destroy the copies of the altered will and hand over all documents he had created over the last two decades for Seaton. James forced Rainn to write out a confession of the intended fraud, naming both Adolphus and Theo as the men who had instructed him to perpetuate it.

By then, Drake had arrived. James had his friend and two of the sailors accompany Rainn to his offices, where Drake collected everything related to the Duke of Seaton, including the original will. A lone clerk who was still in the office was told that Mr. Rainn was retiring immediately, due to health concerns, and the clerk was given instructions to contact all clients and close up the office. Drake had taken it upon himself to ask the clerk of reliable solicitors, and he had been given three names. When pressed, the clerk had chosen the best of the three, naming a Mr. Peabody.

His first mate had told the helpful clerk once the office had been shuttered and all files handed off to clients, he was to report to the Strong Shipping offices if he sought new employment. The clerk, a Mr. Handiwell, readily agreed and said he would accept any position offered at the shipping offices.

After that, Mr. Rainn was escorted to the rooms he rented, where he was told to pack his things and leave London, else charges would be filed. He did so readily, and Drake assigned the two sailors to stay the night and then put the solicitor on a mail coach early the next morning. The destination would be Mr. Rainn's choice.

While that ensued, James had then met with Mr. Barclay, who had been Adolphus' choice to head Strong Shipping. Barclay proved a harder nut to crack, but after an hour of questioning him, James made it clear that Barclay would spend the rest of his life in prison for the chicanery he had practiced while in charge of the shipping line, all at Adolphus Strong's behest. The threat of prison—and even being transported to a penal colony in Australia—finally broke Barclay. He confessed to a long list of deceptions, including altering manifests and ledgers and selling goods and not reporting those profits.

Barclay had claimed a percentage of the illegally gained profits, while the bulk of the funds had gone into Adolphus' pockets.

James seethed at hearing this, wanting to punish his uncle and cousin, but knowing how the law favored the small segment of society that Adolphus belonged to. He might not have a title, but he was the brother to a duke. That, and the wealth which he had siphoned from his bedridden brother, would insulate him from the justice James sought.

He had told Barclay to never return to the Strong Shipping offices, having two more of his sailors see Barclay home. He, too, was told to pack and then the sailors placed him on a ship bound for Baltimore the next day. James had warned Barclay never to return to England again, telling Barclay that he was a marquess and would soon be a duke—and that if he found Barclay had returned to England, he would destroy him.

James had spent this morning at his new solicitor's offices. Though he had no appointment, Mr. Peabody was more than happy to meet with the Marquess of Alinwood. James and Drake had brought all the papers which had been collected at Mr. Rainn's the previous day, and then James explained how his uncle and cousin had exploited the illness of the Duke of Seaton while James had been out of the country for several years. He didn't see the need to explain his sordid history to Peabody, and the solicitor had wisely refrained from asking too many questions.

By ten o'clock this morning, Peabody had officially been retained as the new solicitor to the Duke of Seaton and was in possession of all files and documents which contained His Grace's business affairs. James liked the solicitor, who had a sharp mind and keen wit. He told Peabody more questionable practices had occurred at Strong Shipping.

The solicitor offered to take two of his clerks and go to the office immediately, examining the ledgers and rooting out any discrepancies. James had taken Peabody up on his offer, and he and Drake had accompanied the solicitor and clerks to Strong Shipping.

Now, he returned after being gone to Mrs. Grant's, and he wondered what had been found.

Arriving at the offices, he paid his cabbie and entered. Drake had remained behind, and James had given him full authority to dismiss any employee who appeared to be attached to Adolphus and his schemes.

His friend was sitting at a desk with a clerk when James entered.

Rising, Drake said, "My lord, this is Mr. Compton. He is the only person we have retained. Everyone else is gone, including the former manager of the warehouse."

Mr. Compton, a thin man in his mid-thirties, scrambled to his feet, bowing. "My lord. I am grateful you have returned to England. Mr. Andrews informed me that you are now in charge of Strong Shipping."

"Why grateful?" he asked.

"As I have shared with Mr. Andrews—and Mr. Peabody and his clerks—Mr. Strong was exploiting his position to behave in a nefarious way."

"Compton has been very helpful, my lord," Drake told him. "He has worked at Strong Shipping for almost fifteen years. He knows how it was run before your uncle stepped in."

"I didn't want to turn a blind eye to the unscrupulous practices that were implemented," Compton said. "I kept records of the wrongdoing and have provided these to Mr. Peabody and his people."

Drake nodded in confirmation. "Mr. Peabody has found the records Mr. Compton kept to be quite helpful. It will still take several days to sort out the mess, but we are headed in the right direction."

"I like hearing that," he declared. "Would you be capable of running Strong Shipping once things are straightened out, Mr. Compton?"

The clerk looked flabbergasted. "You wish for *me* to run your family's company, my lord?"

"Are you competent enough to do so?" he asked.

Compton grew thoughtful. "I know everything that goes on here, my lord. I have experience that cannot be bought or found if you brought in someone else."

James could see the man's confidence growing as he spoke.

"While some might say that I am just a clerk, I have been involved in every facet of Strong Shipping over the years. Yes, my lord," Compton said, nodding his head. "I am capable of what you ask. And grateful for the chance to prove my worth."

"Then I will have Peabody draw up a contract," he said. "You will work closely with me, but I will give you the authority to hire new workers for the office and warehouse."

Compton now beamed. "I will not disappoint you, my lord. The bones of Strong Shipping are still here. With good leadership, we can right this ship, so to speak, and make the company something you can again be proud to own."

"Thank for agreeing to helm the wheel," James said, sticking to sea terms because they were what he knew best.

He met briefly with Peabody, telling the solicitor of his decision to retain Compton as the new head of Strong Shipping, and asking that a contract to that effect be drawn up. In return, Peabody would finish going through the records with Compton and his clerks and even lend the two clerks to Compton until he was able to hire competent help of his own.

James bid Compton farewell and told him he would be back in two weeks' time in order to see what changes the new manager had implemented.

"I won't let you down, my lord," Compton promised.

He left the offices with Drake, telling his friend, "We are to sail *Vesta* the day after tomorrow to Greenwich."

"You are still committed to doing so, my lord?"

He grimaced. "If you call me that in private one more time, Drake, I shall have to soundly thrash you. I'm sure you don't want that pretty face of yours marred. The women have always been drawn to it."

Drake grinned. "All right. James it will be when it is just the two of us," he agreed. "But you don't need to go to Greenwich. I can handle it."

"I know you can," he said evenly. "I have another reason to wish to do so."

Understanding dawned on Drake's face. "It is not about *Vesta*. It is about Mrs. Grant. You have taken to her. But you are her competitor now, James. Beyond that, you are a bloody marquess. You'll need to marry a blue-blooded woman and have little lords and ladies. After all, you'll be a duke, probably sooner than later."

"Mrs. Grant is a viscount's daughter," he revealed.

"Hmm." Drake pondered that a moment. "But she didn't marry anyone with a title, James. And she's ruined what little reputation she has by taking over for her husband and dirtying her hands, running Neptune Shipping Lines."

"There are but a handful of dukes in all of England," he said softly. "And from what little I know, dukes are a law unto themselves. Polite Society be damned."

Drake's jaw dropped. "You're going to woo Mrs. Grant, aren't you?"

"I believe I am," he said. "She doesn't know yet that I'm a duke's son. For now, it will be Captain Jones who shows his interest in her."

His friend shook his head. "Be careful, James. You are playing with fire. Something tells me that Mrs. Grant would be none too happy for you to keep from her who you truly are."

"Leave that to me, Drake," James said.

He had grown in confidence over the years, especially so after he had become captain of *Vesta*. Now that he knew his true origins, self-assurance soared.

He had no interest in wedding some young chit angling to snare a duke.

No, James Strong, Marquess of Alinwood, wanted a woman who would be a partner to him in life. One who matched him in wits and intelligence.

That woman was Mrs. Grant.

And he planned to win her heart and mind.

Chapter Ten

Sophie arrived at the London docks a few minutes before six, eager for the short trip to Greenwich aboard *Vesta*.

And the time she hoped to spend alone with Captain Jones.

Her hansom cab driver helped hand her down, and then he retrieved her small trunk. By the time he did so, Captain Jones was coming down the gangplank.

"I'll get that," he said, easily lifting the trunk and placing it atop one shoulder.

Sophie paid the cabbie and then followed Captain Jones up the gangplank, enjoying the view she had of his broad shoulders.

Handing off her trunk to another sailor, he said, "We will be leaving shortly since you are here." He paused, his gaze searching her a moment, causing her to grow warm by the attention.

"Though we had touched upon this briefly, Mrs. Grant, I wanted to reiterate that I am going to allow Mr. Andrews to manage a good portion of this brief trip. I hope that you will consider him for a captaincy with your shipping line."

"If you commit to another voyage as *Vesta's* captain and have Mr. Andrews as your first mate, he should gain the remaining experience he believes he needs to take a position as a captain at Neptune Shipping."

He snorted. "Mr. Andrews is more capable than any sailor I've ever known. He taught me most of what I know regarding sailing vessels."

"Have you known one another that long?" she asked.

"Aye. We met when I was but eight, and he was just shy of twenty. Mr. Andrews has served more as an older brother to me, as well as my good friend."

"No wonder you wish to see him do well with Neptune."

An odd look crossed his face, and then he asked, "Would you like a cup of tea before we sail?"

Sophie had been too excited to eat or drink anything this morning, but she thought it a good idea to have tea now.

"That is a lovely suggestion, Captain."

He escorted her to the ship's galley, where one of the sailors she had previously met placed a pot of tea and two cups in front of them.

"I'm afraid there's no sugar for your sweet tooth," Captain Jones teased. "You will have to rough it a bit while you are traveling aboard *Vesta*."

He smiled at her lazily, the teasing light in his eyes suddenly becoming heated. The look caused her to shiver in the most delightful way, and Sophie knew her choice of this man to introduce her to the pleasures of the flesh was the right one.

Now, she only had to address the delicate request with him.

Once they had drunk their tea, he took her back up on deck, where he gave the order for the crew to draw up the anchor and make for Greenwich. She noted Mr. Andrews at the ship's enormous wheel and went to stand next to him while the captain was busy supervising his crew.

"I hear that you will be the one steering us to our destination, Mr. Andrews."

"Aye, Mrs. Grant. The captain wants me to get as much experience as possible, in ways both small and large."

She couldn't help but like this first mate, with his pleasing demeanor and good looks. He would make an excellent captain for *Vesta*. That is, if Captain Jones agreed to her offer and changed ships.

They set sail down the Thames, and she stood at the bow, pointing out various sights to Captain Jones. In turn, he regaled her with amusing stories from his time at sea. Sophie liked the fact they stood so close together, and his shoulder brushed against her several times. Each touch brought a deep yearning within her, and her lips ached, longing to brush against his.

They arrived in Greenwich and were greeted by Mr. Purdy himself, along with one of his engineers who would be in charge of the repairs made to *Vesta*.

"It is good to see you again, Mrs. Grant," Mr. Purdy said in greeting. "We are making progress on your new ship."

"I am eager to show her off to Captain Jones, here, Mr. Purdy. I am trying to tempt the captain into taking her on once she is built."

"You won't find a better designed nor better built ship, Captain Jones," Mr. Purdy said confidently. "My architect, Mr. Fex, may be my son-in-law, but he is the most knowledgeable architect I have come to know. We can go and meet him and see what's been done so far on the new build once you lead us through *Vesta*, and we discuss her repairs. I understand that time in dock costs you money, Mrs. Grant, and I assure you we will address the needed repairs promptly."

"I would like my first mate, Drake Andrews, to escort you and lead this discussion, Mr. Purdy," Captain Jones said.

They followed the first mate around the ship, and Mr. Andrews gave a detailed, very thorough explanation as to how the damage had occurred and what he believed should be done to remedy it. Sophie knew he was drawing not only from the report she had completed, but also his own experience at sea. When the time came, she would have no qualms turning over a Neptune vessel to Drake Andrews.

As they went about the ship, she was always conscious of Captain Jones at her elbow. He assisted her as they moved about, taking her elbow sometimes or placing his hand against the small of her back to guide her. Every touch brought a sizzle through her. She could only imagine what it would be like to actually couple with him.

They agreed upon the ways to fix *Vesta*, and Mr. Purdy said he would finalize the cost. Thanks to Sophie's report to him, Mr. Purdy had already sent a strong estimate, and she did not think the cost would rise much beyond what he had already spoken to her about.

"Shall we go to the offices and collect Fex?" Mr. Purdy asked.

Mr. Andrews spoke up. "Is the crew to be dismissed now, Captain?"

He turned to Sophie. "I will leave that up to Mrs. Grant since *Vesta* is her ship."

"I do not believe you and the crew will be needed further, Mr. Andrews. You do still have the funds I gave you to see you back to London?"

The first mate nodded. "I do, Mrs. Grant, and I thank you for them, as well as those to bring us back to Greenwich again. Simply send word, and I will bring the same crew members to sail *Vesta* back to London for you."

"Thank you, Mr. Andrews," Sophie said, dismissing the sailor.

She and the captain followed Mr. Purdy to his offices, which she had visited before on several occasions with Josiah. A bit of sadness ran through her, thinking her husband would no longer accompany her to Greenwich, nor would he see the new ship he had desired brought to fruition.

Inside the offices, they went and met Mr. Fex. He was a man of small stature with a large brain and an obvious talent for ship design.

Fex greeted them, thanking Sophie again for the business she had brought their way.

"Mr. Grant always had his ships built at Mr. Purdy's shipyard. I would be remiss if I did not continue to do so." She indicated the captain. "Might I introduce Captain Jones to you, Mr. Fex? I am hoping the captain will wish to take the new ship on its maiden voyage and beyond."

The two men shook hands, and Mr. Fex said, "If anything will tempt you, Captain Jones, it will be this ship. We are using the latest in design and materials, and she will be the most solidly built ship we have ever put on the waters. Let me show you the plans before we see her in person."

Mr. Fex led them to a drafting board and showed them a series of complex sketches.

"You can see the sleek lines, Captain. This ship will also have a few more sails than others we have built, increasing its speed and maneuverability."

Sophie watched the captain, seeing the admiration on his face.

"You have designed quite a vessel, Mr. Fex. How long will it take to finish her?"

"Our goal is eighteen to twenty months, Captain Jones, but since she is the first of this design, we simply don't know for certain. It may take a little longer, or we may complete her in record time."

Fex looked to Sophie. "Have you decided upon the name yet, Mrs. Grant? We like to use it during our builds."

She felt her face flush. "No, Mr. Fex. That has not been determined at this point. My husband had suggested a name, but it is not in line with the theme of the names we choose for Neptune Shipping."

She looked to Jones. "Mr. Grant liked having all his ships named after Roman gods and goddesses. For instance, Vesta is the goddess of hearth and home."

"I did know the origin of the name. Mr. Andrews and I are fond of reading. We have traded books back and forth over the years, and we've read several on Greek, Roman, and Norse mythology."

"Enough talk," Mr. Purdy declared. "Let's go see her."

The four went to the shipyard, and a thrill ran through Sophie again, seeing the size and scope of the new Neptune ship being built.

For a moment, tears stung her eyes, knowing Josiah had so wanted this ship—and wanted it named for her.

Fex led them to each of the stations and discussed the progress that had already occurred, along with what the next several stages would involve. Both Sophie and Captain Jones peppered the architect with questions, which he was more than happy to answer.

"I hope what you have seen and heard will help convince you to take her on, Captain," Mr. Purdy said. "Whatever her name may come to be."

A wistful look entered the captain's eyes as he gazed at the early stages of the ship. "The man who takes her on will be lucky, indeed."

She couldn't help but wonder why Jones seemed torn about assuming control of a new ship. Perhaps he was tired of the sea. Or it was possible one of her competitors was trying to lure him away. It wouldn't surprise her if Strong Shipping, her strongest competitor, did so. For years, Josiah and Sophie had respected the manner in which Strong Shipping was managed. While their competitor, they were still friendly with those who managed the company.

In the past few years, however, things had changed drastically at Strong Shipping. Almost everyone in the offices had been let go, replaced by new workers. Sophie had not been above listening to gossip and learned that the Duke of Seaton, the head of the Strong family and owner of Strong Shipping, was quite ill. His brother, Adolphus Strong, had assumed control of the family's finances, since he was the duke's heir apparent. From everything she could tell, this Strong brother did not have the moral character or strong ethics of his brother. Sophie hoped if she lost Captain Jones, it would not be to Strong Shipping. If he told her he planned to jump to the line, she might have to warn him it might not be the most prudent move.

They returned to the main office, where Sophie saw her trunk and the captain's haversack sitting there.

"I am glad Mr. Andrews thought to place our things here. He certainly has an eye for details."

"How long will you be staying?" Mr. Purdy asked.

She replied, "I believe two or three days will do it, Mr. Purdy. I want to spend a little more time watching the build and hopefully persuade Captain Jones that this is the vessel for him."

"You know of the inn near the shipyard," Mr. Purdy said. "Will you be staying there again as you have in the past?"

"Yes, we will if they have room for us. Might you have someone drive us to it, please?"

"I have a little business in town," Mr. Fex said. "I would be happy to drop you at the inn."

Captain Jones bent, hoisting her trunk on his right shoulder and placing his haversack over his left. "Lead the way, Mr. Fex."

They went to a wagon Fex indicated, and Captain Jones placed their luggage in its bed. He then captured her waist, his hands easily spanning it, and lifted Sophie to the driver's bench.

The sudden movement had stolen her breath and again, all she could think of were his strong fingers running up and down her body. She turned away, hiding her flaming cheeks.

"I'll ride in the bed," Captain Jones told Mr. Fex. "The driver's bench will only fit the two of you."

She glanced over her shoulder and saw Captain Jones stride to the rear of the wagon. He hopped into the bed, his long legs dangling.

It only took ten minutes for them to reach the inn. Mr. Fex bid them farewell, saying he would see them again tomorrow. Captain Jones claimed their luggage, and they entered the inn.

The innkeeper recognized her and greeted her by name. "Mrs. Grant, it is so good to see you again. No Mr. Grant this time?"

She swallowed the lump in her throat. "We lost Mr. Grant last month," she said quietly. "I have come to Greenwich with Captain Jones. His ship, *Vesta*, is being repaired in Mr. Purdy's shipyard. We are also here to see the progress of the new vessel being built for Neptune

Shipping. The captain might take on command of her once she is completed."

The innkeeper clucked his tongue in sympathy. "I'm sorry to hear of your loss, Mrs. Grant. Your husband was a fine gentleman. He will be missed. I suppose you'll be needing two rooms then."

"Yes," she said. "I will be paying for them both since Captain Jones is an employee of Neptune shipping. Please have the one bill made up for me."

The innkeeper retrieved two keys. "Do you know how long you might be with us?"

"Two or three days is my best estimate," Sophie told him.

They followed the innkeeper up the stairs, and he unlocked a room, awarding her the key. Captain Jones brought her trunk inside the room and placed it on the ground at the foot of the bed.

The bed she hoped they would both be in by night's end.

"These rooms connect, Mrs. Grant, but as you can see, there is a lock here," the innkeeper showed her. "This will ensure your privacy."

She recalled that from past stays at the inn. She and Josiah had always taken separate rooms, but they had left the door unlocked between them in case they needed to speak to one another.

"Thank you very much," she said. "Would it be possible for us to have a quiet, private supper? It has been a long day, traveling from London and then spending many hours at the shipyard. I know you have a supper room upstairs which Mr. Grant and I have been able to use previously."

"I can oblige you, Mrs. Grant. If you will go there now, I'll have my wife bring up a meal for you."

The innkeeper looked to Captain Jones. "Wine for the both of you, Captain, or would you prefer whisky?"

"Wine will be fine."

"Then here is your key, Captain. You already know you are next door to Mrs. Grant. If either of you have need of anything, you have only to let me know."

Captain Jones looked to Sophie, and she felt herself tremble slightly.

"I'll place my things in my room, Mrs. Grant, and give you time to unpack. Shall I call for you in ten minutes? You can show me to this supper room."

"Yes, Captain. I will see you soon."

After the two men left, she opened her trunk. The room had no wardrobe, and she used the only chair to rest her gowns upon. She did decide to change her shoes, removing the practical, sturdy boots she had worn all day for more comfortable slippers.

A knock sounded at her door, and she answered it. Awaiting her was Captain Jones. Determination filled her at seeing him again. She was a successful businesswoman. She would handle him as she did any client of Neptune Shipping. She would make her case, and then it would be left up to him to decide whether or not to take her up on her unusual offer. Sophie determined to address the matter with him after they had supped.

After all, even she knew a man with a full stomach was much more compliant than a hungry one.

Chapter Eleven

James had come into this dinner wondering how to begin his courtship of Mrs. Grant.

The woman continued to intrigue—and impress—him. Today, she had shown just how much she knew about ships. It wouldn't surprise him if Mrs. Grant even decided to design her own ships one day.

He was glad he had been first attracted to her intellect, but sitting with her now, he couldn't help but notice her beauty. Her heart-shaped face was expressive, causing her brown eyes to light with interest. He longed to loosen the golden-brown hair and run his fingers through it. While her gown was more demure than most women wore, he couldn't help but notice her ample bosom. He had already discovered how small her waist was from having lifted her into the wagon earlier.

So, the woman appealed to him physically and intellectually. Certainly, that was a good start. But having had no family other than Drake for many years, James longed for an emotional connection. If he were to take a wife, and he must since he would need to pass his title along to a son, he wanted a closeness with the woman he chose to wed. He didn't want to admit it, but what he had in mind was a love match.

Could that be possible with the practical Mrs. Grant?

He didn't even know her first name. She oozed practicality and competence. He wondered if she had a softer side to her.

He finished the soup, which the innkeeper's wife had brought to them, tearing off another piece of the bread.

"Tell me more about the ports of call you have made during your sailing career, Captain," Mrs. Grant said, spooning more soup into her mouth.

His gaze fixed upon that mouth, the lips the color of pink roses.

James wanted his mouth on hers so badly that he ached.

The innkeeper's wife appeared again, carrying a large tray. She set plates in front of them, and the smell of beef wafted up to him.

"Anything else you need, Mrs. Grant?" the woman asked. "If not, simply leave your dishes when you're done. I'll collect them."

His companion thanked the woman, and James watched as Mrs. Grant studied the plate a moment before cutting into the meat. He liked that about her. She observed things around her and took in details that others seemed to miss.

Cutting into his own beef, he savored the first bite. "Very tender."

"Yes, the food here has always been good."

"You have made several trips before?" he asked.

"We do a good amount of business with Mr. Purdy. Josiah—my husband—always believed forming a personal connection with a client made for a better professional relationship. I will continue to keep to that as I run Neptune Shipping."

"You seemed to have learned a great deal from Mr. Grant."

"I did. While I have always had patience, he helped me to understand attention to detail is important. Upon our marriage, I began to learn about Neptune through examining the ledgers and then being responsible for keeping the books. I've always had a way with numbers."

"That was a large undertaking, I'm sure," he pointed out.

"Indeed, it was, Captain. I became responsible for billing clients. Collecting fees. Paying for the salaries of all our employees, including the crews we hired on for every voyage."

"But you have done more than that, haven't you?"

She took a bite of her peas and chewed thoughtfully. "Eventually, I became involved in every aspect of Neptune Shipping. I understand now that my husband was preparing me for the day when I would run the line."

"Did you ever think to bring in someone to do so for you after his death?"

Mrs. Grant looked at him as if he'd sprouted two more heads. Then laughing, she said, "Never. I enjoy what I do. But tell me more of the South Seas, Captain. It sounds like paradise on earth."

They ate as he told her of some of his favorite places around the globe. The longer they were together, the more appealing she became to him, the candlelight softening her features, making her appear almost dreamlike. When he had been on shore leave, the places he frequented had women who angled to couple with sailors, especially handsome ones like himself.

This situation was altogether different. James had no idea how to approach Mrs. Grant and tell her he was interested in her. She seemed so devoted to her company. He also had to consider the recent death of her husband. She'd been a widow less than two months. Perhaps she needed time before he approached her regarding a courtship. Even then, she was so business-minded, he worried she would flatly refuse any offer he made for her.

He poured more wine for her, and she sipped it, looking at him intently. Something stirred within him.

Perhaps she was aware of him as a man. He was certainly aware of her as a woman.

"Were you able to tend to the family business you mentioned, Captain? I know you mentioned that your father was in poor health and that he needed you to take on more responsibility."

"Yes, he is quite ill. I had not seen him . . . since he suffered an attack of apoplexy. He is bedridden."

"Oh, I am dreadfully sorry to hear that," she said, her sympathy genuine. "My husband feared that very thing. He was much older than I was, and he worried about apoplexy or his heart giving out, turning him into an invalid to be cared for."

"I know you mentioned he passed away last month. Was it a lingering illness?"

"No, thank goodness. We were at the office, discussing the new ship. I had agreed it was a good idea to expand, and as we talked it over, he was struck with heart pain." She paused. "Within five minutes, he was gone."

"I hope he did not suffer much."

"Josiah lived a good life. He came from nothing and made a name for himself and a fortune men only dream of building. Though in pain, he slipped away with a smile on his face, satisfied at all he had accomplished."

Mrs. Grant took a deep breath and then reached for her wine, downing the entire contents.

"A little liquid courage," she said.

"You are the bravest woman I have ever met," James told her. "I think there are but a handful of women who could have taken on what you have and met with success."

"But even women who are skilled in business have needs, Captain."

The atmosphere in the room changed. He looked at her, wondering if she meant what he thought she did.

"I am sure you understand what I speak of," she continued. "You have spent long stretches of time at sea. When your ship comes into port and you go on shore leave, I am sure you have taken care of . . . those needs."

"I have," he said carefully, wondering where this conversation was headed.

"Women, too, have certain needs," she said. "As a widow, I have . . . a bit more freedom in seeing that mine are . . . met." Clearing her throat, she said, "I am asking as delicately as possible if you might wish to explore those with me, Captain Jones. I do not expect any type of commitment from you. In fact, I do not want anything of the sort. You are here for a limited time, and then you will be gone. I am lonely. I stay busy with my company for long hours, but I long for some . . . physical companionship."

She wet her lips nervously and gazed at him beseechingly. "Would that be a possibility?"

"I am flattered, Mrs. Grant," James said, his thoughts swirling.

He hesitated, though. He had wanted her to want him for himself, the ship captain that he had been, and not the marquess he had become. More than that, he wanted her for more than a brief encounter or two. He wanted—needed—a wife.

And he could think of no more suitable woman than Mrs. Grant.

She mistook his silence and said, "I have offended you. I am sorry." Her eyes widened. "Oh, my goodness. You are married. You have a wife. And possibly even children. I had thought to ask you and then became caught up in my business proposal to you."

"Business proposal?" he asked, not bothering to hide his smile, amused that she thought what would pass between them as a business transaction.

Her face turned bright red, and she sprang to her feet. "My apologies, Captain. I—"

"Don't," he said, rising quickly and clasping her by the shoulders. "No, Mrs. Grant. I am not married. There is no Mrs. Jones, nor are there little Joneses toddling about."

Relief swept across her face, but then she stiffened. "I understand that we have a professional relationship. I am your employer, and you are an employee of Neptune Shipping. It was inappropriate for me to—"

James cut her off with a kiss.

He broke it, feeling her startled reaction.

Picking up where she left off, she said, "I didn't mean to imply there would be an exchange of money. I merely thought as two consenting adults, we might—"

He kissed her again.

This time he lingered, his lips on hers, which were soft and pliant. Her mouth was firmly closed, though, and he guessed she had done no open-mouth kissing.

Breaking the kiss again, he saw a yearning in her eyes.

For more . . .

"I understand we are both adults, Mrs. Grant. That you want something temporary from me, is that correct?"

She nodded, words apparently beyond her.

James wanted permanent—but he would settle for temporary. For now.

"Shall we return to where we have more privacy?" he suggested, his voice low. "I would hate for the innkeeper or his wife to interrupt us. After all, you have a reputation to maintain."

"Yes," she agreed quickly. "Yes, I do." She paused. "Thank you, Captain. I know you come and go across the world. For all I know, you have a sweetheart in every port of call who waits for you. I do not want to infringe on any relationship you have. I merely am suggesting that we . . . enjoy the next few days."

"There are no sweethearts anywhere, Mrs. Grant," he assured her. "Yes, I do seek female companionship when my ship rolls into a harbor. But I have no lasting attachments."

She smiled brightly. "This will be a brief time in our lives then. Something I hope both of us might enjoy."

Already, he was intoxicated by her. The curve of her neck. The scent of roses clinging to her. The sparkle in her eyes.

Offering her his arm, James said, "Shall we?"

She reached for her reticule and slipped it over her wrist. He escorted her to her door and though no one was nearby, quietly said, "I will go to my room. You may turn the lock to open the door separating us." He gazed down at her. "Take five minutes to think on things. I want you to be sure about this. If you change your mind, I will not be offended."

"I won't," she said, determination in her voice and face.

She produced her key, which she withdrew from her reticule. He took it, unlocking the door for her. Entering her room, she turned to look at him.

"Goodnight, Captain Jones."

"Goodnight, Mrs. Grant."

James watched the door close and then went to his own room to wait.

And listen for the lock to be thrown.

Chapter Twelve

Nerves flittered through Sophie, coupled with anticipation. She touched her fingertips to her lips, marveling that they had been against James Jones' lips only a minute ago.

She twirled in a circle several times, glee filling her.

He did not have a wife or children.

She was so thankful. It had been something which she had worried about, especially with him mentioning his family, but then she had been so nervous that she had forgotten to bring it up before she awkwardly blurted out what she wanted from him.

She wondered what would pass between them. Her imagination was limited by her lack of knowledge in this area. Though she and Josiah had talked about a great many topics during their marriage and he had taught her a great deal about all manner of things, their conversation had never turned to what happened between a man and a woman. He had not wanted physical intimacy with her. She thought it likely had to do with his age, but she didn't really understand why.

Tonight, she would unravel those mysteries and see for herself.

And possibly become with child.

Panic suddenly seized her. She had lost track of time. The door was still locked. What if Captain Jones had tried to enter her room, only to find he could not gain entry. He would believe she had changed her mind.

Quickly, Sophie rushed to the door, turning the lock. She stepped back, her breath coming rapidly as she watched.

A light tap sounded. Before she could find her voice, the door slowly opened.

Captain Jones stepped into the room, closing the connecting door behind him.

He turned and smiled, a smile that caused her toes to curl and her belly to turn upside down.

"You are certain?" he asked.

Nodding, they both took a step toward the other. His hand cradled her cheek, and she nuzzled it, overwhelmed by his size and the masculine scent she inhaled.

"Might I know your first name?"

Breathlessly, she said, "Sophie. I am Sophie."

"Sophie," he echoed, his other hand also touching her cheek.

She felt the long fingers framing her face, as well as the calluses on his fingertips and at the top of his palms. He radiated heat, and she longed to move closer. Afraid to do so, she merely stood, drinking him in.

"I am going to kiss you, Sophie. For a long time."

She shivered in anticipation. "I would like that, James."

He smiled. "I like hearing my name come from your lips. Lips that I long to possess."

He bent, touching his mouth to hers. James kissed her, his thumbs caressing her cheeks. The pressure varied, as if he were testing the waters.

She broke the kiss. "May I touch you?" she asked shyly.

"I am yours tonight, Sophie. You may do whatever you wish."

His words caused something to ripple through her, and she decided it was desire. Desire for this man. In this moment.

Placing her palms flat against his broad chest, she felt the hard muscle, knowing it had come from laboring on ships since he was a boy.

His mouth met hers again, the pressure harder now. One of his hands slipped to her nape. The other glided along her spine, bringing a rush of delicious tingles where it touched. Then his arm went around her waist and drew her closer to him.

The kiss grew more insistent. Sophie knew he wanted her to do something. She could not figure out for the life of her what, though. She felt inadequate and small and broke the kiss.

"I am disappointing you," she said, their lips barely apart, their breath intermingling.

"You have not kissed much, have you?" he asked gently.

"Not at all," she admitted.

James pulled back and studied her. "I know there are some men who do not favor kissing. Was your husband one of them?"

"I don't know," she replied honestly. "He only kissed my cheek. Never my mouth."

"Ah. Then that changes things."

She was afraid he would change his mind. "I can learn," she said quickly. "I have always been a fast learner. I learned to read when I was four. I began playing the violin at six. And when I—"

"You play the violin?"

"Yes. It relaxes me to do so. I play it every night when I come home from the office. Music soothes me."

"I like music. Would you play for me?"

This conversation was not going at all as she had expected. "If you wish."

"I do."

He dipped his head, and once more their lips touched. He pressed soft kisses to her mouth and then lifted his head.

"Since you have no experience in kissing, I must teach you how to do so."

"What more does it involve?" she asked, puzzled. "I thought we have been kissing."

He smiled enigmatically. "Oh, there is so much more to kissing, Sophie. And I am eager to teach you. I want you to be open to whatever happens next. Can you do so?"

She would do anything to remain in his arms like this. "Of course," she said confidently.

"Good."

His mouth came down on hers then, hard and demanding. She could feel the power within him as he held her to him. She got caught up in the kiss.

Until he ran his tongue along her bottom lip.

Sophie gasped, jerking away. "What are you doing?"

He grinned. "Be patient—and you'll see."

Reluctance filled her as her nerves began to fray. This was a terrible idea. This man was a man of the world. She might have been a wife, but she was still innocent of the ways between a man and a woman. She should tell him now.

She opened her mouth to speak, and James pushed his tongue inside her mouth. He began a leisurely exploration of her. Sophie could taste the wine they had shared, along with something deep and dark and mysterious.

Again, she broke the kiss, but before she could speak, he said, "Do. Quit thinking, Sophie. Just be."

She had a thousand questions, but James obviously wasn't in a mood to answer them. She decided to take his advice and stop thinking about everything he did. Instead, she would let nature take its course and merely respond.

His tongue toyed with her lips, outlining her mouth, then slowly dragged back and forth over her bottom lip. Then his teeth sank into her lip, and she squeaked—even as desire poured through her. She could think of only him now as his tongue again eased into her mouth, playing hide-and-seek with her own, teasing, toying, warring with hers.

The kiss was something she had never expected, and yet it was perfect. It quickened her heartbeat and pulse. It brought new sensations throughout her. She wished it could go on forever.

Quickly, she learned what she liked and began imitating what James did. He groaned as she bit into his bottom lip, then licked it with her tongue in a soothing motion.

He broke the kiss, his lips hovering above hers. "You do learn fast, Sophie."

Even as she smiled and his lips devoured hers again, she could feel his own smile.

And everything seemed so right.

James didn't just kiss her mouth. He kissed her nose. Her eyelids. Her brow. His lips slid from her cheek to her temple to her ear, where he tugged on the lobe with his teeth, sending fresh chills through her. Then his tongue found her ear, outlining the shell, dipping into it. She giggled, and he chuckled low.

Suddenly, she found herself swept into his arms, his mouth still on hers. Her heart began beating wildly as he crossed the room and placed her on the bed. He removed her slippers and then sat on the bed, pulling off his boots and shrugging from his captain's coat. He stacked the two pillows so they rested on the wall, and then he sat, his back against them.

He pulled her into his lap and commenced kissing her again. Sophie no longer thought. She only reacted to his kisses. Kissing was simply marvelous, and she couldn't believe she had missed out on it for so long. She grew bolder, pushing her fingers into his thick hair, hair that looked as if it had been kissed by the sun. She held onto his locks, kissing him with everything she had within her, using her new knowledge to its limits.

Then his lips trailed down her throat, nibbling at it, causing her to shiver in response. As he kissed her, his hand slipped into the bodice of her dress, cupping her breast. The rough, callused palm against her delicate skin was such a contrast. She wriggled against him, and he moaned.

"Careful, love. It's not time to go there just yet."

She had no idea what he was talking about, and her face must have revealed her thoughts.

"Sophie," he said, his gaze pinning hers. "Did you make love with your husband?"

Heat filled her cheeks. "No," she said quietly, her gaze falling.

James lifted her chin until their eyes met. "Why did you not tell me?"

"I . . . . I didn't know how. It was hard enough trying to convince you to couple with me. I have never had to embark on such a conversation before."

"You told me you had needs which must be met."

She huffed. "I do! I know there's something inside me. Something that yearns for what I don't even understand. I have no idea what happens when a man and woman come together, only that Josiah was thirty-five years my senior and said he was no longer interested in it. He was so kind to me when he didn't have to be. Brought me into his world and taught me about business. It was enough when he was alive."

She began to sob. "But it isn't anymore. I want things I don't even understand. I know I have missed out on them. I am already six and twenty. My youth is fading fast. I simply wanted to appease my curiosity. And you are so big and handsome, quite breathtaking for a man. I thought if you were willing to let me explore a few things, then I wouldn't be in the dark."

"And you asked me—besides the fact that I am handsome—because I would be leaving London soon?"

Sophie nodded, tears still cascading down her cheeks. "I am not asking for any kind of commitment from you, James. I know you are, in truth, married to the sea. She is your mistress and commands your loyalty. I merely wanted to understand the urges inside me. Let you help me understand them. Then you would be gone, and I would be satisfied, having learned about what happens when a man and woman come together."

"You say you have these urges. Have you done anything to soothe them?"

She frowned. "No. What would I do?" she asked, frustration pouring from her.

He used the pads of his thumbs to brush away her tears. "Even when a man is nowhere in sight, a woman can pleasure herself."

"She can?" That thought had never occurred to her. "But I am a virgin, James. Is it possible to . . . I don't know what!" she cried.

He laughed, a low rumble in his chest. "I am going to kiss you some more, Sophie Grant. Then I am going to touch you where no man has done so. Once I show you what to do, *you* will be able to do the same."

She pondered his words. "You mean like when you have kissed me and then I kiss you back the same way? Like that?"

"Yes. But you are going to have to trust me. Can you do so?"

Sophie didn't know this man well. What she did know was that he was a good man.

"I trust you, James."

His response was to kiss her. The kiss went on and on. He tugged on her head, pulling it back some, and the kiss deepened. His kisses caused her body to feel on fire, as if her very blood had been lit by a match and burned within her.

She barely noticed when his hand began stroking her leg. When she did, she realized the touch made her belly feel excited and nervous at the same time. Then James' hand crept under her gown. He massaged her calf, his touch sensual and slow. Her core tightened as new feelings rushed through her.

His fingers made their way to her knee, and he lightly touched it, causing the butterflies in her belly to explode. Gradually, he moved higher, stroking her thigh, his fingers alternating between light brushes and firm caresses.

Sophie knew his final destination, and anticipation filled her as he finally reached it. He dragged a finger along the seam of her feminine sex, causing her to gasp.

"You like that, don't you?"

"Yes," she gasped, her breathing shallow.

He smiled lazily at her. "You'll like this even more."

His gaze pinning hers, James pushed a finger inside her. She was scandalized by the action—and reveled in it.

She licked her lips. "What now?"

"I touch you. Learn what you like."

"Oh."

He stroked her, deep and long.

"Oh!"

She gave over to the touch. He teased her, another finger joining the first. She began breathing hard, then mewling, the sensations new and exciting.

"This is your sweet bud of pleasure," he told her, his thumb encircling a point on her, pressing against it.

Sophie began writhing. Panting. Soaring.

"Don't think. Just be," he reminded her, and she gave over to the sensations rising within her.

Then she was flying, high as the clouds, moving against his hand, crying, laughing, her back arching as she shattered.

Sophie cried out, but James had anticipated that. His mouth covered hers, the sound muffled as he kissed her.

She came back to earth after her brief visit to the heavens, still enjoying his kiss.

When he broke it, she protested, but it came out so weak. She had never felt as spent as she did now. She would be hard pressed to raise even a hand.

"Tired?" he asked.

"Yes," she said, completed, sated.

"You have been exposed to a great deal tonight. I think our lesson is at an end."

"No," she protested, grabbing his wrist as he tried to move from the bed. "I want more."

James chuckled. "Love, you couldn't handle any more right now."

"Stay," she urged. "At least until I fall asleep."

"All right."

Sophie closed her eyes, feeling him leave the bed. He lifted her slightly, moving the bedclothes down and then bringing them back up, covering her. He slipped under them, his arm coming around her shoulders, drawing her into his chest. She snuggled against it. Against him. His warmth drew her in.

"Sleep, Sophie," he urged.

She did.

CHAPTER THIRTEEN

WHEN SOPHIE AWOKE, she felt rested as she never had before. Then she recalled having asked James Jones into her bed and quickly sat up.

The handsome sea captain was gone, obviously leaving her sometime during the night. She fell back against the pillows, turning and cradling one, catching the masculine scent he had left behind. Sophie inhaled deeply, hugging the pillow to her.

Kissing had proven to be something utterly delightful. She could have kissed Captain Jones until eternity came, but that would not have been long enough. She was also aware now of her body in a way she never had been before. Her cheeks heated as she recalled his fingers touching her between her legs, causing her to pant and writhe. The incredible sensations were something she would never forget. She recalled he told her she could do the same for herself, but she doubted she would be brave enough to attempt to do so.

There was a lot more to what went on between a man and a woman than she had suspected. Kissing was a good example of that. She had merely thought you pressed your lips against someone else's, and that was it. Little did she know just how involved—and seductive—a kiss could be. She looked forward to more explorations with Captain Jones.

At least she had let him know her intentions by explaining this was only a temporary arrangement. He seemed happy to comply with her request, and so she must get out of him what she could now. The inn they stayed at offered them a modicum of privacy. Sophie worried, though, that the innkeeper had placed them in these rooms because he knew exactly what they would be up to. That the locked door would not remain locked between them. She still had her reputation to maintain, and she hoped there would be no gossip from her stay here with Captain Jones.

Sophie washed and dressed, using water that the innkeeper's wife must have placed in her room while they supped the previous evening. She put on her boots and heard a knock at her door. Answering it, she found Captain Jones in the corridor, looking so handsome that her teeth ached at the sight of him.

"You look ready for the day," she commented. "Even freshly shaved."

She remembered the slight stubble on his cheeks from last night, forcing herself to keep her hands by her side and not reach out to touch his face.

"If you are ready, we can go downstairs and eat," he told her.

"I am ravenous," she said. "Lead the way, Captain."

They ate a hearty breakfast and then decided to leisurely stroll to the shipyard, which took a little over half an hour to reach. Mr. Purdy greeted them effusively, and asked what they might wish to see today.

"We don't want to take up any more of your time, Mr. Purdy," Sophie told the yard's owner. "If you don't mind, we will simply wander about and see what projects are going on."

"You're free to go wherever you wish, Mrs. Grant. If you have need of Fex or me, please come and find us."

They went to the far end of the massive shipyard and saw two other ships currently being built. One vessel was about halfway completed, while the other looked to be almost ready. The supervisor overseeing its work was happy to give them a tour of it.

It was easy being with James. They had much in common with their knowledge of ships. Sophie still hoped he would take command of her new vessel being built, but would not push him on the matter, not knowing what responsibilities now lay at his doorstep with his father being so ill.

Eventually, they made their way back to her ship, and he asked, "Why haven't you gone ahead and named her? You said Mr. Grant had a name in mind."

"I also said that it did not fall into line with the usual naming of our ships," she reminded him. "I am reluctant to place the name he wanted because of that. And other reasons, as well," she said quietly.

She was aware of this man now, even more than she had been before, his body close to hers as they stood at the rail and watched the building process.

"Would you share the name Mr. Grant wished her to be called?" James asked.

A blush tinted her cheeks as she said, "*Sophie*. Josiah wished to name the ship *Sophie*. After me."

"I think it would be a great honor to have a ship named after yourself," he mused. "Even though Sophie is Greek for wisdom."

"You know that?" she asked, surprised by the depth of his knowledge.

"My taste is eclectic in regard to reading," he admitted. "Besides mythology, I have studied many topics over the years, both on my own and with Drake. While being a seaman is hard work and fills a sailor's days, there are still long hours in which you have nothing to do other than stare out upon the waters, no land in sight. I used that time to better myself. For myself. Drake and I educated ourselves and each other, constantly sharing books and talking late into the night regarding many topics. I always enjoyed standing watch with him at night because it gave us time to discuss so many things we'd read about."

"I believe you and Mr. Andrews are quite unique as far as sailors go," Sophie observed.

"Perhaps we are," he agreed. He hesitated. "I think you should honor your late husband's wishes, Sophie. Name the ship as he wished."

"I want to, but it seems so . . . self-absorbed. What would people think when they learned of her name?"

"Are you a woman to truly care about the opinions of others and what they think of you?"

"I used to be," she admitted. "My background is quite different from the few women who enter into business. You see, my father is a viscount. That means I come from what is termed Polite Society. Of course, when I wed Josiah, I was cut off from it. My husband may have been as wealthy as Midas, but he never would have been welcomed into a *ton* ballroom. The fact that I helped him in his business and now run it on my own? I, too, will never receive an invitation to an event during the Season."

"I gather that the Season is for this small portion of society to come together."

"It is. Oftentimes, the Season is a large part of the Marriage Mart. That is when a young lady makes her come-out—her debut—into Polite Society. These young women seek a husband, and titled gentlemen are looking for wives in order to get heirs off them."

"What is the Season like?"

She shrugged. "I know a little about it from having grown up in that world, but I never made my own come-out because I wed Josiah before it began. It involves several months of social events. Balls. Routs. Garden parties and musicales. Trips to the theatre and opera. I did go to both of those, however. My husband knew how much I enjoyed the fine arts, and he would take me on occasion to see a play or opera. But we were never invited to any event by anyone, not even a dinner party. My marriage to Josiah Grant cut me off from Polite

Society."

"Do you regret that?" he asked, his gaze intense.

"Not really. I gained so much more by marrying my husband. He taught me about a world I never knew existed. He let me see that I was more than a pretty young thing who played a musical instrument. I have been able to use my head. I make decisions that affect dozens to hundreds of others. Do I miss having contact with others? I'll admit that I do. I have no friends. They all gave me up upon my marriage, and I can only imagine what the *ton* makes of me now.

"I simply do not fit into any world, James," she continued. "Polite Society will have nothing to do with me. The clients I deal with would never think to extend an invitation to me. In fact, more than one have jokingly mentioned how their wives are jealous that I spend so much time in their company, so I must draw firm lines between business and social relationships. I must be satisfied by the work I do and the shipping line I manage."

"I am sorry, Sophie."

"No, I do not want your pity. I am sorry if you thought I was angling for it. I enjoy my life. Yes, perhaps I am a bit lonely, but I am living life on my terms, with no man telling me what to do." She smiled. "Not even Josiah dared to tell me how to think. He knew I was my own person."

"Name the ship *Sophie*," James insisted. "Mr. Grant wished to honor you in that regard. Who cares what others might say? *Sophie* will be the best vessel sailing the high seas, a fitting tribute to the woman who runs a business empire."

"All right," she agreed. "Shall we go and tell Mr. Fex of this decision?"

They left the shipyard and went to the offices, where they found Mr. Fex at work on a new design.

"We have come to share the ship's name with you, Mr. Fex," Sophie said. "She is to be called . . . *Sophie*. It was my late husband's dying wish to name the vessel after me, and I realize I must honor it, no matter what others say."

The architect smiled broadly. "Jolly good for you, Mrs. Grant. I shall make certain the workers know how to refer to her now. I will also work on the font we will use for the name. Of course, you will see all these and be able to make your choice accordingly."

They bid Mr. Fex farewell, and James asked if she was hungry.

"After all," he said, a twinkle in his unusual eyes, "we want to make certain you have enough sustenance to make it through the day—and night."

Sophie shivered in anticipation of what was to come between them and accompanied him to a cart, where he purchased meat pies for them. They found a bench and sat upon it, eating their pies as they watched passers-by.

When they finished eating, James said, "I think we should go back to the inn. Our rooms should have been cleaned by now. I suggest that if anyone asks, you tell them you have a megrim and are retiring to get some rest."

"But I never have megrims," she protested and then paused. "Oh, you want me to have an excuse to be in my room this afternoon."

"You catch on quickly, Mrs. Grant," the captain said, a teasing light in his eyes.

They returned to the inn. James told her that he would stay downstairs and have a glass of ale, making certain they knew not to disturb her.

"I will be up for you as soon as I can," he promised, and they parted.

Once in her room, Sophie used her tooth powder, understanding now how she wanted her breath as fresh as possible for the kisses to come. She also unlocked the connecting door and even opened it a bit. Perching on the end of the bed, she waited, her heart beating wildly in anticipation of what was to come.

A quarter-hour later, James appeared in the doorway. He came to her, taking her hands and pulling her to her feet. His arms went about her, and his mouth came down on hers, hard and possessive, causing a thrill to ripple through her. She would do as he had suggested and not think of what was to come. She would revel in the here and now.

He kissed her a good, long while, his mouth insistent, eventually moving to her throat. Her breasts seemed to swell as his hands caressed them. He freed one, lifting it from her gown. His mouth closed over it, sucking hard, bringing a dizzying thrill. Sophie clung to him, wanting to do for him as he did for her.

He lifted his head and smiled at her, a smile which would melt glaciers.

"You know just how handsome you are, don't you?" she asked.

"As long as I am pleasing to your eye, Sophie, that is all that interests me now."

He took her mouth again with his, the kisses deep and fulfilling, even as his hands roamed her back.

Finally breaking the kiss, James said, "I can wait no longer, love. I want to feel your skin against mine. I want to touch you simply everywhere."

"I want to *be* touched everywhere by you, James," she said, feeling like a wanton—and not caring that she did.

"Undressing one another can bring a level of satisfaction," he informed her. "Especially if you kiss as you shed your layers of clothing."

It took them a good half-hour to remove one another's clothes, many kisses traded between each piece of apparel removed.

Sophie had thought she would be self-conscious once she was laid bare to him, but she found that was not the case at all, thanks to his admiring gaze.

"You are simply perfect, Sophie Grant," he said, the pads of his thumb grazing her nipples, which pebbled in need.

"I must say that you, too, Captain, are a fine sight to behold."

She reached and grazed her fingertips against his hard, muscular chest, slowly dragging them to the flat of his belly. The muscles bunched as she did, dancing beneath her, delighting her. Her eyes fell to his manhood, jutting at full attention. Fascinated by this, Sophie grasped it, hearing James groan.

"You like that," she said in wonder, stroking her thumb up and down his shaft as she held it firmly in place.

He growled, saying, "I like that more than you know. But let me continue my exploration of your body."

He caught her up in his arms and placed her gently onto the bed, joining her.

Sophie lost track of time, as James' mouth and fingers took their time exploring her. Each touch brought new sensations, and she felt a quickening within her, anticipating the feelings she had experienced last night when his fingers had entered her.

He rose from the bed and retrieved a hand towel and a handkerchief. Raising her hips, he placed it beneath her.

"Why did you do that?" she asked, curious about everything they were doing.

"When I make love to you for the first time, love, it is going to hurt."

"Hurt?"

"Aye. I will break through your maidenhead and for an instant, there will be pain. I don't want you to be surprised by that. Only know that it hurts the one time and never again."

"Ah, there will be blood when you do this breaking," she said in understanding. "Like when my courses come."

"Yes." He cradled her cheek tenderly. "I wish it didn't have to hurt, but I promise the pain is fleeting."

"I trust you," she told him. "I also thank you for making me aware. I will be more prepared now."

"That's why I told you. But I hope I have a few surprises up my proverbial sleeve."

She laughed, leaning to kiss his muscled forearm, tanned from days in the sun.

James began kissing her again, his hands everywhere. Running along her arms. Her legs. Teasing her thighs apart. His fingers found her core, and his tongue pushed into her mouth as his fingers entered her, both in the same thrilling motion. Again, she reached the peaks of pleasure, her cries swallowed into his mouth, her body bending as a bow, shuddering, then collapsing.

He buried his face against her neck as he parted her again, his manhood pressing against her. Then, with one push, he was inside her. Sophie gasped, but the pain was quick, as he'd told her it would be. He hovered above her now, not moving.

"Get used to me," he rasped. "I am filling you like nothing ever has."

She did feel full, but she itched to move and did so.

"Ah," he said. "Now, that felt good to me."

"It did?" she asked, pleased.

"Do what comes naturally to you, love. Move how you wish. Touch where you want."

"And don't think," she teased. "Just do."

"Aye," he growled, thrusting into her again, his mouth covering hers.

They began a dance, Sophie matching her rhythm to his, her hands moving along his sleek, muscled back, down to his hard buttocks. She stroked him as he stroked her, loving the feel of him against her, touching her, being inside her.

Then the rhythm changed. The speed increased. He pumped into her with unbridled enthusiasm, and she soared high again, laughing, tears of wonder and joy escaping. Suddenly, he withdrew, grabbing the nearby handkerchief. Groaning, he expelled something into it and then wadded it up, collapsing atop her. She welcomed his weight, her arms going about him, clinging to him, needing to stay close. Needing his warmth. His scent.

Needing him . . .

He rolled to his side, and they faced one another. His hand stroked her hair.

"Are you all right?" he asked.

"I am more than all right, James," she assured him.

"Was it what you expected?"

She giggled. "I had no expectations. No mother or friend to tell me what the experience was like." Sophie sighed. "Frankly, I doubt anyone could have conveyed to me what just went on between us."

He leaned in for a slow, sweet kiss. "I hope I satisfied you."

Sophie's fingers caressed his cheek. "I am very content, Captain Jones. I only hope you got something out of our coupling."

A slow, lazy smile spread across his handsome face. "Aye, that I did, Mrs. Grant."

He kissed her again and then touched his lips to her brow. "Let's get you cleaned up."

James eased the cloth from beneath her, and Sophie saw the small bloodstain upon it. He wet the cloth and then bathed her. The gesture was intimate—and very, very sweet.

Climbing into the bed again, he wrapped his arms about her, pulling her back to his chest, his lips tenderly kissing her nape.

"May I ask what you used the handkerchief for?"

"My seed. If I had released it into you, it might result in a child being made. Not always, but I couldn't take the chance."

"I wouldn't have minded that, James," she said softly.

His lips stilled. "What?"

"Before my marriage, I always assumed I would be a mother. That possibility did not exist during my marriage to Josiah. I have been thinking on it, however. Why build Neptune Shipping into a behemoth, only to have no one to inherit it and keep it going once I am gone?"

Sophie sat up. "I would like to have a child, James. A boy or girl. It does not matter. But I would see my company passed on to my own flesh and blood. The only question is, would you be the one to help me with this?"

Chapter Fourteen

To say James was overwhelmed by Sophie's bold request would be an understatement.

What he did know was that this woman continued to astonish him. And move him. Making love to her had been an incredible experience, knowing he was the first to touch her body... and hopefully, her soul.

It made him even more determined to make her his wife and eventual duchess.

Yet he had yet to tell her his true identity. He wanted to, but he feared everything would change between them when he did. She had been treated abominably by what she called Polite Society. To know he was a member of it and that he would eventually become a duke and one of the *ton's* leading members might ruin everything building between them.

For now, he would refrain from mentioning he was Lord Alinwood. He still must answer her, though.

"I am honored and a bit astonished by your request, Sophie," he said, his hand resting against her belly, the belly he hoped one day would swell with the child they had made.

"It is a lot to ask of you. I understand that, James. In fact, let's not discuss it now. You need time to think about it. I understand that. I do want you to know I would hold you under no obligation, however. I would raise the child. You would not have to contribute financially in any way."

Anger filled him. He turned her in his arms. "You think I would ignore my own child?"

Her eyes widened. "No. I just want to make clear that I would have no expectations of you helping to raise him or her. This is something I am perfectly willing to do on my own. I just need . . . a bit of help. In conceiving a babe."

"I don't wish to discuss this now, Sophie," he said firmly.

Yes, he wanted her to carry his child. He wanted to marry her, for goodness' sakes. He wanted to love her—and suspected he already did.

"I am sorry to have brought this up," she apologized. "We do not have to address the issue now. I still have years left in which to bear a child. Why, we might even address the subject when you return from *Vesta's* next voyage."

"Who is to say I wish to take *Vesta* out again?" he countered.

"Oh."

She fell silent, and he could almost feel the wheels turning inside her.

"You have mentioned your family obligations. I do not wish to pry, James, but do you think they will prevent you from sailing as *Vesta's* captain? Or even *Sophie's*?"

Of course, his responsibilities would keep him ashore. He couldn't tell her that now because he didn't want to get into it. He still wanted this woman to like him—to want him—for himself. For James Jones and not the Marquess of Alinwood.

"I cannot answer that just yet, Sophie. I will know more after I return to London," he said, hoping to put off further discussion.

"Are you angry with me?" she asked quietly.

James tried to get his body to relax. "No, love," he said, brushing his lips against her nape.

"Good. I thought you were."

"I could never be mad at you, pet."

James moved his palm against her belly, caressing the tender flesh. Sophie sighed. He inhaled the scent of roses which clung to her, savoring it. Savoring her.

His hand moved lower, a finger pushing into her. She whimpered. He continued to kiss her nape as he let his fingers do his talking. He brought her to orgasm, feeling her shatter in his arms.

"James," she sighed, her trembling finally ceasing. "James," she echoed sleepily.

"Close your eyes, love," he said, and moments later, her breathing evened out.

What was he going to do?

He fell asleep as he worried, only waking when Sophie stirred in his arms. He turned her to him, kissing her, wanting her all over again. Worried that she would be too sore.

She found his cock and began massaging it. He was used to taking care of his partner's needs and was touched how she wanted to cater to him.

Rolling onto his back, James said, "It is time you explored me, Sophie. I am yours to do with as you wish."

The corners of her mouth turned up. "I will try not to be too tentative. I also want you to tell me if you like something in particular."

"I like you," he said, smiling up at her. "I will like everything you do."

Mischief flashed in her eyes. "Promise?"

"Promise," he repeated.

Sophie took her time, her fingers investigating the contours of his body. Examining. Probing. Searching.

"You are so hard everywhere, James," she marveled, her fingers skating up his forearm, squeezing the muscles of his biceps. "I cannot imagine what work you have repeatedly done to be in such superb condition. Perhaps I should seek out other sailors and compare them to you."

Even though he knew she was teasing, jealousy roared within him. James quickly flipped so that Sophie was on bottom and he was on top of her. Her eyes widened as his mouth sought hers, his body covering hers, desire rolling through him. He pinned her wrists together above her head with one hand, leaving the other free to tease and torment her. James brought her to orgasm again with his fingers, Sophie half-laughing, half-crying as he did so. His mouth savaged hers as he pushed inside her, deep thrusts that told her she was his.

He wanted her. He needed her.

He decided he must have all of her. Damn the consequences.

This time when he reached his climax, James did not pull away. He spent himself inside her, his seed filling her. A heady satisfaction filled him, knowing he had made Sophie all his.

Tenderly, he framed her face with his hands, resting his body weight on his knees and elbows so as not to crush her.

James wanted to tell her he loved her.

So he did.

"I love you."

He kissed her through her protests, quieting them by overwhelming her. She quit trying to speak and responded to his kisses, her nails digging into his back, her legs wrapping around his waist, drawing him to her.

Finally, he broke the kiss.

Was he sorry for what he'd said?

Absolutely not.

Gazing down at her, he said it again. "I love you, Sophie. I have never said that to another woman, but I am saying it to you."

He saw conflict in her eyes.

"You might think you do, James, but—"

"No buts, my darling. I simply do. And no, this is not a poor sea captain trying to coerce his very rich employer. I care nothing for your wealth. What I do love is your body. Your mind. Your inquisitiveness. Your sweetness."

Sophie shook her head. "James, this is so sudden. I cannot . . . why, I am barely a widow. I shouldn't . . ." Her voice trailed off.

He pressed a kiss to her brow. "I am not asking for a commitment from you now, Sophie. I only ask that you don't turn me down outright. That you give me a chance."

"A chance at what?" she asked, clearly confused.

"I want to marry you, Sophie Grant," James proclaimed.

"*Marry* you?" she echoed.

"Yes, marry you," he said firmly.

He kissed her again and rose from the bed. "I have to leave now, else I'll want to make love to you again. You are far too tender for me to do so. Besides, you are a thinker—and you have quite a bit of thinking to do."

As he dressed, James told her, "I will sleep in my own room tonight."

Bending, he brushed his lips against her brow. "Get some rest, Sophie. I will see you in the morning."

He passed through the connecting door, closing it behind him.

>>><<<

SOPHIE DRESSED IN her night rail and slipped into her dressing gown, belting it tightly. She paced the small room, frustrated at herself and James Jones.

Why had she asked him to father her child?

While the request had not strictly come out of nowhere—at least on her part, because she had previously thought about getting with child—*his* unexpected offer of marriage took her completely by surprise.

And the fact that he had told her that he loved her.

He couldn't possibly love her. They barely knew one another. Had only met a handful of times. Yet her heart told her that she knew everything she needed to know about the handsome ship captain. He was intelligent. Honorable. Thoughtful. Not to mention the physical intimacy that had passed between them, which was something she still couldn't quite comprehend.

Yes, coupling with Captain Jones had changed absolutely everything.

But she couldn't let the buoyant feelings overtake her good sense. Sophie had always been someone who thought with her head and not her heart. She was methodical. Practical. Even as a girl, she had never been one for daydreaming. She must also remember that she owned a hugely successful shipping line, rivaled only by that of Strong Shipping. Even then, with Strong Shipping's recent rumored troubles, Neptune Shipping was the premier line in Great Britain. Josiah hadn't built his company from nothing merely to hand it over to his widow, who allowed her head to be turned by the first man who came along.

No, she could never wed. Because that would mean giving up Neptune. British law would make the company her new husband's. He would own its wealth. He would have the choice of running it himself or hiring someone to do so for him. He could even sell it, not needing her permission. While she thought Captain Jones intelligent, she could not, in good faith, walk away from what Josiah Grant had built for a man who said he loved her.

Even if James truly had fallen in love with her, Sophie could never do the same. She couldn't wed the handsome ship captain and lose everything.

She would have to end things between them.

Of course, that meant she wouldn't get the child she so desperately wanted, an heir to Neptune Shipping. Then again, James had remained inside her when he had made love to her. His seed could be growing inside her.

The thought of never kissing him, never touching him, never having him in her bed almost did her in. Perhaps she could persuade him to bed her one more time before they returned to London. If no child resulted in their coupling, then she could find another man to solve her problem.

Yet Sophie's heart told her that no man was James Jones. No man was as honorable—and physically appealing—as *Vesta's* captain.

A knock sounded at her door, causing her heart to race. She hurried and opened it, finding the innkeeper standing outside, a tray in his hand.

"Captain Jones told us of your megrim and that you needed sleep this afternoon." He peered at her. "You do look as though you seem much better, Mrs. Grant."

"I am. Much better." She eyed the tray. "Have you brought me supper?"

"I have. Would you like it here?"

"Yes, please. On the table if you would. I shall eat and go straight to bed again. I will certainly be myself by tomorrow morning."

He left the room and she moved the chair to the table, attacking the soup and bread as if she hadn't eaten in days. Once it was finished, she dabbed her mouth with the napkin and then placed the tray outside her door, not wanting any further interruptions from the couple who ran the inn.

Sophie heard no stirring in the room next to hers, so she determined that James was still out. Perhaps he dined downstairs. She sat in the hard, wooden chair. Waiting.

An hour passed. She stared at the connecting door, willing it to open. Then she realized she needn't wait.

She could go to him.

It was the perfect solution. She would be in his bed, naked, waiting for him to return. She could have one last, sweet session of lovemaking. If she became with child, so much the better. If she didn't, she would still create lasting memories, ones which she believed would sustain her over her lifetime.

Going to the door, she smoothed her gown and took a deep breath. James had closed the door when he left her, so she didn't need to unlock it.

Surprise rushed through her when the door did not open.

James had locked the door.

From his side.

His action helped to clear her mind. Resolve filled her. She must end things with him. She couldn't marry him and give up everything Josiah had worked so hard for and entrusted her with, no matter how much she yearned to be with him. Protecting Neptune Shipping must always be her priority.

Quickly, Sophie redressed and packed her things and headed downstairs. The inn had a few people supping, but a quick glance about the room told her James was not one of them.

Finding the innkeeper, she said, "I forgot that I have a very important business meeting tomorrow morning. I must return at once to London. Can you help find a coach to take me there?"

He frowned. "I don't know of a coach, Mrs. Grant. My sister's boy works at a livery two blocks over, though. Perhaps something could be rented. It wouldn't be fancy. Most likely a wagon."

"Could you please send word? And ask him if he could drive me?"

He nodded. "I can go myself. Wait here a few minutes."

Sophie did so, her heart in her throat, worried that James would return and catch her sneaking off. Usually, she was quite brave in business matters, but this quick affair of the heart had turned her resolve into mush. If she caught a glimpse of him, she would have no control over her emotions, much as a drunkard had no control over imbibing.

The door opened, and she breathed a sigh of relief. Stepping to the innkeeper, she asked, "Were you able to arrange things?"

"Yes, Mrs. Grant. My nephew is waiting out front with a horse and cart. It will be a bit bumpy, but he can get you back to London. Shall I fetch your trunk?"

"Please."

When the innkeeper returned, she stepped outside with him. After he placed her trunk in the cart, she slipped him several notes.

"This should cover my room and that of Captain Jones. Obviously, he will be staying here tonight."

"Does the captain know of your meeting?"

"No," she said, guilt rushing through her. "I only recalled it. Would you please tell him where I went tomorrow morning?"

"I can do so. Or tonight if I see him."

She shook her head. "I would prefer Captain Jones get a good night's sleep. Please let him know in the morning that I am safely in London."

He frowned but agreed to her request. "It was good seeing you, Mrs. Grant. I hope we see you again soon."

"Thank you."

The innkeeper handed her up into the cart, where the driver tipped his hat to her and said, "I've lit the lantern for us, Mrs. Grant. It may take us several hours, but I will get you safely back to London."

As they pulled away, Sophie glanced over her shoulder, knowing she could never return to this inn—or James' arms—again.

Chapter Fifteen

James awoke after a restless night. He had longed to go to Sophie, but he was reluctant to do so after he proclaimed his love for her, as well as the marriage offer which had spilled forth from him unexpectedly. Actually, he hadn't truly asked for her hand. He had simply told her he loved her and wanted to marry her. He didn't know much about women in her position, but James figured that she would want to be courted more before committing to him.

Yet why waste time on that process when he knew what he wanted? By God, he wanted Sophie Grant.

He almost went to the door that connected their rooms, but he stopped himself from doing so. He had made certain the lock was in place yesterday, mostly to remind himself that he shouldn't go to her, but also to keep her out of his room, as well. James knew they both needed time to digest what he had said, as well as time for Sophie to recover and rest after their vigorous lovemaking.

He readied himself for the day and then went and knocked on her door. She didn't answer, and he wondered if she had been hungry enough to venture downstairs without him.

Suddenly, the door swung open, and the innkeeper's wife appeared, a bundle of bedclothes in her arms. James glanced over her shoulder, not seeing Sophie in the room.

"Looking for Mrs. Grant?" the woman asked. "She's already gone,

Captain, back to London."

Maintaining his composure, he said, "I see. When did she leave?"

"Around suppertime last night. Poor thing remembered an important meeting she had in London. Don't worry, Captain. Mrs. Grant paid the bill for you."

"You may clean my room if you wish since I will also be heading back to London this morning."

James returned to his room and threw things in his haversack. Slinging it over his shoulder, he went downstairs, where the innkeeper greeted him.

"Good morning, Captain," the man said as James handed over his key. "I suppose you'll be leaving us today."

"I heard from your wife that Mrs. Grant has already gone back to town."

"She did, indeed. My nephew drove her. I know you sailed your ship from London to Greenwich, but you'll need to be getting back on your own. There's a livery to the east, where you can rent a horse."

He had a vague impression of being atop a horse, but he wouldn't trust himself on one and said, "I'm a seaman, sir. Not a horseman."

The innkeeper chuckled. "Then there's a coach that heads to London twice a day. If you hurry, you can catch it."

The man gave him instructions as to where the coach departed from, and James quickly went to the location, purchasing the last available ticket on the morning run. The coach was crowded, and he was a large man, not looking forward to riding in the cramped quarters.

The driver must have seen his dilemma because he asked James if he wished to ride atop with him. He quickly accepted the offer and climbed aboard.

During the journey to London, his thoughts were a jumble. He hadn't taken Sophie to be a coward, yet she had done the very thing cowards do.

Run.

Perhaps he was judging her too harshly. Men and women had vastly different temperaments. While he was used to confronting problems head on, Sophie might have a much different way about her. He also had to consider that she had been a virgin widow. Having never made love before opened a new world to her, one she was an infant in. She had much to learn, and yet he had foolishly tipped his hand and told her he loved her. She was still having to grow accustomed to having her husband gone, and here James had gone and wanted her to up and wed him less than two months after Josiah Grant's demise.

Still, he would have thought she would wish to discuss the matter with him instead of fleeing. It was definitely going to make his pursuit of her more complicated.

But James was determined to have her as his wife.

They arrived in London, and he hailed a hansom cab to take him to Mayfair. He wasn't up to speaking to Drake at this point. His friend would have too many questions, which James wouldn't be able to answer.

He paid the driver and approached the door, wondering if he should knock since he now lived there. Deciding it would be more appropriate than entering on his own, he did so. Dursley, the footman who had first greeted him, received him.

"Mr. Powell wishes to speak with you, my lord," the footman informed him. "If you will wait in the parlor, I will send him to you."

James went to the room just off the foyer and waited until the butler appeared.

"Good morning, my lord," Powell said. "Things have taken a turn for the worse regarding His Grace. Dr. Nickels was here all night and is still with His Grace. I thought you should prepare yourself."

A plethora of emotions swirled within him, but he stoically said, "Thank you, Powell. I appreciate the warning. I will go to His Grace now."

James climbed a flight of stairs and found a sobbing Georgina sitting on the stairs at the landing. Quietly, he joined her, placing an arm about her quivering shoulders. Georgina buried her face in his chest.

He sat with her a few minutes and then felt a presence behind him. Effie took a seat on his other side, slipping her arm through his.

"Mama has told us that Papa will be gone soon," Effie explained. "Uncle Adolphus did not allow us to see Papa these past three years. It was only after you came and sent him and Cousin Theo away that we were able to visit Papa."

Effie swallowed, shaking her head. "It has been hard to see him this way."

Georgina lifted her head, tears staining her cheeks. "It is not as if Papa ever really loved us. Even before he became an invalid, we rarely saw him. But not being allowed to visit him all this time was distressing. Knowing now he will soon be gone hurts my heart, James."

"I understand how you feel. Even I recall that His Grace was a distant father to me when I was a child. Not one to show much affection. Still, I realized I had missed him, being gone all these years. It is hard for me to come back and know I will never have any kind of relationship with him, since he will soon be gone."

He smiled gently at Georgina. "But we will have each other, Georgie. You have your mother, your sisters, and cousins. And now me. We will get through this together."

Effie squeezed his arm. "We are so glad you found your way home, James. You should go see Papa now before it is too late."

"Go bathe your face, Georgie," James told his sister. "Effie, go with her."

The three came to their feet, and James made his way to the ducal rooms, hoping his father had been moved to them since his uncle had left the household. He entered the first room, an antechamber, and found Pippa, Mirella, Allegra, and Lyric all sitting in it. The girls leaped to their feet and surrounded him. He gave them hugs and told them, "I know you are sad about losing His Grace, but you have each other. You also have your mother and me. We are here to comfort you. I promise you will not be neglected."

They wiped away tears, nodding at his words.

"Georgina is very upset. Effie is with her now, but they could use your company."

"We'll go to them now," Mirella said, and the girls left the room.

James steeled himself for what lay beyond the next door and went through it, entering the ducal bedchamber. He spied his father in the bed, with Dinah seated on one side and the doctor opposite her.

He moved toward the bed and introduced himself. "I am Alinwood. Tell me His Grace's status."

Nickels' grave expression said it all. "As you can see my lord, His Grace is quite ill. There is nothing more left to do for him."

"Then I will stay until the end," he promised, pulling up a chair and joining Dinah for the vigil. He took her hand and squeezed it as they sat listening to the labored, final breaths of the Duke of Seaton.

A quarter-hour later, those breaths ceased.

Dr. Nickels asked the duchess, "Is there anything I can do for you, Your Grace? Perhaps a draught to help you sleep?"

"No," she replied, wiping away her tears with a handkerchief. "Thank you for everything you have done for His Grace these past three years, Doctor. You have been so kind to us."

"I will inform Powell of His Grace's passing as I leave," the physician said, exiting the room.

Dinah placed her free hand over her husband's. "He was not the best of husbands, but he was certainly not the worst. Most importantly, Seaton gave me four wonderful daughters. For that alone, the marriage, in my mind, was a successful one."

She turned and gazed up at James. "*You* are now Seaton, Your Grace. I hope you have completed your business as Captain Jones, because your family needs you to step up as the new duke."

"I have done so, Dinah," he confirmed. "My ship will have a new captain named, and he will be responsible for *Vesta's* return to London. Hopefully, it will be my friend, and *Vesta's* first mate, Drake Andrews."

He glanced at his father, then turned his attention back to Dinah. "What is next? Where is Seaton to be laid to rest?"

"He would want to be buried at Shadowcrest," she told him. "I have wanted you to see the estate anyway. I assume you will accompany us to Kent."

"Yes. As head of the Strong family and now Duke of Seaton, I am fully committed to my responsibilities. We should leave for Shadowcrest in the morning. I know it will take some planning and several carriages will be needed to convey all of us and His Grace's body."

"I believe the girls and I will remain in Kent after the funeral," she said. "We have all missed country living and can return next spring for the come-outs which need to be made. I will tell you all about what that involves, James. You, too, will be expected to attend the Season. You will need to find a bride for yourself on the Marriage Mart and get an heir off her."

He kept silent, not wishing to share that he had already decided the woman he would marry.

"I will go and meet with Mr. Peabody now and return later."

"Take the carriage, Your Grace. It is yours now."

James went downstairs and told Powell he needed use of the carriage and also let the butler know that the family would depart in the morning for Shadowcrest and the duke's burial.

"I will send word to Shadowcrest to expect you, as well as notify the vicar of His Grace's passing, Your Grace," the butler said.

"Thank you for taking care of that, Powell. I suppose I should hire a secretary soon to handle such matters."

He thought if Charles Timmons could maintain his sobriety, his old tutor would make for an excellent secretary.

"Her Grace said she and the girls will remain in the country until next spring. I, on the other hand, will return to London soon."

"Very good, Your Grace," the butler said.

James went to his new solicitor's office and was immediately granted entrance to Peabody's office.

"Ah, Lord Alinwood, it is good to see you again. I have several things to share with you about what we have found at Strong shipping."

"I want to hear what you have to say, Mr. Peabody, but I am here to inform you of His Grace's death this afternoon."

Sympathy filled the solicitor's eyes. "I am sorry to hear this news, Your Grace," he said, and James saw how smoothly the man transitioned into addressing him in a different manner.

"What needs to be done regarding my claiming the title and inheriting?"

Peabody went through the legalities of the situation, and James knew the solicitor would handle everything seamlessly.

"As to His Grace's will, almost everything goes to you, both entailed and unentailed estates. Except for one. His Grace designated Crestridge for Her Grace's use. It is a property about ten miles from Shadowcrest. A manor house sits on the property. It and the land will be where Her Grace may reside. Of course, she can also live part of the year in the dower house at Shadowcrest. The two of you will have to work things out."

"That won't be a problem," James assured the solicitor.

"There are also dowries His Grace provided for his four daughters."

"Are those dowries of an equal amount?" he asked.

"They are, Your Grace," Peabody confirmed.

"I wish you to draw up whatever papers are necessary to provide the same amount for my two nieces, Misses Allegra and Lyric Strong. They are under my care now. Their father has had little to do with them their entire lives, and I want to see them have the same advantages as my sisters do."

"I can certainly take care of that for you, Your Grace. I will also draw up your will. Will His Grace be buried at Shadowcrest?"

"Yes, we are leaving for Kent tomorrow morning. If you have need of me, I will be there for several days. We can discuss anything regarding Strong Shipping upon my return."

"An excellent idea, Your Grace. By then, my clerks should have completed their review of all the documents. If I may say so, Mr. Compton is going to be an excellent head for the company. His years at Strong Shipping have provided valuable experience, which could not be replicated by another candidate assuming the position."

James said his farewells, then directed his coachman to head to the address he had obtained from Powell before they left the house. While he had learned from Powell that his uncle had given up his rented townhouse when he moved the family to the Duke of Seaton's townhouse, Adolphus had sent word to Powell where to deliver his and Theo's things. The townhouse they now arrived at was small but elegant. With no income, James wondered how long his uncle and cousin would be able to live here. Then again, he had no idea how much Adolphus had stolen and squirreled away. It might be enough to live with ease for the rest of his life.

He knocked upon the door, and a butler answered.

"I am here to see both Mr. Strongs," he announced.

The servant's eyes flicked over James, who still wore his sea captain's uniform.

With disdain, the butler asked, "Do you have a calling card, Sir?"

James stood proudly, towering over this servant. He wouldn't be bullied by his uncle or any of Adolphus' staff. "I am His Grace. The Duke of Seaton. And I will see my uncle and cousin at once."

The butler's jaw dropped. He began sputtering, but James cut him off.

"Tell them that I am here and will not be kept waiting," he ordered, hoping he sounded sufficiently ducal. Glancing to his right, he said, "They are to come to this parlor."

He brushed past the butler and entered the parlor, thinking it best that he made his relatives come to him. James prepared himself, knowing his uncle would come in on the attack.

Going to the window, he stood looking out, clasping his hands behind his back. He did not want to appear meek or humble, as if he were waiting for the pair.

Minutes later, he heard angry footsteps crossing the tiled foyer, and he sensed his uncle's presence.

"What nonsense are you spouting, James?"

Slowly, he turned, seeing Adolphus was red-faced. Theo stood nearby, looking unsure of himself.

Using his height to full advantage, James strode across the room and glared down at his uncle.

"You are to address me as Your Grace," he said, steel in his voice. "Your brother passed away earlier today."

"Impossible!" cried Adolphus, grasping at straws.

"My father has been in poor condition for quite some time. Then again, you wouldn't know firsthand, simply because you never visited him." His eyes narrowing, James added, "And you forbid his own daughters to see him."

"Yes, he was ill," Adolphus said. "But—"

"No buts, Uncle," he interrupted. "You took extreme advantage of your own flesh and blood's poor health. You moved into his house and all but claimed the title from him. I have proof from both Rainn and Barclay that you and Theo drained funds from the family's estates and businesses, especially Strong Shipping."

Adolphus was speechless, and James saw Theo turn white.

"I am not above handing over the evidence of your crimes to the authorities," he added.

"You wouldn't dare," his uncle said. "It's an empty threat. You wouldn't embarrass the family that way. There are all those girls to be married off. No suitable gentleman would want to entangle himself in a family filled with such a sordid scandal."

"Ah, but I am a duke. Everyone always wishes to cozy up to a duke. Be his friend. Marry his sisters or daughters. Rainn is gone. Barclay was put on a ship bound for America. You—and Theo—are no longer a part of the Strong family. You acted in a manner unbecoming a gentleman. Falsifying His Grace's will. Leaving his wife and daughters penniless."

"You know about that?" Theo asked, fear clearly in his eyes.

"Quiet, Theodore!" barked Adolphus.

"I want you gone from London," James said evenly. "You stole enough money. Buy yourself a small place in the country—and stay there, Uncle. Else I will have to bring your misdeeds to light."

"You wouldn't dare."

"Oh, believe me. I would. And the *ton* would like nothing better than a juicy scandal to sink their teeth into. It's over, Uncle. Your little reign of terror is done. I don't want to see you or Theo. I don't want to hear about you or from you. If I so much as catch you in London, I will beat you until you are half-dead and can no longer walk nor talk."

James cracked his knuckles. "Don't think I won't do it. Duke or not, I will always be the seaman I have been all my life." He smiled evenly. "I merely have the power of being a duke to go along with my uncouth ways."

"We'll leave," Theo declared. "We'll be gone by tomorrow morning. You won't hear from us again, James." He swallowed. "Your Grace."

"Make it happen," he commanded. "I will be back this time tomorrow, along with several of my crew. If you are still here? Then the fun will begin."

James knew he would be on his way to Shadowcrest tomorrow,

but he was not going to share that bit of information with these two.

"Yes, Your Grace," Adolphus said through gritted teeth.

Smiling pleasantly at the pair, he said, "Have a good day, gentlemen," and sauntered from the room and back to his waiting carriage.

Chapter Sixteen

James sent word to the waterfront inn where Drake had said he would be staying, asking his friend to come and see him, letting Drake know Seaton was dead. By the next morning, he still had not heard from his first mate, which troubled him. Of course, Drake was popular with women, and most likely had either spent the night in a new acquaintance's bed or had brought her back to the inn with him and had had no time to reply to any messages.

He breakfasted with Dinah now. Usually, the girls all came down for breakfast, but the duchess said it was a madhouse upstairs this morning, with last minute additions being added to trunks, including which treasured items not to be parted from.

"I've had tea and scones sent up to them," Dinah told him. "They know we are leaving after breakfast today. Miss Feathers will make certain everything is loaded and every girl accounted for."

"Who is Miss Feathers?" James asked, having barely begun to learn the names of various servants in the London townhouse, wondering if he might recognize from his youth any servants still at Shadowcrest.

"Miss Feathers' title is that of governess, but she is much more than that. She has been with us five years and handles the girls beautifully. They listen to her and never object, as they sometimes do when I suggest things." Dinah smiled. "There are times when I have asked Miss Feathers to help me in encouraging one of the girls in small matters. Getting one to try a certain color of gown or play a particular piece on the pianoforte. Miss Feathers gives a subtle suggestion—and it is accepted."

"She sounds like the ideal governess and companion to the girls in the house."

"I agree," Dinah said. "Miss Feathers has certainly made my life easier since she arrived five years ago."

A footman entered the breakfast room and spoke to Powell, who came to James.

"Mr. Andrews has arrived, Your Grace. He said you sent for him."

"Have him join us, Powell." He turned to Dinah. "Mr. Andrews is First Mate of *Vesta* and my closest friend. He helped see Mr. Rainn from town."

"Oh, I already like him," she said, taking a sip of her tea.

"Mr. Andrews," Powell announced two minutes later, and Drake entered the breakfast room. He came toward James and paused.

"What do I do? Or say? I'm new at having a duke as a friend."

Dinah's laughter tinkled softly as she and James rose, and she said, "It would be appropriate to bow slightly, Mr. Andrews. No, that is too much. Try again."

She had Drake bow three times until he got it right in her eyes.

"You have to strike the right balance between respect and fawning over him, Mr. Andrews," she explained. "I believe you have mastered a proper bow, though." She smiled at him.

"We have not been introduced," Drake said, returning her smile.

James sensed the shift in the air. Was his friend *flirting* with his stepmother? And she with him?

"May I introduce the Duchess of Seaton? Mr. Andrews, Your Grace."

Drake's eyes lit with amusement. "Am I also to bow to you, Your Grace?"

"You may," she said, her eyes merry. "It would also be appropriate to take my hand and kiss it."

"Kiss it. Your hand."

"Yes, Mr. Andrews. Unless you do not wish to do so."

Drake's smile widened. "I very much would like to do so, Your Grace."

He bowed and then took the hand she offered, brushing a kiss against her bare knuckles. James noticed Dinah's cheeks pinkened slightly. It struck him that Dinah and Drake were close in age, both very attractive, intelligent, kindhearted people. Knowing Seaton had been a good twenty-five years older than Dinah, and that his youngest sister was five and ten years of age, it possibly had been many years since Dinah had coupled with a man.

The way the pair looked at one another now, it wouldn't surprise him if they excused themselves and found the nearest empty bedchamber.

Clearing his throat, James said, "Would you like some coffee? Or tea?"

Drake finally released Dinah's hand. "Yes, I would like... tea. That sounds very good."

"Have a seat," James told his friend, who first seated Dinah before himself.

A footman brought a cup and saucer, and Dinah herself poured out from the pot sitting on the table.

"Would you like cream or sugar, Mr. Andrews?" she asked, her voice pitched lower than usual.

The sailor gave her a wink. "I'll take it the way you do, Your Grace."

She chuckled. "I hope you won't regret saying that, Mr. Andrews. I have quite the sweet tooth."

"A sweet lady should have a sweet tooth," Drake quipped.

James cleared his throat again, and it seemed to break the spell between the two.

"*Vesta's* repairs are well underway," he said. "I think in another week, she'll be ready to sail back to London. I want you to be the one to steer her here."

His friend frowned. "Wouldn't that be Mrs. Grant's choice?"

"Of course," James said quickly. "I will be leaving for Shadowcrest in the next hour. It is where we will bury His Grace. After a few days of seeing the estate, however, I will return to London. I need to speak at length with Mr. Peabody and Mr. Compton regarding Strong Shipping. I will take time to visit with Mrs. Grant and resign my position from Neptune Shipping Line. When I do so, I will recommend that you be my replacement."

"I am grateful for that," Drake said. "I won't expect it to happen, though. I lack the experience most men named to be a captain should have."

"If His Grace feels you are ready, then you are definitely ready," Dinah interjected. "And if this Mrs. Grant is truly the clever businesswoman they say she is, she will also realize that, Mr. Andrews."

A blush rose on Drake's cheeks, shocking James. He couldn't have imagined any situation which would cause that to occur.

"I simply wanted you to know why and how long I would be out of town, and that I would speak with Mrs. Grant regarding your employment when I return from Kent."

His tone was dismissive, and Drake picked up on that. Rising, he said, "I appreciate the good word you will put in for me, Your Grace. I bid you and Her Grace a good day."

"Goodbye, Mr. Andrews," Dinah said. "I hope we see you again soon."

James wanted to say more, but with four footmen and Powell in the room, he realized private conversations at mealtimes were a thing of the past. He would need to get Dinah alone, however, and see what she had meant by flirting with his closest friend.

The door flew open, and three of the girls hurried in.

"We're all packed, Mama," Mirella said. "And the carriages are being brought around now."

"There is so much!" Pippa declared. "Why, you would think we were carrying half of London home to Shadowcrest with us."

Lyric added, "Miss Feathers said that she has shown Powell what is to be sent in the next trip. That not everything can travel with us this first time."

James had been shocked when Dinah had told him how many carriages would be taken to Shadowcrest. Just to convey the family alone, they would need two carriages. Then there was one which would carry the body of the deceased Duke of Seaton. It and another would hold servants, and a final vehicle would be loaded with trunks. Trunks would also be placed atop all the carriages carrying passengers.

"Go tell the others it is time to depart," Dinah said. "His Grace and I will join you outside."

The girls rushed from the room, like a whirlwind which had set down for a moment and then picked up of its own accord again.

"Powell?" the duchess said as she stood. "Are you ready?"

"Whenever you are, Your Grace," the loyal butler said.

Powell had asked James and Dinah if he might accompany them to Shadowcrest, keeping watch over the duke's body on the journey and attending the funeral. While Dinah had told James it was an unusual request, they had agreed to it, the butler being a steadfast servant and leader in the duke's household for many years.

Sutton would also be coming to Shadowcrest with them, serving as valet to James. When James had protested, Dinah cut him off, saying it was expected for any gentleman, and especially a duke, to have a valet. James had said there was nothing Sutton could do for him that he couldn't do for himself. Dinah explained that if he insisted on doing for himself, then Sutton would be unemployed.

"You are expected to employ a great number of servants, both in town and at your various country estates. Yes, part of it is for show, but these staff members are valuable cogs which keep the estates running."

Her words had caused James to see things in a different light, and he had agreed to keep Sutton on. Already, the valet was proving invaluable. Since James had no wardrobe beyond his sea captain's clothes, Sutton had gone into the many wardrobes of the Duke of Seaton. Before the apoplexy struck, Seaton had been a man full of vim and vigor, close to James' height and weight. Already, Sutton had begun altering clothes to fit James.

Dinah said that would do for now, but she'd already given James express instructions that when he returned to London after the funeral, he was to see Seaton's tailor and have an entire wardrobe made up for him. She again explained that it might seem like far too many coats and trousers and pairs of boots, but it kept others employed.

She emphasized how a duke was a leader of society in all manner of things, from his dress to his speech to the opinions he spouted. She wanted James, as the new Duke of Seaton, to cut a fine figure and be an unquestioned leader.

He didn't mind wearing new clothes, but he doubted he would be leading anyone in Polite Society. He might now be a duke, but he would never lose the rough and tumble sailor within him.

James helped Dinah, Allegra, and Georgina into the first carriage, where he would ride until they stopped to trade out horses on the journey from London. Mirella, Pippa, Lyric, and Effie rode in the second carriage. Those carriages carried the seal of the Duke of Seaton on their doors. The remaining carriages were plain black. Dinah told him the one carrying the duke's body was rented from a nearby livery, while the other two were used in various capacities when the family was in town.

The journey to Shadowcrest would take about three hours total. The estate, located in Kent, was southwest of Maidstone, the closest city, though a few other villages were nearby. It would be in Crestview, the closest village to Shadowcrest, where the duke would be laid to rest in a family plot next to the local church.

During the first leg of the journey, Dinah was quiet. She had told him the brief trip would help him to get to know the girls better.

"I play rather well," Georgina said. "I am not bragging about that, Seaton, but ask Allegra about my singing."

Knowing Georgina must be joking, he solemnly asked his cousin, "How is Georgie's singing?"

"Atrocious!" Allegra said, laughing so much she had to hold her sides. "Both dogs and cats will flatten their ears and hide. Servants will find rooms on the far side of the house to dust. Don't ever let Georgie sing for you, Seaton."

James didn't like that the girls were referring to him this way, but he supposed it was ingrained in them from a young age how to address titled peers.

"What about you, Allegra? What are you fond of, besides making fun of your cousin's terrible voice?" he asked.

Allegra laughed again. "Oh, I enjoy singing and do not annoy servants or animals," she told him. "I also like playing the pianoforte and adore long walks in the country. I am so ready to be at Shadowcrest."

When they stopped to exchange the teams, which Dinah had told him all about, including the fact that Seaton kept horses at the changing stations so he would always receive his own fine beasts and not merely rented ones. James knew nothing about horseflesh, but he could see the horses pulling their carriages were first-rate.

As he watched the exchange, Pippa joined him. "Do you like horses, Seaton?"

"I might. I don't know much about them. I think I rode as a boy at Shadowcrest, but I'm not certain."

"I live to ride," she said. "I will teach you. A groom taught me, and he is now head of the stables at Shadowcrest. I may not seem a likely instructor, but when it comes to horses, I have all the patience in the world."

"I hope that will extend to patience with human dukes who haven't the slightest idea how to ride a horse."

Pippa giggled. "I like you, Seaton. It's nice to have a brother. And I will teach you how to ride. You will have to know how to do so. Riding is the way to get around in the country. You'll want to visit your tenants. I can go with you."

"I would appreciate that, Pippa."

They returned to the second carriage, and he traveled with new companions the rest of the way. He learned that Mirella loved singing and dancing, but her true devotion was to painting landscapes. Effie was bubbly, but admitted to being a bit stubborn at times.

"Stubborn?" Pippa asked. "You are argumentative, Eff. Especially when you are fighting to bring home a new stray."

Effie stroked the cat in her lap. "Animals need someone to advocate for them. Take Daffy here, for example."

"Daffy is short for Daffodil," Lyric told James. "Because of her yellow color."

"Daffy was tossed out like rubbish," Effie continued. "She was covered in lice and had a broken leg, her fur matted and filthy. But she was mostly starved for affection."

"Then I am glad you rescued her," he said. "I am sorry you had to leave a few of your pets behind."

"Oh, they will be spoiled, with or without me," Effie assured him. "The maids and footmen love to play with them. Besides, I have plenty of animals at Shadowcrest waiting for me." She frowned. "I do hope they'll remember me," she fretted. "We have been gone for so long."

Lyric slipped an arm around her cousin. "They will, Effie. No one could ever forget you."

While her twin had sable hair, Lyric's was a deep russet shade. He learned that she created pottery and was fond of gardening.

"I cannot wait to get to Shadowcrest and see the gardens," Lyric told him. "I can take you on a tour of them, Seaton. They are remarkable. The best you will ever see."

"I look forward to that, Lyric," he said.

"We're here!" cried Pippa, lowering the window and leaning out. "This is the turn, Seaton. It's another mile or so along this lane, and then the house will come into sight."

Anticipation filled him, having seen glimpses in his mind of his childhood home. When the carriage pulled in front of it, however, awe filled James.

The structure was larger than his London townhouse, the brick neat, the landscaping impeccable. Two long lines of servants lined the drive.

"Why are they all outside?" he mused aloud.

Mirella told him, "They are ready to receive the new duke. Look ducal, Seaton," she teased.

James got out of the carriage and helped the passengers from it. A man stepped toward him.

"Your Grace, I am Forrester, the butler at Shadowcrest."

Forrester was in his late thirties, with gray hair at his temples. He indicated a woman who joined him. "This is Mrs. Forrester, your housekeeper, and my brother's widow."

Neither servant looked familiar to him. "It is good to meet you both," he said. "Shall I meet the rest of my staff?"

Forrester led him down each line, introducing each servant by name and what they did at Shadowcrest. Once he had met all of them, he addressed them briefly.

"I am humbled to have become the Duke of Seaton, and I am grateful for your service to the previous duke. The family will be staying in the country until next spring. I hope you are as happy they are home as they are to be here."

"Lady Effie's pets will be glad to see her," Forrester said. "They have been well-cared for, my lady."

"Thank you, Forrester," Effie replied, stroking Daffy's head. "I do hope they'll take to Daffy."

"We should get inside," Dinah declared. "It's a bit cold."

Organized chaos ensued, with servants unloading and carting in trunks. Powell supervised the duke's coffin being carried inside, where Forrester had set up a parlor for visitors wishing to view His Grace's body before tomorrow morning's funeral.

James watched how efficient everything unfolded, and then he noticed a tall man striding toward him. His chestnut hair gleamed red in today's sunshine, and as he approached, James saw he possessed the Strong eyes. Immediately, he knew the identity of the newcomer.

Offering his hand, he said, "Cousin Caleb. It has been a long while since we have been in one another's company."

Shaking hands, Caleb also inclined his head. "It is good to see you again, Your Grace. You are one of the few pleasant memories of my childhood. I remember how patient you were with me when we built things with blocks." He chuckled. "Especially when Theo would knock down our bridges and castles."

"I had forgotten that," he admitted. "You have jogged my memory, though, Caleb. I hear that you are steward at Shadowcrest."

"I am, Your Grace. It was at my father's request." He smiled ruefully. "Actually, his demand. The Shadowcrest steward was set to be pensioned off, and after Uncle's apoplexy attack, my father stepped in. He thought I could learn more as the steward here than at university."

"How long were you there?"

"Only a year." Caleb sighed. "I wish it could have been longer. I enjoyed the academic life. But I will admit that learning about Shadowcrest and how to run a large estate has been a lesson that continues each day."

"I look forward to going out on the estate with you, Caleb. Seeing it. Meeting my tenants."

His cousin smiled. "I will be happy to take you, Your Grace. You have a lot to see and be proud of. We should go in, though. Mrs. Forrester will have tea ready for the family."

"Lead the way."

They went to the doors of the great house, and James looked over his shoulder, seeing the manicured lawn and mature trees which lined the lane leading up to the house.

Who would have thought a former cabin boy would one day own such a grand estate?

He looked forward to seeing every inch of it.

And bringing Sophie here. As his duchess.

Chapter Seventeen

Sophie climbed the stairs from the warehouse and entered Neptune Shipping, greeting the clerks she passed as she made her way to her office. Mr. Barnes brought her a cup of tea and asked if she needed anything from him at this time.

"No, thank you. I do have some figures that I may want you to look over when I am done with them, however," knowing the secretary had nearly as good a head for figures as she did.

"Happy to oblige, Mrs. Grant."

The secretary left, and Sophie sat back in her chair, restless as she had been for the last week since she had left Greenwich. She still regretted doing a very un-Sophie-like thing, turning coward and leaving without speaking to James.

While the days had been hard, she had forced herself to concentrate on the business at hand. The nights, however, were long. She had gotten little sleep. All she could think of was James' hard body pressed to hers. His lips against hers. All the ways in which he had made her feel treasured.

Even loved . . .

She should not have run. She should have stood her ground. Told him she couldn't love him or marry him, but that she hoped they might continue their brief affair until he returned to sea. A tear escaped from the corner of her eye, and she angrily wiped it away.

Though she could admit it to no one, like James, she also wanted more. Not an affair.

Something lasting. Something permanent.

It would do no good to cry over spilt milk, though. She had not heard from him in the week she had been back in London and doubted she would. She wondered if he might sign on at Strong Shipping, her chief competitor. Sophie had read in the newspapers about the death of the Duke of Seaton, and how his son was the new duke.

That had surprised her because she—and all of London—had been under the impression that the heir apparent was Seaton's twin brother, Adolphus Strong. While Adolphus had not held the title these past few years, he had acted in his brother's stead, making decisions for Strong Shipping and she supposed the family, as well, due to the duke being incapacitated in some way. She wondered why this son had not stepped in and prevented his uncle's poor decision making. Then again, she wasn't privy to the gossip of the *ton*, so she had no idea of why the heir apparent had been absent. Perhaps there had been some falling out between father and son, and the ducal heir had had little to do with his father and family.

A light tap sounded on her office door, and she said, "Come."

Mr. Barnes entered. "Mrs. Grant, word just came from Mr. Purdy. *Vesta's* repairs have been completed, and she is ready to be returned to the London docks. Shall I send word to Captain Jones?"

"Captain Jones will not return *Vesta* for us," she told him. "Instead, it will be Mr. Andrews, the first mate. I am going to offer him command of *Vesta*."

The only reaction Barnes had was one eyebrow rising slightly. "Shall I send a message to Mr. Andrews to come see you now?"

"Please do so. Tell him at his earliest convenience, but convey that it is urgent."

"Yes, Mrs. Grant."

Sophie was able to bury herself in work, grateful she had something else to concentrate on besides the mistake she had made with James Jones.

An hour later, Mr. Barnes again entered her office, saying, "Mr. Andrews has arrived."

"Send him in," she told her secretary. "I will not need you since our meeting will be brief."

Mr. Andrews entered her office, and she told him to close the door behind him. He was quite nice-looking himself, and for a moment, Sophie considered asking him if he might be interested in coupling with her because the resulting child would hopefully have his good looks.

She refrained from doing so, however, knowing she had already lost one excellent captain over such foolishness. She wasn't willing to lose Mr. Andrews, too.

"Won't you have a seat, Mr. Andrews?"

"Good morning, Mrs. Grant. I was happy to hear from you. I hope it is good news and that *Vesta* is her usual self again."

"Mr. Purdy has assured me that all necessary repairs have been completed. I need you to assemble your skeleton crew again and bring *Vesta* back to London."

He studied her a moment. "You wish for me to do so?"

"Yes, I do, Mr. Andrews. I also would like to offer you the position of captain of *Vesta*. I hope you will accept my offer."

Andrews beamed at her. "I may be foolish in doing so, Mrs. Grant, but I am more than happy to take on this new role with Neptune Shipping."

"I am delighted to hear your decision, *Captain* Andrews. I know you had worried a bit about not having the necessary experience, but you have spent your entire life at sea. You have been around several men who have shown you what true leadership is, including Captain Jones." Sophie hesitated a moment and then asked, "Have you spoken to Captain Jones since Greenwich?"

"I supped with him last evening," Andrews informed her. "He returned to London yesterday afternoon."

"And . . . was he in . . . good spirits?"

Her new captain's face gave nothing away. "Aye, he seemed to be. He's very busy with his family, so I was happy we had a chance to catch up."

"I would like to give you one of our shorter routes to begin with, Captain," she said crisply, forcing her thoughts back to business. "It is late September now. Let us look at some of the routes *Vesta* might travel, taking weather into consideration."

She retrieved a folder and led him to a nearby table, where a map of the world was laid out for easy reference. Over the next half-hour, she explained the various routes to him and the ports of call on each route. They decided which route would be best for his ship.

"I can have the cargo loaded onto *Vesta* once you sail her back. Because of the journey we have chosen, everything that would need to be loaded onto *Vesta* is currently in my warehouse."

"I can leave within the next hour for Greenwich, Mrs. Grant," Andrews assured her. "We can sail her back this afternoon, and loading can commence tomorrow morning. How long will that take?"

"A full day. Loading goes faster than unloading because I already have the manifests in hand and the designated crates all grouped together, ready to go, unlike when a ship returns from her voyage and manifests must be closely examined, with each crate being opened and checked for its contents. How long will it take for you to assemble a crew? I have experience in hiring them and am happy to help you with this task."

"I have been thinking about it ever since we spoke. I would like to use a majority of the crew which sailed on *Vesta's* most recent voyage. I will only add a handful of sailors to that roster. Having sailed around the world with these men, I am familiar with them and have a good idea how to handle them."

Sophie thought a moment. "If you bring her back today and we load the cargo tomorrow, would you be able to sail the day after with first tide?"

"Yes, Mrs. Grant. I can make that happen. Most of the crew has remained close by, knowing *Vesta* would leave soon after her repairs were made. I will go to the waterfront now and collect my skeleton crew. I'll also find a reliable sailor who will spread the word about our plans on when we will set sail. By day's end, most of the crew should have returned and can come aboard *Vesta*. They can help with loading the cargo tomorrow. It will help speed things along."

He rose, and Sophie did the same, offering her hand.

Andrews shook it. "Thank you for giving me this opportunity, Mrs. Grant. If all goes well—including the weather—I should be able to bring *Vesta* back to England by late July or early August."

"You will need to be fitted for your captain's uniforms," she told him. "Once you return from Greenwich this afternoon, go to this tailor."

Sophie turned and scribbled the man's name and his shop's address onto a piece of parchment and handed it to her new captain.

"He keeps a line of uniforms ready for us, in varying sizes. When you see him later today, he might have to make a few slight adjustments, but you should be able to leave his shop with all that you need."

Andrews frowned. "Do you know what that might cost? I hope I have the funds to cover such an expense."

Not wanting to lose this capable man over something as trivial as the cost of a few jackets, she said, "Oh, Captain Andrews, this is a company expense. We wish for you to present yourself in the best light to your crew, especially since you are representing Neptune Shipping Lines."

Relief crossed his face. "Thank you, Mrs. Grant. That's quite generous of Neptune to cover those costs."

The company had never done so before, but Sophie decided that would be a new policy, where Neptune Shipping paid the cost for captains' uniforms.

She bid her new captain farewell. Once he had time to leave the premises, she gave the note she had just written to Mr. Barnes.

"See that this is delivered to the tailor we use. We will cover the costs of Captain Andrews' uniforms, and that will be what we do in the future for all new captains. If any of our current captains go in for replacements, Neptune will also pay for those, as well."

Mr. Barnes nodded sagely. "A wise decision, Mrs. Grant. I'll see the note is delivered at once."

She told him the trade route she would send Andrews and the vessel on and said, "We will commence cargo loading early tomorrow morning. Please notify our warehouse supervisor so that workers will be sent to the docks with cargo first thing tomorrow morning. In the meantime, see that all manifests are pulled and checked to make this process run more smoothly."

"I will take care of that," the secretary promised.

Sophie returned to her office and made notes on *Vesta* and the merchandise the vessel would carry on its upcoming voyage.

The rest of her day went smoothly, and she was pleased that she was able to concentrate as well as she did. Being busy was the best medicine for a broken heart, and she admitted to herself that was the condition she suffered from. Sophie didn't think she loved Captain Jones, but she missed him terribly. It was best, however, that they had parted ways because she feared it would have been very easy to fall in love with him.

She decided to pen a note to him and took out fresh paper, beginning to write.

Dear Captain Jones —

I regret the haste in which I left Greenwich. I have never been a coward before, and I apologize for my speed in leaving you without us having a final chat.

I hope you will accept my sincere apologies for my rude behavior. Since I have not seen you, I will assume that you no longer have an interest in sailing for Neptune Shipping Lines.

I did meet with Mr. Andrews today and offered him the position as captain of Vesta, which he graciously accepted. Thank you for bringing Captain Andrews to my attention. I believe he will perform at the highest levels and represent Neptune Shipping well.

I do lament how things ended between us, but I wish you the best in your future endeavors, and I hope your family is well. Whether you realize it or not, you changed my life for the better—and for that, I am grateful.

Sincerely,
Mrs. Sophie Grant

She allowed the ink to dry and then folded the letter, realizing she had no idea where to send it. She slipped it into her reticule, not wanting it to be laying about the office. Not that she suspected any of her employees would be going through her things, but she would like to keep private matters private. When she saw Captain Andrews tomorrow, she would ask if he knew the address of his friend's family, so that she might send the letter to him. If not, Captain Andrews would most likely be generous enough to deliver it in person the next time he saw James Jones.

Sophie tidied her desk, something she did every evening before she left, and then exited her office, telling her secretary goodnight. She made her way through the warehouse and outside, coming to a sudden halt.

James Jones stood waiting for her.

Her heart began beating rapidly, and the butterflies in her belly exploded.

He closed the distance between them. "Good evening, Mrs. Grant.

Might you be available to dine with me this evening?"

He no longer wore his captain's uniform. Instead, he had on a well-tailored coat and pair of breeches. The coat fit him to perfection, emphasizing his broad shoulders, while the breeches defined his muscular legs. She supposed his family was quite well off if he were able to dress in such a fine manner. Even his cravat was expertly tied.

Finding her voice, Sophie said, "I was not certain I would ever see you again, Captain Jones."

She opened her reticule and withdrew the letter she had so recently penned, handing it to him.

"This is my apology to you for my abominable behavior in Greenwich. Know that I regret my actions, and I hope I am never such a gutless mouse again."

He slipped the letter inside his coat. "I will read it later, Sophie."

Just hearing her name on his sensual lips caused her to shiver.

"You haven't answered my question yet. Are you available to dine with me this evening?"

She told herself it would be a terrible idea, spending time alone with him. And yet every fiber of her being longed to do so.

"My cook was . . . making a stew for me tonight. Would . . . would you . . . care to come to my home for dinner?"

He gave her that sunny smile, which had stolen her heart. Sophie finally admitted to herself that she was in love with this man.

"I would be happy to accompany you to your home and share the meal with you," he said. "I have a hansom cab waiting to convey us there." He indicated the vehicle standing behind him. "Shall we?"

She allowed him to hand her up, his touch sending feelings through her which she had pined for during the past week. James gave the driver her address, and then he climbed in bedside her. The fit was snug because he was a large man, and she relished their sides resting against one another.

He didn't try and start a conversation on the way home. She appreciated that. She had so much to say to him—and yet she did not know where to begin.

They reached her small house, and he paid the driver, handing her down. Sophie removed her key from her reticule and let them in.

"Please have a seat in the dining room," she told him, pointing to the room opposite the parlor, where she had entertained him at tea. That seemed a lifetime ago. "I will set another place."

She left him, entering the kitchen and smelling the stew. Cook always knew the time Sophie would arrive home, and she would leave a plate warming or a bowl of stew or soup in the warmer. She took out a bowl and split the portion of stew between them, seeing James had the larger amount, knowing it would be hard for her to eat more than a few bites.

Setting the bowls on a tray with a spoon, knife, and napkin for him, she retrieved the freshly-baked bread and a crock of butter, also placing these on the tray. Then she added wineglasses and carried the tray to the dining room. Before she left, she lit the stove, which had a large pot of water sitting atop it.

James sat patiently waiting, but he quickly came to his feet and took the tray from her.

As she began placing the items on the table, he asked, "Shouldn't your servants be doing this?"

"They are gone," she told him. "Mr. Grant came from humble beginnings. Even after he made his fortune, he did not believe in wasting money. We lived very simply, and I continue to do so. My maids are two sisters who live together and come to the house each day. One of them makes me tea and toast each morning, and they stay several hours to clean. Cook actually works next door for a widower. She cooks for him and brings me a part of that meal each evening. She was kind enough to prepare tea for us . . . when you came."

Sophie allowed him to seat her. She poured the already opened wine into his glass first and then hers.

"The stew smells wonderful," he said. "You get used to a meaner fare of food aboard a ship. This stew and bread are a feast." James paused. "Then again, you are a feast for my eyes, Sophie."

A hot blush filled her cheeks. "You are still complimenting me. Even after I abandoned you. My abysmal behavior." She shook her head, shame filling her.

He spooned a bit of stew in his mouth and made a satisfied sound. "It was—but I have forgiven you for it."

James casually buttered his bread and took a bite of it. "Your neighbor's cook is to be commended. The bread is heavenly. Almost as good as the company."

Sophie placed her spoon down. "You do not have to flatter me anymore, James. I was awful to you. I am sorry for that." She hesitated. "I am not quite sure why you are here."

His gaze was so intense, she felt it down to her very soul. "You know exactly why I came, Sophie. I had to see you. And get an answer to my question."

Her heart slammed against her ribs. "What question is that?" she asked quietly.

"I suppose it's two questions. One—do you think you could love me as I love you? And two—will you marry me?" He smiled at her. "But you don't have to answer either until after we've finished supping."

Chapter Eighteen

James knew he'd taken a huge chance simply showing up at Neptune Shipping out of the blue. He'd waited over two hours for Sophie, not knowing when she would leave.

He had wanted to come to her sooner, but his new duties called. He had spent five days at Shadowcrest with his relatives. It was apparent how happy the girls were to be back in the country. His reunion with Aunt Matty had been one for the ages. She had aged since James had last seen her, but she still had a quick wit and ready smile for him. He looked forward to spending more time with her in the near future.

Shadowcrest had been opened for guests, and a large portion of the community turned out for the reception following the duke's burial. He recalled a few of the titled gentlemen who called from years past, when they had visited his father. Numerous citizens from the local village also had come. Some, he knew, did so in order to pay their respects to the late duke; others were simply curious, wanting to meet the new duke. No one dared ask him, though, where he had been all these years. James realized being a duke insulated him from such things.

He had spent many hours in Caleb's company, enjoying his time with his younger cousin. Caleb was bright and personable and from what James could tell, his cousin had done a terrific job stepping in as the Shadowcrest steward. They had reviewed ledgers from the past decade. Caleb had explained the crops which were produced on Shadowcrest lands and the livestock that were a growing part of the estate.

Pippa, true to her word, had given him a few horseback riding lessons. Her instruction enhanced whatever memories he had because James did feel comfortable atop a horse and took to riding with ease. It had allowed him to ride about the estate with Caleb, as well as Pippa and Effie. Both girls proclaimed they were more comfortable on horseback than walking and had desperately missed riding while in town.

After seeing every corner of the estate, he had taken two days to call upon various tenants, Caleb and his two sisters accompanying him. The girls were well-known in the community, and it seemed Caleb had the respect of the tenants.

James had asked Caleb if he intended to remain at Shadowcrest, acting as its steward. His cousin asked if that would be possible, saying he'd come to love the estate in the three years he had been working on it. James readily agreed but told Caleb if he chose to go back to university, his education would be paid for. Caleb thanked him but said being a steward was his calling in life and as long as James allowed him to continue using the family's library, he would be content to remain in that capacity.

He'd left Shadowcrest for London, meeting with Peabody and his clerks, as well as Compton. It seemed while his uncle and cousin had used Mr. Barclay and a few crooked clerks to drain a few accounts of Strong Shipping, the company was still in a good position and quite profitable, despite those misappropriated funds. James suspected Uncle Adolphus had only taken limited funds since he thought the title and its wealth would soon be his anyway. Mr. Peabody agreed that dragging the two Strongs into court would be a messy affair, and he doubted that James would be able to recuperate the stolen monies in full. Both men decided it was better to let sleeping dogs lie and limit the amount of gossip.

That was especially important to James because he doubted Sophie would even consider marrying him if he were under a cloud of gossip. Not that the *ton's* talk seemed to matter much to her, but he did know she valued her business reputation. It was spotless, and he wanted to help her maintain it.

He sat now, eating of the stew the cook had left, Sophie watching him surreptitiously. She hadn't answered either question he'd posed. In fact, she hadn't said a word.

It didn't matter. He was in her company. For now, that was enough.

They both finished their bowls of stew, and James took a final sip of his wine. Nervously, she downed the remaining wine in her glass. He recalled how she had called it liquid courage when she had first asked him to couple with her.

"Since you've no help in the house tonight, do we leave the dishes here?"

"No," she said, pushing back her chair. "I always take them into the kitchen and wash them. It is the courteous thing to do."

Sophie placed her bowl and bread plate on the tray, along with her silverware, followed by her wine glass and the bottle of wine. She corked it since it was still half-full. James also placed his dishes on the tray and carried it to the kitchen. He was surprised by how small the house was. She had entertained him in the parlor when he had come for tea. Then there was the dining room and this kitchen. One other small room that was next to the parlor. He supposed it to be a study which Josiah Grant had used.

She went to the stove, which had a pot of water simmering atop it. "Cook leaves water for me to heat so that I can wash the dishes. You don't have to worry about helping to wash them. It won't take me long."

"I will stay with you," he said firmly. "I want to do my share."

"I would prefer you go to the parlor and wait for me, James."

At least she had finally called him by his given name and not Captain.

"You can read my letter to you," she added.

"All right," he agreed, vacating the room and going to the dining room first. Removing the candelabra on the table, he took it to the parlor so that he might have light to read by. He set down the candelabra and removed the letter from the pocket of his coat, which Sutton had made over.

The valet was skilled with a needle and thread and after having James try on several coats of Seaton's, said it would take him a short time to tailor the coats for the new duke. Sutton had insisted, however, that he return with James when he left Shadowcrest. The servant had taken James this morning to the Duke of Seaton's tailor, where his measurements had been taken. When asked for his preference regarding styles and materials, he had been overwhelmed. Sutton had seen that and had told James to go about his business. That he and the tailor would make certain the wardrobe made up would be elegant and befitting a duke.

Breaking the seal, he read Sophie's letter to him, hearing regret in every line she had written. He read it again and then refolded it, placing it in his pocket. While not a love letter, it was her first correspondence with him other than a message summoning him to her. Because of that, he would keep it. James had never thought himself sentimental, but when it came to Sophie Grant, he found he wanted every piece of her, even if it were a letter she had penned.

He thought about how to approach her. What he might say. He struggled, though, not knowing what argument would be best.

Then the air changed. He caught the scent of roses. Anticipation filled him. Turning, he saw she stood in the doorway, looking a little unsure of herself.

"Have you read the letter?" she asked.

"I have. Thank you for your apology."

She stepped into the room. "It was out of character for me. I am known for my practical nature and meeting things head-on. In business, I study things carefully. Look at it from all angles. Then I make my decision and stick to it." She frowned. "I did not do so with you."

Sophie took a seat in the chair next to the settee he sat upon. "Honestly? I panicked, James. I had already strayed far from my usual, familiar situation in asking you to . . . couple with me. You were more than kind to satisfy my curiosity about lovemaking." Her cheeks reddened. "I never imagined what it was like. I am certain you are very good at it and have had much practice."

"Those days of finding an available woman are done, Sophie," he told her. "Yes, I would seek out female companions whenever we came into port. The trysts were brief. Some satisfying. Many not."

James reached and took her hand, threading his fingers through hers. "What I did not expect was just how meaningful it would be to make love to you. It was never like it was with others. The way we were together. It was something new—and wonderful. Something I can't quite define. All I know is my feelings for you are immeasurable.

"I want to always be with you, Sophie. I want you in my bed and by my side. I want to make love to you every day and night. I want to build a life with you. Share in everything."

Tears filled her eyes. "I cannot do that, James. I want to, but I mustn't share everything with you."

He came to his feet, pulling her to hers. His arms encircled her, his mouth descending to hers. The moment their lips touched, sparks occurred. Together, they hungrily kissed one another as if starved. Her palms flattened against his chest, then she began kneading him as if she were a kitten.

James tilted her head back, deepening the kiss, a kiss that consumed them both, as if a pyre had been lit. He felt the flames flash through him and knew she felt the same.

Breaking the kiss, his lips hovering just above hers, he rasped, "Bed?"

"Upstairs," she said breathlessly, and then he was kissing her all over again, the need filling him.

He swept her into his arms, his mouth still fused to hers, blindly stumbling until he found the stairs. He opened his eyes long enough to make his way up them.

"Left," she said, her own voice hoarse, when he reached the top.

Only one door lay that way, and he went to it, opening it. The room was dark, but he caught the outline of the bed and carried her to it. Slowly, James undressed her, kissing her as he did so. Each kiss was more precious than the one which came before.

When she was bare, he quickly doffed his own clothes, climbing atop her, his lips nuzzling her neck. He touched her everywhere, hoping his caresses conveyed the depth of his feelings for her.

He reached her calves, stroking them, his tongue running along them. "You have beautiful calves," he praised.

"You . . . you cannot see them," she sputtered.

"Ah, but I can, my darling Sophie. Beauty can be touched as well as seen."

James made love to her, branding her as his. When he reached his climax, he chose again not to withdraw. He hoped they did make a babe because he wanted nothing more than to see Sophie's belly swell with his child.

Afterward, he cradled her in his arms, glad they didn't have servants to deal with. Of course, he would need to be gone before morning came and her maids arrived.

She stroked his forearm absently as he kissed her temple. James envisioned many nights of them this way, coming together in love.

"May I have the answer to my questions now, Sophie?" he asked.

She was quiet a long moment, and he thought perhaps she had fallen asleep until she said, "Let us dress. We can talk then."

They did so, and she left the bedchamber quickly. James followed her as she returned to the parlor. He took a seat as she began pacing. She finally stopped and took the seat she had before.

"You asked if I could love you as you love me. I won't question whether you love me or not, James. Though I think it is much too soon for you to say those words, I believe you do have feelings for me. Perhaps it is love. I have never been in love, so it is hard for me to say."

She paused, her eyes welling with tears. "I do have tender feelings for you, though. I do not wish to define them, though." Sophie swallowed. "That leads to your second question. My answer is no, James. I cannot wed you. Not now. Not ever."

"Why?" he demanded, trying to tamp down the anger that rushed through him.

"It is because of Josiah," she told him. "My husband came from humble means. Through a tremendous amount of hard work, coupled with a good deal of luck, he built Neptune Shipping Line. It is his legacy—and he entrusted it to me."

She looked at him in sadness, and he asked, "What does that have to do with anything?"

Sophie blew out a long breath. "It has everything to do with us. Don't you see?"

"Apparently not. Explain it to me."

Her jaw tightened. "If we were to wed, I would have nothing."

James looked at her blankly. "I don't understand."

She studied him carefully. "I suppose you don't. Have you spent your entire life at sea?"

"Yes. Since I was a young boy of eight."

"Ah." She nodded to herself. "You have no knowledge of how British law works. As a widow, I have the right to own land. A house.

A business. I can run Neptune Shipping as I see fit. I do so now to honor Josiah. He changed my world. My father, Lord Galpin, is a terrible man. He never loved me or my mother. When I became of age, I was sold into marriage. Fortunately, Josiah treated me with respect. Courtesy. Honor. He taught me everything I know about business."

James frowned. "And?"

Sophie placed her hand atop his. "If we wed, James? The law says that everything which is now mine goes to you. Neptune Shipping would be yours. So would this house and all the funds I have in the bank. Not only would I be penniless, but I would have no control—no say-so—over the very company Josiah left to me."

He was thunderstruck. "You would lose everything? How is that possible?"

She smiled ruefully. "Because men write the laws, James. And women suffer because of them. You could be wooing me—pushing me to wed you—so that you could gain control of Neptune Shipping."

"Sophie, I would—"

"I do not believe you have ulterior motives, James. You have done nothing for me to suspect that is the case. But even a good man can be tempted by vast wealth. Yes, I may live humbly, because that is how Josiah liked things to be, but I am one of the wealthiest women in Great Britain. I own a fleet of ships which trade all over the world."

She looked pained as she said, "Even if you love me. Even if you tell me I could still run Neptune, it is an empty promise. The moment I speak those vows and sign the wedding license, I am powerless. And I can never do that."

He reeled at what he had learned. Then again, what Sophie said made sense. James could protest, telling her he would never try to take over Neptune or take it from her.

But she would never believe him.

Unless he told her who he truly was.

James had wanted her to say yes to his marriage offer so that he would be certain she wanted him for himself and not because he was a duke. That was no longer possible. He was going to have to admit to her that he was Seaton.

As he opened his mouth to tell her the truth, a loud banging sounded on her door, startling them both.

Quickly, Sophie hurried to the door. James thought it best he remain out of sight, not wanting to compromise her reputation in any manner since they were alone in the household together.

"What is it?" she cried.

"Mrs. Grant, there's a small possibility your warehouse might be in danger," a male voice said. "The warehouse of Strong Shipping is on fire, and the danger of it spreading throughout the waterfront is a distinct threat."

James ran from the parlor, seeing the man who had brought the news. "Strong is afire?" he demanded.

"Yes, sir," the man said.

Without stopping, James ran from the house. Spying the hansom cab in front, he leaped into it, shouting, "To the waterfront! Now!" he commanded, and the frightened driver drove off.

Chapter Nineteen

James saw the unnatural glow against the night sky as they drew closer to the waterfront. Then the acrid smell of smoke slammed into him.

The driver pulled up, halting the hansom cab, saying, "This is close as I get you, my lord. The crowds will keep me from going closer, and the horse will be frightened."

He leaped from the vehicle and tossed a coin to the man, running toward the docks and Strong Shipping's warehouse. When he reached the area, it was jammed with people. He saw two handcarts, a type of fire engine which had men manually operating the pumps aboard them. He supposed the riveted leather hoses were drawing from the nearby Thames, and he was grateful the warehouse was located so close to the water.

The hoses reached into the building. Strong Shipping Lines' office sat on one corner. Across from it, on the opposite corner, stood the company's enormous warehouse. It was built of stone and seemed to be holding up, but it was the inside which was ablaze. He supposed the fire had poked through and destroyed the roof since he'd seen the light from the fire at a distance.

James also saw lines of men passing leather buckets, even recognizing some of his crew members from *Vesta* as a part of these lines. It looked as if many sailors and dock workers were trying their best to save what they could of the merchandise stored within the warehouse.

Racing to the building, he entered. His heart sank when he saw the size of the fire the brigades were fighting. He spied a man shouting directions to those who held the hoses spraying water.

Hurrying toward him, James said, "I am James Strong. I own this warehouse."

The supervisor waved him away. "Get out! Let us do our job."

Stripping away his coat, James tossed it aside, and shouted, "I'm here to help. I'm large and strong and have more endurance than most men. Tell me what to do."

The man ordered him to one line of men, and James helped hoist the heavy hose and hold it up so the water would flow from it more freely. The group of men moved as one, and he could tell they had experience fighting fires together. It let him know they were no volunteer group but one which was trained.

Gradually, he rotated up the line as exhausted men near the front fell away. Others joined in from time to time, giving brigade members a rest, but he refused to allow anyone to take his place. Eventually, James found himself at the front of the line, aiming the firehose at the blaze. He could see that they were finally getting the fire under control, though they still had to dodge falling debris from time to time. Relief swept through him. Yes, much had been lost or damaged, but there was still a good deal of merchandise within the warehouse which had been saved.

He, too, had to fall from the line eventually, his strength having ebbed from managing and aiming the hose for so long a time. He stumbled from the warehouse, and the man he had first spoken with came toward him.

"Are you Seaton?" the man asked, worry on his face.

James collapsed to the ground, fighting for air. Each breath he took hurt, and he knew inhaling the fumes from the fire had weakened him.

A tankard was shoved into his hands, and he downed its entire contents, grateful for the cold, refreshing ale. He handed it back and saw none other than Drake Andrews had given it to him.

Smiling weakly, he said, "I hear you are now *Vesta's* captain." He began coughing, wishing he hadn't drunk all the ale.

"I am," Drake confirmed. "I didn't think you would mind me taking her on, especially since you'll be a landlubber from now on."

Drake helped James to his feet, and the man who still lingered nearby said, "I'm Swan, Your Grace. Head of the fire brigade for your insurance company."

"What exactly is that?" he questioned. "I've only recently become the Duke of Seaton."

"Strong Shipping—both its warehouse and office—are insured. That means you pay a yearly fee, and we place a fire mark upon each building which has met the fees. When a fire breaks out, we are notified and respond to the scene."

Swan looked about. "Many of our fire brigade are composed of former sailors. Oftentimes when fires break out near the waterfront, not only do we respond, but dock workers and sailors will also pitch in, as well, forming a bucket brigade. They know their livelihood depends upon the very places which might be ablaze, and they are happy to lend a fire brigade a helping hand."

"Do you have an idea yet how this fire began?" James wanted to know.

Swan nodded grimly. "We will investigate, Your Grace, but since the blaze was confined inside the warehouse itself, the likelihood of it being deliberately set is a distinct possibility."

A hot wave of rage rippled through him. He knew who had set this fire.

Adolphus or Theo.

He doubted either man had physically been present. Rather, they would have hired someone to start the fire in their stead.

"It looks as if you have an idea who the culprit might be, Your

Grace," Swan said. "Are you willing to share the name with me?"

"My uncle. Adolphus Strong. Or his eldest son Theodore Strong. They are angry I've returned to England. My uncle believed he would be the next Duke of Seaton, and Theo would follow after him. My sudden appearance squashed those dreams.

"I believe this is the way they have chosen to seek their revenge."

Swan shook his head. "Finding proof of how the blaze started will be fairly easy. Attributing guilt to your family members will be much harder, Your Grace. And bringing charges against them?" Swan paused. "You—and they—are among the swells. I doubt you wish for such grievances to be aired publicly. Think of the scandal."

"They must be punished," he declared vehemently. "Just because Adolphus is the son of a duke, he should be held accountable for his actions."

Swan placed a hand on James' shoulder. "Calm yourself, Your Grace. Your warehouse is insured. That means an investigation will be conducted, which I will be a part of. No matter who started the blaze or for whatever reason, the goods inside the warehouse itself are protected by the policy you hold. You will be reimbursed for your losses. That is how insurance works. It has for over a hundred years, guaranteeing buildings can be rebuilt if a policy is held. You are very fortunate, though, since it is only recently that items inside buildings have been covered under these policies."

It all seemed too much. He shook his head, coughing again. "Do you have further need of me, Mr. Swan?"

"Not as this time. I suggest your friend get you home and you have a physician look you over. You need rest after fighting this fire on the front lines. After I complete my report for the insurance company, I will be happy to meet with you once that occurs."

"Thank you, Mr. Swan. I am grateful for what you and your brigade did this evening."

Swan smiled. "You are the one who has paid the premiums, Your

Grace. Your building held the fire mark. That is the only reason we went in, trying to save as much as we could and contain the fire."

"You mean if the building had not been marked in such a manner, you wouldn't have lifted a finger?" he asked, incredulous.

Swan shrugged. "That's the way things work. If you will excuse me, I have much to see to."

He strode away, and James felt his legs turning weak again.

"Ease me down, Drake," he instructed. "I'm so exhausted, I cannot move."

His friend lowered him to the ground, and within moments, James was surrounded by various crew members from *Vesta*. Each man came and patted him on the shoulder, then seated himself in a circle around him in a show of unity.

He gazed at the small group gathered about him and addressed them.

"Thank you for coming to the aid of Strong Shipping's warehouse," he began, coughing again several times.

"Another tankard," Minnix called, and James found one pressed into his hand.

He sipped on it this time instead of downing the entire contents as he had previously done.

"Captain Andrews told us he'll be at the helm when *Vesta* sails in two days' time," Thomas said. "Where will you be, Captain Jones? And why did you fight so hard to save your competitor's warehouse?"

"Changes have occurred in my life which sound as if they have been made up," he began. "It's a long story, my friends, but I learned when we came ashore two weeks ago that I am a Strong. James Strong."

He gazed out at the startled group. "And I am now the Duke of Seaton."

SOPHIE COULD NOT understand why James had taken off in such a mad dash.

Unless he was now employed by Strong Shipping and was concerned about the goods in the company's warehouse if he had signed on for an upcoming voyage.

Still, his odd behavior puzzled her.

"Let me collect my reticule and lock up," she told her nightwatchman. "We can then go down to the waterfront."

They walked a short way before engaging a hansom cab to deliver them to the docks. The cabbie got them as close as he could, and they walked the rest of the way. Strong Shipping Lines was set up slightly different than Neptune, in that its office was across the street from their warehouse. She saw how crowded the area was and the two fire engines in the street next to the warehouse.

It looked as if the outer structure of the edifice had held, with only a little damage to it. Obviously, the roof was gone because flames rose from it, lighting up the sky. She glanced about and saw many sailors and dock workers which she recognized. They had formed bucket brigades and passed buckets of water to the head of the lines, which snaked inside the warehouse. The buckets were painted with the name and address of their owners, and they would be left at the largest tavern in the area so that they could be retrieved tomorrow. She knew among those buckets would be ones from her own warehouse, as she saw many of her workers in line.

She spied the long hoses, ones attached to the pumps on the hand trucks, and they also disappeared inside the building, where the fire brigade would be guiding them, trying to put out the flames from the blaze.

For over two hours, exhausted men poured from the warehouse, while others on the brigade took their places. The bucket brigade continued at a steady pace, a valuable contribution from those assembled volunteers. She never spied James, though, and wondered where he might be.

Finally, the fire died down, and she knew the danger had passed. Fortunately, the fire had remained contained within the Strong warehouse. Seeing the fire mark carved into the building, she knew it was insured, just as her own Neptune Shipping Line was.

She spied Captain Andrews and moved toward him, but the seaman ran closer to the warehouse. Sophie saw why he did so, as James staggered from the building. His face and clothes were covered in soot, and he coughed deeply. She wanted to rush to him, but something held her back. She had always been a person who observed everything around her, and she knew she might discover answers to her questions if she remained in place.

The pair spoke briefly before they headed toward a man whom she knew to be the head of one of London's fire brigades. Sophie watched and waited. James had a conversation with Swan, and she wondered why he did so. Was he asking about merchandise within the warehouse that he would take out on his next voyage? It was certainly not his place to be meeting with Swan. It still troubled her that James had rushed into the warehouse and fought the blaze.

Something didn't add up.

Eventually, the conversation between the men ended, and Swan headed off. A group of men who had ringed the trio as they spoke now moved in.

Sophie moved closer now to hear what she could. James' back was to her, so he had no idea of her presence.

He began to speak to those gathered around him, and she recognized men from his old *Vesta* crew, ones she had seen as they collected their pay from their most recent voyage. But what she learned as James spoke sent shock waves through her. James was not James Jones.

He was James Strong. The Duke of Seaton.

She couldn't help it. She gave a cry of dismay, apparently loud enough for James to hear.

He glanced over his shoulder. His eyes widened as their gazes met.

Whirling, she raced away. She heard him call her name but knew he was too weak to catch her. Sophie ran away from the docks. Away from James, who had lied to her.

Finally, she came upon a hansom cab and engaged him to take her home. He helped her into the vehicle, and she gave him her address, her teeth chattering as she did so. Sophie trembled all over. Her thoughts were a jumble. She could make no sense of what she had learned tonight.

They arrived at her house, and she paid the driver. It took her three tries before she successfully fit her key into the lock. She entered her house, dropping her reticule onto a nearby table, and stumbled into the nearby parlor, where she collapsed onto the settee. Confusion filled her—but one thing was clear.

She had fallen in love with a man who had repeatedly lied to her. A man who was her chief competitor.

Sophie now knew that the sweet words James Strong had uttered to her were meant to dupe her. Sway her. Convince her that he loved her. She could not believe she had given her body to him. And her heart. He had quickly offered marriage to her, and she now knew why. If they had wed, he would have absorbed Neptune Shipping into his own company, and a true shipping empire would have been born.

Bitterness filled her, along with the hurt, as she forced herself to climb the stairs. She fell onto her bed, hot tears spilling onto her pillow, as she realized what a fool she had been.

Chapter Twenty

James awoke in a bed, not knowing where he was. His head ached terribly. He blinked, his eyes stinging. Swallowing let him know he had a raw, scratchy throat. His entire body ached.

"You are awake, Your Grace."

He turned to his right, seeing a man by the bed.

Timmons.

Yes, that was his name. He knew him, but he wasn't sure from where.

"Drink this," Timmons said, offering him a bowl.

Discarding the spoon, he tilted it, drinking the warm chicken broth. It hurt to swallow. He realized he was also a bit short of breath, as if he had run a great distance.

"How did I get here?" he asked, still not quite sure where *here* was.

"Captain Andrews and a few sailors brought you home," Timmons answered.

The door opened, and he saw Sutton and another man enter. The man looked vaguely familiar, but James couldn't place where he had known him from.

"He just awoke, Dr. Nickels," Timmons said. "He drank some of the broth, but he still seems a bit confused."

Now, he recalled the man. Nickels was the duke's physician. James frowned. Wait. Something was off.

"Excellent," the doctor said, stepping to the bed. "How are you feeling, Your Grace? You had us worried."

Your Grace?

"Are things a bit muddled?" Nickels asked.

"Yes," he said carefully.

"Let me look you over, Your Grace."

As the physician peered into his eyes and ears, a kaleidoscope of memories flooded him. He remembered now. He was the duke. His father was dead and buried.

And then he remembered the fire.

"The warehouse?" he asked, sitting up. "How is it?"

"Settle down, Your Grace," the doctor ordered. "Please open your mouth. Hmm. Your throat is still quite red. Your pulse is also rapid, as is your breathing. Do you feel short of breath?"

"Aye," he said, so tired he could barely keep his eyes open.

"Your symptoms are a result of inhaling smoke at the fire," Dr. Nickels said.

James began coughing, and Sutton helped him sit up and drink from a mug. It was lukewarm tea, but it felt good going down.

"Your sinuses are still irritated. Do you still have the headache you complained of, Your Grace?"

He didn't recall any complaining, but he said, "Yes."

"What about chest pain?" pressed the doctor.

"No. None," he confirmed.

The physician beamed. "That's very good news, Your Grace. You will still need rest for another few days. The cough will linger, but the runny nose and sore throat will clear up soon. You will sound hoarse for several more days. I suggest resting your voice as much as possible. I shall be back to see you tomorrow morning."

Nickels looked to the other two men. "The more broth and tea you can get down him, the better. Soft food if he is up to it. Mashed peas or carrots would be good. Send word if you have need of me before tomorrow morning."

The physician left the room. James had questions, but it took too much effort to think about what they were, much less voice them. He closed his eyes.

The next time he opened them, the room was no longer light. The drapes had been closed. Candles burned beside the bed. His throat was parched.

"Drink," he managed to say.

The mattress sank next to him. He saw Dinah had sat next to him.

"Here's some tea," she told him, holding a mug to his lips.

James drank greedily, some spilling and running down his chin. She wiped it with a handkerchief.

"Take your time," she encouraged. "Better."

He finished the tea, and she set down the mug. "When did you come to London?"

"Captain Andrews came to fetch me," she said.

A flash of memory sparked. He recalled the two sitting at breakfast, flirting with one another.

"He told me about the fire and how you fought at the front of the brigade to save what you could inside the warehouse."

She dipped a cloth in a basin of water beside the bed and wrung it, bathing his face. Her soothing touch felt like a tonic.

"The girls all wanted to come," she told him. "I said no. You did not need six of them hovering about you, chattering like magpies, asking endless questions."

"When will you go back . . . to Shadowcrest?"

"When I think you no longer need me," she said crisply.

"Can you help me to sit up more?" he asked.

"Of course."

Dinah leaned him forward, stacking the pillows behind him. James fell back into them, already drained of energy.

"I don't need a nursemaid," he said sullenly. "I'm a grown man."

"Who is suffering from the effects of smoke inhalation," she reminded him. "You are weak, James. You will need to build up your strength. Dr. Nickels has assured me you suffer from no chest pains. That was his chief concern."

Then what had tugged at him, whether conscious or unconscious, finally surfaced.

"Sophie..."

Dinah frowned. "Sophie? Who is that, James?"

He closed his eyes, shaking his head. "The woman I love."

"What?"

Opening his eyes again, he said, "I've bungled things badly with her, I'm afraid," he rasped.

"Rest now. Close your eyes. Your body—and your voice—need rest. We will talk about this Sophie when you can tell me more."

Again, he plunged into the darkness.

When he next awakened, it was daylight again. Dinah no longer sat next to the bed, but Sutton was there and alert.

"How do you feel, Your Grace?"

He thought a moment, swallowing and finding the pain gone. "Better," he said, hearing his voice only slightly hoarse. "I am still aching all over, but it will pass."

"Are you hungry, Your Grace?"

"Very," he decided, his belly growling loudly.

"You have slept for two days," Sutton informed him. "You should be hungry."

The valet rang, and Powell showed up.

"It's good to have you back with us, Your Grace," the butler said.

"Breakfast for His Grace," Sutton told the butler. "Poached eggs. Toast with marmalade. Tea."

"I need more than that," James declared. "Also, a rasher of bacon. Coffee."

"At once, Your Grace," Powell said, quickly exiting the room.

Sutton helped James up so he could relieve himself. His legs wobbled a bit, but he wasn't as weak as he'd been the last time he was awake.

Dinah arrived when his breakfast did, saying, "I will make certain His Grace eats well, Sutton. Have hot water brought up to His Grace's dressing room. He is in dire need of a bath. And fresh sheets will need to be put on the bed, as well."

Though he was famished, he ate slowly, taking a sip of coffee or tea between each bite to keep his throat moist. Dinah talked of the girls and things happening at Shadowcrest as he ate.

"Once you are back on your feet, I will return there," she told him. "I miss all my sweet babes."

He chuckled. "Those babes are grown women for the most part," he told her.

"Yes, we will need to prepare for next Season with care. All but Effie will be of age. The others will need to make their come-outs. It will be quite an expense, launching five girls during the same year, but I believe your coffers can handle it, James. At least I hope you don't mind if Allegra and Lyric make their debut with Pippa, Georgina, and Mirella. Do you know Adolphus has yet to write a single letter inquiring about them?"

He set down his teacup. "Does that surprise you, Dinah?"

"It shouldn't. It does disappoint me."

"How are Allegra and Lyric getting along without their father?"

She smiled. "Splendidly. They both have always loved the country. Over the years, Adolphus has seen them very little. They have spent more time with me and at Shadowcrest than with him. And they are happy to be reunited with Caleb. The two of them are more like their mother, while Theo is Adolphus made over."

"I believe the two of them are responsible for the fire at the warehouse," he revealed.

She pressed her lips together, her disapproval obvious. "I had suspected as much. What do you plan to do?"

"I am supposed to receive a Mr. Swan. He is investigating the matter for the insurance company. I had no idea those even existed. I'm only glad we had the policy in place." He sighed. "As to my uncle and cousin? Swan seemed to think I should sweep the entire incident under the rug. He thought the scandal which would result would be too disheartening to the family."

Dinah mulled over his words and then said, "I am afraid this Mr. Swan is correct, James. Especially with the girls due to make their come-outs before Polite Society next spring, any hint of scandal could lessen their chances at making a good match."

"Intellectually, I agree with you, Dinah. But I have such loathing for them in my heart. I want them punished. They have stolen money from the family and now tried to burn down our company's warehouse. They should encounter some kind of justice."

"I understand why you believe so, James, but you cannot think purely of yourself. You have the girls to consider. They are under your care now. They live under your roof. You will be the one who decides who their husbands will be. Of course, I will weigh in with my own opinion, but in the long run? It is for the Duke of Seaton to determine who will wed his sisters and cousins."

James hated to have that kind of responsibility on his shoulders. "I'm not the one marrying these men. Shouldn't the girls decide?"

She laughed. "Oh, I do not doubt you will get an earful of what they think. I believe you will listen to them, but you also will discern which suitors will make the best husbands for them."

Dinah saw he was through and lifted the tray from him, placing it on the ground.

"Shall we speak of Sophie now?" she asked.

He sighed. "I will be blunt. I am in love. The last thing I thought would ever occur. Sophie is Mrs. Grant—of Neptune Shipping."

Her eyes grew large. "*The* Mrs. Grant? Oh, I knew you had spoken of her in admiring tones, but I had no idea you had fallen in love with her."

"It was sudden. As if I tumbled headfirst and could not stop myself." He hesitated. "I had wanted her to say yes to the sea captain and not the duke, so I had not told her of my title."

"James!" Dinah chided. "You must. Hiding that from her is wrong."

He shook his head. "That cat is out of the bag. She was on the docks the night of the fire. Actually, I had dined with her that evening. When a messenger came to warn her of the fire on the waterfront and said it was at Strong's warehouse, I fled without a backward glance."

She looked at him with disdain. "Not very gentlemanly of you, James."

"I realize that now. I had just asked her for an answer to my marriage proposal. You should know she had turned me down."

Dinah said, "Of course, she did. You were a sea captain with a limited salary and resources. My goodness, James. Sophie Grant is one of the wealthiest women in England. The moment she married you, she would lose everything. *I* would have turned you down myself, even if you are a handsome devil of a man."

He raked a hand through his hair. "I had no idea of the laws of Britain. How would I? I never completed my education. I have lived at sea most of my life. When Sophie told me why she couldn't wed me— for the very reasons you just stated—I knew I must tell her that I was the Duke of Seaton and didn't need her money. I had a shipping company of my own."

"But you bolted from her house when you heard of the fire at Strong shipping."

"Yes. And it gets worse, Dinah."

"I dread hearing this, but tell me."

"After I came from the fire, I collapsed on the ground. Several of my former crew members had been among those who formed a bucket brigade. They surrounded me, wanting to protect me." He paused. "They were also curious as to why I would risk life and limb to fight the fire at Strong when *Vesta* was a part of Neptune Shipping. I told them—and Sophie was nearby. She heard that admission."

"No!" she cried. "Oh, James, you poor thing. And Sophie, too. That must have been quite the blow." Determination filled her face. "You must make things right between you, James."

"I don't know if they can ever be right. She will think I lied to her. Which I did. Not deliberately, but a lie of omission, all the same." He groaned. "I cannot live without her, Dinah. I want Sophie as my duchess. No other woman will ever do."

She stood, dusting her hands together. "Then I suggest that you eat something and hop into that bath, Seaton. I will also send for your tailor. He has already sent a message that several pieces of your new wardrobe are completed and only needs you to try things on to see if any adjustments need to be made. I can have him come here and dress you in something appropriate to go and woo a widow." She chuckled. "On your knees, I'd imagine. You will need to beg her for forgiveness."

"You're right," he agreed. "I must see Sophie in person and explain what a fool I have been. I only hope she will have the courage to take a chance on me."

CHAPTER TWENTY-ONE

SOPHIE FINISHED UP the reports she had been working on for a few days. It was a list of voyages which would leave during the next three months and the trade routes they would follow, along with the merchandise they would carry. She had made a few adjustments because of *Vesta* taking a different route from its usual one. She felt good, though, about Captain Andrews taking the ship's command.

She set the reports aside, making a note for three copies to be produced. She would retain this original, while Mr. Barnes would also keep one of the copies. Another one would be given to their warehouse supervisor so that he would know what cargo needed to be pulled for each of the ships and when. The final copy would go to the captain of each of those vessels.

Satisfied that she had accomplished such a large task, Sophie sat back for a moment. It was in these moments of stillness that she had time to think.

About James.

Learning that he was the Duke of Seaton had been a tremendous blow to her. Knowing now that he had only plied her with sweet words to gain control of Neptune Shipping caused her to harden her heart and doubt herself in many ways. Still, that very heart had been shattered by him. Sophie had believed James when he told her he loved her, and though she had no plans to accept his offer of marriage, she admitted to herself that she had loved him in return.

Her courses had come early yesterday morning, so she knew she was not carrying his babe. Part of her had been relieved when they started, and yet another part of her grew sad, knowing she would not produce an heir to Neptune Shipping. At least not with James Jones. No, she chided herself. James Strong. The Duke of Seaton.

She would not give up on the idea of having a child, though. What she had voiced to James was true. It would be wrong not to have Neptune Shipping continue after her death. She would not wish to see Josiah's company broken up or taken on by someone who was not a family member. That meant at some point, sooner rather than later, she would need to find a man willing to father a child with her. One who would step away and not claim any parental rights. She wanted to raise her son or daughter in her own way, helping him or her to learn about the shipping business and honor Josiah's legacy.

But who might that man be? She had a severe distrust of men, especially now after what had happened with James. The only men of her acquaintance who might be suitable for this endeavor were those whom she did business with, and they were always wary around her because of their jealous wives. She supposed she might seek another captain employed by her shipping line, but then it would possibly be awkward once she produced a child. Her dilemma would need to be solved, though, because Sophie was determined to pass Neptune Shipping to her son or daughter.

A light tap sounded at her door, and she called, "Come."

Mr. Barnes entered, looking bewildered. It was possibly the first time she had seen him in such a state.

"Whatever is wrong, Mr. Barnes?" Sophie asked.

"You . . . have a visitor, Mrs. Grant."

"I have no appointments listed in my diary today," she pointed out. "Who might this caller be? A client we haven't dealt with before?"

"It is . . . that is, it is . . ."

Suddenly, a woman swept into the office. She was most likely ten or so years older than Sophie was, and quite a beauty. Her hair was the color of molasses, her eyes blue, and her frame petite. Besides her looks, the woman's attire was impeccable, her gown made of the richest fabric.

"Mr. Barnes seems a bit befuddled," the woman said, oozing confidence. "Perhaps you might fetch us some tea, Mr. Barnes. That would be lovely."

The secretary shuffled from the room without a word, and the woman closed the door behind him.

She came toward Sophie, who had stepped from behind her desk, and said, "I am sorry for barging in here, Mrs. Grant, especially without a proper introduction." The woman offered her hand. "I am the Duchess of Seaton."

Manners drilled into her long ago took over, and Sophie swept into what she hoped was an appropriate curtsey.

"Your Grace," she said. "It is nice to make your acquaintance."

She saw the woman's hand still extended and took it, squeezing it briefly.

"I am certain you must be wondering why I have come," the duchess said. "Might we sit and chat a bit if you are free to do so?"

"Of course, Your Grace," Sophie said shakily, indicating the two chairs in front of her large desk.

The duchess took one, and she took the other, sitting tall and straight, wondering why this woman had called upon her out of the blue.

"First, I must tell you that I greatly admire you, Mrs. Grant," the duchess began. "I am raising four girls, as well as my two nieces, and they are all bright, lovely creatures. I hope they can be exposed to more women like you—women who use their intellect and are not cowed by men. They will be making their come-outs soon, over the next couple of years, and I hope they will find men who treat them as equals. Men such as your Mr. Grant."

The duchess gazed at Sophie with sympathy. "I know it must have been very hurtful for Polite Society to turn its back on you after your marriage. I hope that won't be the case in the future."

"I am clearly confused, Your Grace. What are you speaking of?"

"I will admit that I should not even be here, Mrs. Grant. That it probably is none of my business, but I believe if I do not step in, mistakes will be made." The duchess' gaze met Sophie's. "Mistakes which you might regret."

Understanding filled her, and her hackles rose. "You are referring to the marriage offer I received from the Duke of Seaton," she said stiffly.

"No," the duchess replied. "The one you received from a sea captain."

Unexpectedly, Her Grace reached for Sophie's hand, squeezing her fingers.

"I have not been given liberty to share James' story with you. If he knew I were here? He might draw and quarter me. Or have me walk the plank. But I needed to try to see that you at least gave him a chance to hear that story before totally rejecting his suit."

The duchess released Sophie's hand and sat back. "All I am going to say is that my stepson was abducted as a small boy. He went missing for many years and was supposed dead by our family. That little boy, one who was left alone and confused, grew up to be a fine man. A man who made something of himself on his own, in what I can only assume to be a very difficult world."

The duchess paused, smiling slightly. "And that sea captain fell in love with *you*, Mrs. Grant. While that was happening, he did discover he was the heir to a dukedom. James wanted you to love him for himself, Mrs. Grant. Not the duke he would one day become."

"But . . . why . . . how did he—"

"I cannot answer any of your questions, Mrs. Grant. James has been recovering these past few days from the ill effects of the fire he fought at the Strong warehouse. He is finally better today—and determined to come to see you. I am sure he will be able to answer any questions you might have, so I would ask you save them for him. It is more appropriate for him to answer them himself. All I ask is for you to give him a chance to make his case. Would you promise me you will hear him out?"

Sophie's thoughts swirled in her head, confusion reigning.

The Duchess of Seaton stood, so Sophie quickly came to her own feet.

"I told James that he was wrong to have kept his true identity from you once he learned of it. That I myself would not have accepted his offer of marriage because I would not have wanted to lose the business I ran."

Her Grace's gaze intensified, holding Sophie's, as she added, "But I can tell you that James Strong is a man of his word. If he says he loves you, he does. It is not because you own a shipping line. It is because you are the woman you are. One who will challenge him. Be a partner to him."

The duchess took Sophie's hand again and squeezed it. "I hope that we will become family—and friends—Mrs. Grant. I would so much like to see that happen and have you as a shining example to my girls. Good day."

She watched the Duchess of Seaton sail from her office. Sophie collapsed into the chair again.

Could she trust what this stranger had said? Was it true the duchess came on her own and not on the instructions of the Duke of Seaton, trying to lure Sophie in?

Barnes appeared in the doorway with a tea tray. "I see our guest is already gone," he remarked.

"The cup of tea is still much appreciated, Mr. Barnes."

He set the tray on her desk. "Then I will leave you to your tea,

Mrs. Grant."

She handed him her completed reports and asked for him to make the number of copies she needed. Barnes exited the room, leaving Sophie to mull over what little the Duchess of Seaton had revealed.

※

JAMES FINISHED HIS breakfast, forcing himself not to wolf it down. He was still tired and achy, but the shortness of breath had left him. Only a slight cough lingered.

He eased into the bath and allowed Sutton to bathe him in order to conserve what little energy he had. By the time he stepped from the bath and was draped in a bath sheet, Timmons had arrived. When James had returned from the country, he had met with his old tutor, who had remained in the ducal townhouse the last couple of weeks. He told Timmons that he was in need of a secretary and could think of no better person to serve him in that capacity.

Charles Timmons had accepted his offer, telling James how generous he was, promising he would use this second chance in life to make something of himself.

"Your tailor is here, Your Grace," Timmons told him. "Mr. Swan also sent word that he will be here in an hour's time."

"Thank you, Timmons," he said. "I'll see the tailor now and then meet with Swan once he arrives."

For the next hour, James tried on numerous pieces of clothing with Sutton's help. He praised his valet and tailor for the wise choices they had made regarding his wardrobe. It was incredible to put on such clothing made of the finest fabrics available. Everything the tailor brought fit him to perfection, and the man said he would have many more items ready in the next few weeks.

James remained in the last garments he tried on, while Sutton assured him that he would take care of the rest of the garments scattered about the room.

Timmons returned, telling James that Swan was waiting for him in the study.

"Come with me, Timmons," James urged. "As my secretary, you will be privy to all Seaton business."

"I will take notes for you during the meeting, Your Grace."

He greeted Swan and introduced him to Timmons. The two men sat in chairs by the window, while Timmons sat at James' desk, removing parchment to jot down notes.

"What did your investigation find, Mr. Swan?" he asked the investigator.

Swan went into detail regarding what they had learned about the origins of the fire. He had even found two witnesses, both night watchmen at the warehouse. One knew very little, only that he had been struck in the head from behind and dragged from the building before it was set on fire. The other saw a suspicious figure fleeing in the shadows. He had wanted to follow the man, but he noticed the glow in the warehouse and knew a fire had been set.

Instead, this night watchman roused the fire brigade. Still, he had a good idea who the man who set the blaze was.

"How so?" James asked.

"Apparently, the man had a distinct gait. A limp, which the night watchman recognized. We have not been able to locate him as of yet." Swan paused. "The insurance company will pay for the damaged and lost goods and any problems to the structure of the building itself. Because of that, we will not pursue the investigation further."

Swan told James when he could expect the funds and bid him good day. Once the investigator left, James turned to Timmons.

"I believe this man started the fire at the behest of my uncle and cousin Theodore. What avenue can we pursue to find this limping arsonist and link him to my relatives?"

"I suggest that you hire a Bow Street runner, Your Grace."

"What is that?" he questioned, recalling he'd heard the term from Timmons that night in the pub.

"Bow Street runners began as a horse patrol during the last century. They have transformed into a sort of police force, investigating crimes in London and beyond. Whenever someone in the *ton* has the need to investigate something quietly—and achieve quick results—then Bow Street is called in to handle matters. They are not cheap, but they get results, Your Grace."

"That sounds like exactly what I need, Timmons. Can you handle this for me?"

"I think it best if you accompany me to the Bow Street headquarters, Your Grace. Your presence will speak volumes to the urgency of this matter."

Though James was eager to go and see Sophie, he knew this affair could not wait.

"Then tell Powell we need the carriage prepared."

An hour later, they pulled up at Bow Street's headquarters, meeting with a Mr. Franklin. James discussed the delicate nature of the investigation and how he wanted not only the arsonist himself found but where his uncle and cousin now were.

"I told them to leave London. I'm assuming the threat of what I planned to do to them if they didn't leave town caused them to do so. I have no idea where they may have gone."

He provided the address of where they had previously been staying, and Mr. Franklin told James that he would put a team of two runners on the case.

"When can I expect results?" he asked pointedly.

"My men will report to you in three days' time, Your Grace. After that, you will receive regular reports until the three men are found and your issue is resolved to your satisfaction."

"Thank you, Mr. Franklin."

He and Timmons returned to the carriage. James told his secretary he had somewhere else to be, and Timmons said he would take a hansom cab back to Mayfair.

James ordered the driver to take him to Neptune Shipping Lines near the waterfront. He knew Sophie would still be at work since it was mid-afternoon.

He tried his best to prepare a speech but could not think coherently. He didn't know if it were lasting results from the smoke inhalation or fear of what Sophie would say when she saw him.

If she saw him.

The carriage came to a halt, and James disembarked from the vehicle, heading into the Neptune warehouse and up the stairs to the shipping offices. Gathering his courage, he pushed open the door.

To the clerk sitting at the first desk, he announced, "I am the Duke of Seaton. Here to see Mrs. Grant at her earliest convenience."

Chapter Twenty-Two

Sophie had left her door open, wanting to hear when James arrived. Based upon what the Duchess of Seaton had indicated, she thought it would be soon. A few hours passed, though, and she began to fret. The duchess had mentioned that James had been suffering ill effects from fighting the recent fire, and it was only today that he was up and about. She worried that he had suffered a relapse. Still, she had a business to run. It wasn't her place to up and leave Neptune Shipping to go call on a man whom she wasn't sure if she could trust. If he truly wanted to see her, he could come to her.

She heard his voice mid-afternoon, pausing over the document she read. Her heart sped up simply hearing that low rumble of his. An awareness rippled through her, as if her body responded to his voice.

"Be strong, Sophie," she said aloud. "Do not let your heart rule your head."

Lowering her head, she pretended to read the page before her as she saw the shadow at the door and then heard the rap on the doorframe.

Looking up, she saw Mr. Barnes. "Yes?"

"His Grace, the Duke of Seaton, would like to see you, Mrs. Grant." He hesitated and added, "It is Captain Jones, ma'am. But he . . . well, he is dressed like and just might be a duke."

"I am surprised you had not heard that bit of gossip yet, Mr.

Barnes. Usually, you are more well informed than I am. Yes, Captain Jones *is* Seaton. You may show him in."

Rising, Sophie took two, deep breaths, trying to compose herself.

Mr. Barnes returned and said, "His Grace, the Duke of Seaton."

James swept into the room, looking dashing and achingly handsome. He bowed to her.

"Mrs. Grant, thank you for taking the time to see me."

Her eyes flicked to Mr. Barnes, who still lingered in the door, awe written across his face.

"That will be all, Mr. Barnes. Thank you."

"Shall I bring tea, Mrs. Grant?" the secretary offered.

"No tea is required. His Grace will not be here long." She smiled politely until Barnes closed the door and then shifted her gaze back to James. "Please have a seat, Your Grace."

"Thank you."

She perched on the edge of her chair, the desk between them. She needed it to protect her from him. Or protect him from her, as the case might be. She was fighting the urge to leap across it and land in his lap, all the better to gobble him up.

Sophie smiled benignly, though, keeping silent. It would be up to him to explain himself.

James gazed at her longingly, almost causing her resolve to weaken. She dug her fingernails into the palms of her hands, reminding herself to remain quiet.

Finally, he said, "I am sorry you learned of my title in the manner you did. I was about to tell you of it the night we dined together. Before the messenger came and notified you of the fire on the waterfront."

She couldn't help herself. "Oh, you mean the night you rushed from my house and stole my hansom cab. The night you ran off without a word of explanation."

He grimaced. "Yes, that would be the night." He paused, their gazes meeting. "The night I asked you to be my wife, Sophie."

"I would prefer you address me as Mrs. Grant, Your Grace," she snapped.

Anger sparked in his eyes. "And I would prefer to keep to Sophie and James. After all, much has passed between us."

He gave her a knowing look, and all Sophie could see was the two of them together, limbs entwined, James thrusting into her as she mewled her pleasure. She felt her face flame, wishing she could hide under her desk.

Still, she continued to look him in the eye, not wanting to be the coward she had once acted like with this man.

"You thought I was a poor sea captain who wanted to marry you because I would then own Neptune Shipping." James shook his head. "That wasn't it at all, Sophie. I wished to wed you because I cannot live without you."

His voice broke on that last word, and she drew in a quick breath. Her confident demeanor crumbled, and she felt tears spring to her eyes.

James rushed to her, pulling her from her chair, clasping her elbows. They drank in one another, and she longed for his mouth to be on hers.

"I will not kiss you yet," he said, more to himself than her. "I must finish what I came to tell you."

He guided her to the chair he had been sitting in and nudged her into it, taking the seat next to her. His proximity overwhelmed her. His size. His masculine scent. He reached for her hands and held them in hers, even as he now held her gaze.

"Sophie, I was once the Marquess of Alinwood. An undersized boy whose father ignored him and whose mother adored him. Mama died when I was four, and I missed her dreadfully. My father remarried and had twin girls."

She thought of the woman who had been in this office hours earlier, the mother of those girls.

"I cannot recall much of what happened because I was so young when it occurred. I know a man grabbed me near the docks. Beat me when I fought him. Took me to a ship and locked me in its brig. The ship sailed—and I didn't come home to England for a very long time."

Her throat grew thick with tears, seeing the pain in James' eyes.

"Those first few years were a blur. You protest and get beaten. You try to tell someone who you are, and you are beaten again. Finally, I . . . accepted my fate. My memories faded. I was called *Boy* for a good couple of years. I finally earned the right to my name again. All I could remember was I had once been James. I finally took on Jones as a surname after a captain whom I admired."

"You are telling me you were . . . stolen from your family. Kidnapped."

"Aye," he said, nodding. "From what I gather, it was a common enough practice. I started as a cabin boy and worked my way up the ranks until I became a ship's captain. *Vesta's* captain, thanks to you and Mr. Grant."

"In all that time, you never recalled your past?" she asked.

"No. Not really. I would sometimes get flashes of images which made no sense to me. Those ceased after the first few years. Drake was with me back then. He taught me all he knew. We became brothers, if not by blood, then by choice."

James paused, breathing in and out slowly. Sophie didn't rush him, understanding how traumatic it must be to talk about his experiences.

"When I met with you in this very office after returning to London to discuss my future with Neptune Shipping, I did not know I was a marquess. After I left here, though, I did go to the Duke of Seaton's residence. You see, a stranger had come up to me in a pub along the waterfront the night before. He was a drunk, wearing tattered clothes. But he told me that he had once been my tutor. That I had gone missing. That others had looked for me and never found a trace. The family assumed I was dead. This man claimed I came from nobility. I thought his tale outlandish, yet the more I pondered my past, the more images came to me. Ones I couldn't understand because I had no context.

"So, I went to this duke's house, which Timmons, the man who approached me, told me about. And yes, I discovered I was the missing heir apparent. Some of the past has come back to me. Some, I suppose, never will. But I have accepted my new role. My father recently passed, and I inherited his title."

Sophie thought back to when she was a young child. Nothing traumatic had happened to her in those early years, and yet she had very few memories of them, only fleeting impressions. She could understand how James, being forcibly kidnapped and beaten, would have lost sight of who he was.

"You grew up at sea," she said quietly. "You went from cabin boy to captain, which is no small feat, James."

"All I knew was my life as a sailor. Obviously, now, those seafaring days are over. I'm officially a landlubber." He paused. "Which leads to you and me."

She tried to pull her hands from his, but he held tighter to them.

"Sophie, I fell in love with you. James, the captain. Not James, a future duke. I thought if you agreed to marry me, it would be because you loved me, not a title. That is why I kept it from you. And then you told me how incredibly unfair British law is to women who wed."

His hold tightened on her fingers. "I would never want to take Neptune Shipping from you. I am already wealthy beyond my wildest dreams. I own estates left and right, as well as Strong Shipping Lines. I neither want nor need Neptune." He paused, his gaze growing tender. "All I truly want is you. As my wife. Mother to my children. My duchess."

She shook her head. "I do love you, James. I will readily admit it to you. But it doesn't change the law. What is mine will be yours if we wed. I cannot do that to Josiah. Yes, I know he is gone, but Neptune shipping lives on through him. Why, he would roll in his grave—come back to haunt me—if I married his chief rival and gave control of his company to you."

"You don't have to," James insisted. "I have a very clever solicitor, Sophie. A Mr. Peabody. He has already taught me so much. I'm sure he can find a way to help us manage this situation."

"Wait a minute," she told him, an idea coming to her. "I am just thinking aloud here, James. I do not know if this would be possible."

"Tell me," he urged.

"When a couple becomes betrothed, marriage contracts are drawn up. Certain things are settled upon. Arrangements made. These marriage settlements establish the amount of dowries for daughters in the marriage. Sometimes, it settles an unentailed property upon a widow if she outlives her husband."

"Yes, I know of this. Dinah—my father's second wife—received an estate in his will. She has not moved to it since she is still raising my sisters and nieces, but it definitely belongs to her. Do you think our marriage settlements might designate that you maintain control of Neptune Shipping?" he asked excitedly. "You know I do not want or need it. The company is yours."

"I am not certain, but it is most definitely something to look into with your solicitor."

"Sophie," James said earnestly, pinning her gaze. "If that is the case—if we can write up some kind of contract which would allow you to maintain control of Neptune Shipping—even give shares of it to our children—would you consider marrying me?"

She could barely see him because of the tears blinding her. Nodding, Sophie said, "Yes. Yes, James. I would wed you if that were the case."

He leaped to his feet, bringing her with him. His mouth came down on hers, and passion burst from both of them. The kisses she had longed for were no longer an unattainable dream. They were happening here. Now. Sophie returned his kisses with abandon.

Breaking the kiss, James smiled tenderly at her. "Shall we go see Mr. Peabody now?"

"Yes!" she exclaimed, joy spilling from her. "Yes!"

He kissed her again soundly and then beamed at her. "My carriage is waiting downstairs."

She moved away from him, opening a drawer and removing her reticule. Placing it over her arm, she said, "I am ready."

He slipped her hand through the crook of his arm and led her from the office. Mr. Barnes hovered outside the door.

"I am leaving for the day, Mr. Barnes," Sophie said. "I will see you tomorrow morning."

"Yes, Mrs. Grant," the secretary said, peering at her with interest.

James escorted her to his carriage, the most magnificent one she had ever seen, his ducal crest prominent on the door, the vehicle drawn by the finest of horses.

Once inside, he told her, "I would have come to you sooner, but I had to meet with Mr. Swan, an insurance adjustor."

"Did he learn who—or what—caused the fire?"

"It is a who. And I believe I know who is behind the who."

Sophie listened as James told her of how his uncle and cousin had taken over after the duke's apoplexy attack, keeping his daughters away from Seaton, while banning the family from returning to the country.

"Uncle Adolphus even banished my aunt Matty to the country because she stood up to him. He stole from Strong Shipping and possibly my other estates. Not from Shadowcrest, my ducal seat, which is in Kent. Even though Adolphus installed his other son as Shadowcrest's steward, Caleb is too moral to have taken funds from the estate."

James explained how he'd told Adolphus and Theo to leave London upon claiming his title.

"I think they had the warehouse set afire as a means of revenge. Adolphus most likely had no idea that the warehouse and its merchandise were insured. I had never heard of such a thing. Then again, I have never owned anything beyond the clothes on my back."

She ran a fingertip along the sleeve of his superfine coat. "They are very fine clothes, Your Grace."

He shrugged. "They are from my new tailor. Dinah says I must dress the part of a duke and act like one if I am to be one."

"Dinah?"

"My stepmother," James said, chuckling. "In truth, she is only a decade my senior. She tried her best to love a little boy long ago. What she has done is befriend the man I have become. Dinah is a good advisor to me. I trust her implicitly."

Sophie decided to keep quiet about the visit she had received from Dinah Strong this morning. Without her intervention, Sophie doubted she would have even seen James.

They arrived at Mr. Peabody's, and James explained how he wished to wed Sophie, all the while leaving Neptune Shipping in her hands and allowing it to be passed down to their children.

"It is a delicate matter, Your Grace," the solicitor said. "It must be worded just right, but I can make this happen for you and Mrs. Grant."

"Excellent!" James proclaimed. "Who is your solicitor, Mrs. Grant? We must put him in touch with Mr. Peabody so these marriage contracts might be drawn up quickly."

"Are you marrying by special license, Your Grace?" the solicitor asked.

Frowning, James asked, "What is that?"

"I will tell him the ins and outs, Mr. Peabody," Sophie said, smiling.

"Then I will contact your solicitor and began our part of the process," Peabody said.

They left the solicitor's offices, and James said, "Would you do me the honor of coming to meet Dinah now? My sisters and nieces are all in the country. Dinah is leaving tomorrow to be with them, since my health is much improved."

"Yes, I would be happy to meet Her Grace."

He ordered his driver to return home. When they reached the large, elegant townhouse, Sophie had to pause a moment, thinking she would soon live in its grandeur.

"A little overwhelming?" James asked as he handed her down.

"Very," she admitted.

"I can't begin to tell you what was running through my mind when I first saw it."

They entered the townhouse, and the butler told them the duchess was in the drawing room.

When they arrived, James said, "I have someone very special for you to meet, Dinah." He beamed at Sophie. "Your Grace, I would like you to meet Mrs. Grant. My Sophie. This is Her Grace, the Duchess of Seaton."

The duchess' eyes twinkled. "I have a feeling I will soon be the Dowager Duchess of Seaton. How do you do, Mrs. Grant?"

Sophie curtseyed and then took the duchess' hand. "It is an honor to meet you, Your Grace."

Their gazes met—and the two women mutually agreed without words not to mention their previous meeting.

"Sophie has agreed to marry me, Dinah," James said happily.

"Then you must call me Dinah," the duchess said. "And I will call you Sophie. It is almost time for dinner. Let us go in and get to know one another better."

He offered his arms, and Sophie and Dinah each took one, allowing the duke to escort them to the dining room.

The meal was heavenly, much better than anything her borrowed cook had ever prepared. After hearing the benefits of acquiring a special license and where to purchase one, James agreed it was what he wanted, asking Sophie if she thought the same.

"Yes, the sooner we wed, the better," she told him, thinking how glad she would be to be back in his bed.

"Would you rather wed in town or at Shadowcrest?" Dinah asked. "You know all the girls and Caleb will want to be present for the ceremony and wedding breakfast."

James raked his fingers through his hair. "As much trouble as it was to move them all to Shadowcrest, I think it would be easier if we went to them. Sophie?"

"I rather like the idea of a country wedding," she told the pair.

"Then I will purchase this special license tomorrow morning," James promised.

"I will leave tomorrow and make certain everything is ready at Shadowcrest," Dinah said. "Simply send word when you'd like the ceremony to be held. I will have the vicar waiting and ready."

James took Sophie back home after dinner. They adjourned to her parlor and spent a good hour kissing. When she asked him to her bed, he refused.

"The next time I make love to you, it will be to my wife, the Duchess of Seaton." Grinning, he added, "All the more reason to get this special license and make our marriage a reality. Are you sure you can take some time away from Neptune Shipping? We'll probably need to stay in the country for several days. The girls will want to get to know you."

"I have a few things to clear up, but I will be free to travel and stay a while," Sophie assured him. "Between Mr. Barnes and myself, Neptune runs like clockwork. I can afford to be gone a bit."

She thought a moment. "I do want to continue running the business, James. You are allowing me to retain control of it. I don't plan to walk away." She hesitated. "The *ton* will most likely crucify you—and me—once they hear of our arrangement and see that I still am running a shipping line."

James kissed her firmly. "I don't give a damn what they think. We will have each other. That is all that matters to me."

Sophie saw him to the door, with one last, sweet kiss goodnight. She watched him enter his coach and give a wave before the driver took off.

Closing the door, she wondered if this had all been a dream and that she would awake and find that none of it had taken place.

She was set to wed the Duke of Seaton and become his duchess. She would bear his children and still run her shipping company.

Picking up her violin, which had always been a source of comfort to her, Sophie played a piece by Haydn, one which always brought her comfort.

Life was absolutely perfect.

CHAPTER TWENTY-THREE

SOPHIE ENTERED THE offices of Neptune Shipping, greeting everyone, her mood sunny. She asked Mr. Barnes to come into her office and closed the door after he stepped inside.

"Have a seat," she told her secretary. "I have much to share with you."

He looked at her with trepidation, and Sophie said, "It is all good news, Mr. Barnes. I am going to wed His Grace, the Duke of Seaton."

Confusion filled his face. "But . . . I thought Her Grace was the duchess. The lady who visited here yesterday."

Sophie chuckled. "My visitor yesterday was indeed the Duchess of Seaton, but she was wed to the previous duke, who is now deceased. I am betrothed to the new and current Duke of Seaton, which will make our guest yesterday the dowager duchess once I have spoken my vows."

"These relationships in the *ton* are complicated," he said, looking at her earnestly. "I do offer you my heartiest congratulations, Mrs. Grant, but . . . what will this mean for Neptune Shipping? With your marriage, His Grace will own this shipping line and his own. I suppose he will have them merge."

She saw how downcast Mr. Barnes was, and she said, "Have no fears. I am marrying a most unusual man. He is seeing the marriage settlements drawn up, and they will reflect that I will retain sole ownership of Neptune Shipping Lines."

The secretary's jaw dropped. "Are you certain, Mrs. Grant? Why, that is unheard of."

"I would not wed His Grace otherwise. I want Mr. Grant's legacy to shine on for decades to come. I will retain complete and sole ownership of the company, and the marriage contracts will be written to reflect that our children will follow in my footsteps. Upon my death, they will own Neptune Shipping. I hope to teach them everything about the business they will one day run.

"However," she continued, "I will have new responsibilities when I become the Duchess of Seaton. While I want to keep my hand in Neptune Shipping and make the important decisions, I plan to depend upon you even more than I do now, Mr. Barnes, to help run this company on a daily basis. Because of that, I wish for you to hire someone new to act as *our* secretary. I want you to occupy this office. It is the larger of the two, and I will relocate to the one Mr. Grant used during our marriage. When I am in town, I plan to come to the offices as often as possible, but I will also be spending time in the country at our Kent estate. I want you to keep me informed with regular reports, though. My solicitor will draw up a contract, and you will see a substantial boost in your income. Are you agreeable to this, Mr. Barnes?"

Happiness filled his face. "I am delighted to stay on in this capacity, Mrs. Grant, but I would prefer the smaller of the two offices."

"You might think so, but you will be dealing with clients more than I will. This office is far grander, and we have conducted much of our business within it. I insist that it become yours. For now, we need to see about hiring a secretary that we both might share. Do you have any idea whom you might wish to select for the position. Perhaps someone from our group of clerks? Or would you prefer to go outside the business?"

For several minutes, they discussed likely candidates, and they both settled upon Mr. Samuel. The clerk had been with them close to five years, and Mr. Barnes relied heavily upon Mr. Samuel on a daily basis.

"Call him in so that we might offer the position to him," Sophie said. "Things are moving rapidly, and I wish to have everything in place. His Grace is purchasing a special license this morning, and I assume we will wed within the week. We will travel to Kent so I might meet his extended family, and the ceremony will take place there. You and Mr. Samuel will be in charge of the offices while I am gone."

They called in the clerk and offered him the new position. Sophie had always liked Mr. Samuel and thought him most capable. She decided he would be a good choice to step in for Mr. Barnes.

After the two men left, she settled in at her desk, addressing the business of the day. She had only been working for half an hour when Mr. Barnes knocked and entered again.

"You have a visitor, Mrs. Grant," the secretary told her, smiling broadly. "It is Her Grace, the Duchess of Seaton."

Dinah swept into the office, smiling at the secretary. "I am happy to know that you are taking my visit better today, Mr. Barnes. No tea is necessary since I am on my way out of town. I only needed to stop and visit with Mrs. Grant for a few minutes."

"Of course, Your Grace," the secretary said, leaving them.

"What brings you here, Dinah?" Sophie asked.

"I wanted to let you know that I have submitted the betrothal notice to the newspapers this morning. Since most of the *ton* left town once the Season ended, your engagement will not cause quite the stir it normally would have, but I wanted to do everything properly to get your marriage off on the right foot in the eyes of Polite Society. I know you and James will never grovel to them, but there is no reason to deliberately alienate them, especially with so many come-outs occurring in the family in the near future. This way, the newspapers will be delivered to the country, and by the time next Season begins, all in town will know of your marriage to Seaton."

"I don't mind at all," she said, thinking she wanted to shout the news from the rooftops.

"I would be remiss if I did not see you properly attired for your wedding, Sophie," Dinah continued. "Knowing how busy you are, I wasn't sure if you could break away from your business matters, so I brought my modiste and her assistant to you."

The duchess stepped to the door and motioned. Two women appeared, one tall and elegant, the other petite and appearing eager to please.

"Mrs. Grant, this is Madame Dumas," Dinah said, indicating the taller woman. "She is my modiste and will also prepare wardrobes for the girls' come-outs the next few springs. She is here to fit you for your wedding gown and possibly a few other ensembles and wardrobe items."

"It is very nice to meet you, Madame Dumas," Sophie said, having heard the name and knowing the modiste worked with the most elite of clients within Polite Society.

"Her Grace has given me ideas as to what type of gown you might wish for your wedding." The modiste looked her up and down. "I quite agree."

"I know you will also want to express your opinion, Mrs. Grant," Dinah said.

"Not really," Sophie said, laughing. "I have never been one for fashion. I will put myself into Madame Dumas' hands."

"She will make up a few gowns for you now beyond what you will wear on your wedding day," Dinah said. "When the next Season comes, she has also agreed to provide your entire wardrobe for it."

"Then you will be quite busy with the Strong family, Madame," she said.

"I only work with the best of Polite Society, Mrs. Grant," the modiste said haughtily.

Dinah chuckled. "I am leaving you in Madame's capable hands and will head for Shadowcrest now. Remember to send word when you and Seaton are coming. I will see you soon."

Dinah embraced Sophie, kissing her cheek. As an only child, she had always wanted a sister, and she believed she had found one in Dinah Strong.

After the duchess left, Sophie was measured by the assistant from head to toe. A trunk was brought in, and various cloth samples were pulled from it. Madame Dumas also removed a sketchbook, turning through different pages and showing Sophie various styles.

They settled upon one design for her wedding gown, and Madame promised work would commence upon it immediately.

"Her Grace said time is of the essence because of the special license, so I know we must complete the gown quickly. Be glad this is not a busy time for me since most of the *ton* has retreated to the country," Madame said. "We will work on the gown today and tomorrow, and I would like you to have a fitting the day after tomorrow. Would that be possible, Mrs. Grant?"

"Yes, Madame Dumas. I will put it in my diary. Shall we say ten o'clock? And I am happy to come to your shop instead of having you come to me. Please leave the address with my secretary."

Sophie sat at her desk again once the modiste and assistant left. She had never been excited about clothing, but this wedding gown was an exception. She had not had anything special made up for her marriage to Josiah Strong. Her father was already in too much debt by that point, and Sophie had merely worn the best gown she possessed at the time to the ceremony.

This gown would be different—as would this marriage.

THE NEXT AFTERNOON, Sophie met James at Mr. Peabody's office. The solicitor and Mr. Martin, her own solicitor, had written up the marriage settlements. She did not know how long the process usually took, but was pleased that it had already been done. She would now go over the contracts and see if any adjustments needed to be made.

A clerk greeted her. "Ah, Mrs. Grant. It is good to see you. His Grace is already here, as is Mr. Martin. May I take you to the conference room so that you might join them?"

"Of course," she said, following the clerk down a corridor.

Once in the room, James greeted Sophie with a kiss on her cheek, sending tingles through her. The marriage couldn't happen soon enough for her because she was ready to christen it in their bed.

James introduced her to Peabody, and he asked that they all be seated.

Mr. Martin said, "I must tell you, Mrs. Grant, that this has been the easiest negotiation I have ever been a part of. I have hammered out my fair share of marriage contracts the last two decades, and nothing compares to this experience. Of course, I wish for you to read over the documents now, but I will tell you that His Grace has been most generous in every aspect."

She smiled at her betrothed. "I would expect nothing less from His Grace. He is kind to a fault."

Sophie spent the next half-hour reading the documents. As Mr. Martin had told her, they were quite straightforward. She was given complete ownership and control of everything she possessed coming into the marriage, including every facet of Neptune Shipping Lines. She also retained ownership of the house she currently resided in, as well as all funds in her various bank accounts.

Dowries were to be provided for any daughters that resulted from their union, and financial provisions were also made for any sons beyond the heir apparent. The contracts specified that Sophie would always be head of Neptune Shipping and that the company would be passed down to their children, giving her the freedom to decide what role each future child would play and the percentage they would own. It thrilled her to know her children would be a vital part of Neptune and keep it thriving.

"I am ready to sign," she told the two solicitors. "No changes need to be made. I assume I may do so legally because I am of age."

"That is correct," Mr. Peabody said, calling in two clerks to act as witnesses to the procedure.

Peabody showed Sophie where her signatures were required. He did the same for James and within minutes, all copies had been signed. Both she and James received copies of their own, with Peabody and Martin retaining copies, as well.

Business being done, James asked if he could see Sophie home. She readily agreed. Once in his carriage, he asked if she might wish to stop at an inn for dinner, knowing she had already ended her arrangements with the cook next door as far as her evening meals were concerned. She had already told her maids that she would be selling the house she now lived in, and that she would recommend the new tenant retain them. If not, she had promised she would find them a place in one of her future husband's households.

They stopped at one she was familiar with and were taken to a private supper room upstairs, where they enjoyed roasted pork, peas, and carrots, along with a crusty bread.

James escorted her home and asked if he might come in.

"Dare I ask if you have changed your mind about bedding me since our marriage is imminent?"

He laughed. "No, love. I thought you might play your violin for me. You have mentioned doing so, and I would enjoy hearing you play."

"I would be happy to play for you, James."

He took a seat while she retrieved the violin from the shelf it sat upon. She moved her bow across the strings a few times, tuning the instrument slightly, and then played several selections for him, ending with Haydn, her favorite composer.

Placing the violin and bow on a chair, she went to James, and he enveloped her in his arms, kissing her hungrily for several minutes. Finally, he broke the kiss.

"Ah, my sweet Sophie. You continually surprise me. I think I'm going to need you to play for me every day."

"I will play for you anytime you ask, James. Shall I bring my violin with me when we go to Shadowcrest?"

"Aye, love," he said, his gaze warm. "When will your gown be ready? It is the only thing keeping us in London—and me from your bed."

She blushed. "I have a fitting for it tomorrow morning at ten o'clock at Madame Dumas' dress shop. If no adjustments are necessary, we could leave for the country shortly afterward."

"Then I'll plan on that to be the case. I'll send word tomorrow morning of our arrival later in the day. I know the girls will be thrilled to meet you. Caleb, too."

He frowned.

"What's wrong?" she asked.

"I have talked about my family, but we've not mentioned yours. I know you have no siblings, but should we ask your father to the ceremony?"

"He is gone. He died a year after my marriage to Josiah," she revealed. "He thought selling me off would give him the money he needed to live on, but he dropped dead of a heart attack—and had spent every farthing by his death. I have no one on my side, James. Your family will become mine."

He kissed her again. "Then let's hope Madame Dumas has done her job properly and everything fits perfectly tomorrow. I will send my carriage to Neptune Shipping, and you may take it from there to your dressmaker's appointment. Bring your trunk to your office tomorrow morning and then the dressmakers, so we can depart as soon as possible."

"Then I had best pack tonight."

"I will leave you to that. I'll see you tomorrow, Sophie, my darling."

She walked James to his carriage. He gave her a lingering kiss before boarding it.

Sophie returned inside, locking the door behind her. She entered the parlor and retrieved her violin and bow, thinking to take them upstairs and place them in her trunk as she packed.

As she turned, she froze.

Two men stood in the doorway.

One aimed a pistol at her.

CHAPTER TWENTY-FOUR

Sophie was unlike most women of the *ton*. She used her mind every single day, solving difficult, complex problems. She worked with numbers and weather patterns. Figured cargo loads and trade routes. Her work had her deal with everyone from civil, mannered clients to rough and tumble sailors and dock workers.

So, while these men posed a threat, she was already thinking through ways to escape. She knew if they bound her wrists and ankles with the ropes the older man held in his hands, it would be incredibly difficult to get away. That meant she had to keep them from restraining her. She would do her best to talk sense into them. Tell them what they wanted to hear. Promise them things to placate them. And if that didn't work?

She would scream like a banshee and run like hell.

Her grip tightened on her violin and bow. Those could be used as weapons if and when the time came that she needed to go on the attack.

"I am not quite sure why you believe you could simply enter my home," she began.

The younger man snickered. The older one merely narrowed his eyes. She could see they were the same color as James' eyes, an unusual cornflower blue.

Instantly, she surmised the pair to be his treacherous uncle and cousin and knew they were here to do her harm.

"If you hurt me, Seaton will destroy you," she said boldly. "And if you kill me, you will wish you were dead yourselves," she threatened. "He has no love for either of you."

"You know who we are?" the younger man said.

"Of course," she said haughtily. "His uncle and cousin. The ones who stole from the Strong family."

"Watch your mouth," Adolphus Strong warned. "Be a good girl so Theodore doesn't have to shoot you."

But Sophie knew she would be no good to them dead. Most likely, they had seen in the newspapers of her betrothal to James and thought to use her to get money from him since their source of income had dried up.

"You wouldn't do that," she challenged. "A kidnapper needs a live person in order to gain what he wants. I suppose you are after money. Gold, most likely."

Adolphus' gaze bore into her, chilling her. In it, she sensed evil in the man.

"We could also throw your dead body in the Thames and tell Seaton we have you," he mused. "Get what we want from him." After a long pause, he added, "And then kill him."

Her courage waned a bit, and Sophie told herself she must live. She had everything to live for. A man who loved her. The family she would be welcomed into. The babes she would hold in her arms who would grow up and see that Neptune Shipping thrived.

"He would never pay without seeing me. *Alive*," she emphasized.

"He'll get you back," Theodore Strong said. "Even if you may not be quite the same as you were before." He paused. "You have a smart mouth on you, Mrs. Grant. I will be happy to take you down a notch. Why, you and I are going to have a fine time together. I hope Seaton takes his time gathering the ransom. It will mean I can use you up completely."

Nausea filled Sophie at the thought of this man touching her intimately. She knew she must act quickly, while they least expected it. While she wanted to charge Theodore, he held the gun shakily, and she feared he might fire without meaning to.

Instead, she pretended to turn meek at his threat.

"Oh, please. Don't harm me," she pleaded, moving slowly toward the pair. "I will go quietly with you. I promise I won't cause you any problems."

She saw both men relax, dropping their guard as she approached slowly, trying to look at non-threatening as she could.

Adolphus dropped one of the coils of rope to the ground, pulling the remaining one taut between his hands. "Come here, Mrs. Grant. I will bind your wrists together. It is for your own good."

She thought Adolphus old and slow. Theodore would be the greater threat, especially since he possessed the gun. She continued walking slowly toward Adolphus, keeping Theodore in her peripheral vision.

Just as she reached the pair, Sophie whirled, slamming her violin into the side of Theodore's head. It splintered as he yelped, falling to his knees. The pistol fell to the ground and discharged, the noise frighteningly loud. With what was left of the violin, she struck Theodore again in the back of the head, knocking him to the ground.

Releasing the little that remained of the violin, Sophie turned and jammed the bow at Adolphus' face. It plunged into his eye and stuck there. His screams pierced the air.

Suddenly, Sophie heard banging on the front door and ran toward it. Throwing the lock, she opened it, finding James on the other side. She flung herself at him, his large, solid frame bringing her comfort.

"They're here. Parlor," she managed to get out.

James released her and dashed past her, as did another man whom she recognized to be his coachman. Sophie's teeth began chattering as she leaned against the wall, sliding down it, coming to a stop when she touched the ground.

Loud cursing sounded, along with the sound of heavy blows. She knew James might very well kill his relatives. She forced herself to come to her feet and hurried into the parlor.

"Stop!" she cried. "Don't kill them."

James held his uncle by the collar. The violin bow still protruded from Adolphus Strong's eye. The driver was lifting Theodore, placing him over his shoulder.

She moved to James, placing her hand on his forearm. Calmly, she said, "I do not know if a duke would hang if he killed a man, but I would prefer not taking that chance. We have a lifetime to fill, James. Babes to raise. Please, do not throw it all away over these worthless scoundrels. Punish them—but do not kill them."

He nodded slowly. His free hand cradled her cheek, and she leaned into his palm, drawing strength from the warmth.

"It will be as you ask," he promised.

Sophie picked up the separate coils of rope. "You could bind them with these," she suggested.

James nodded. She handed one to the coachman, who dropped an unconscious Theodore to the ground, lashing his wrists behind his back. Giving the other rope to her betrothed, she watched him spin Adolphus Strong and bind him in a similar fashion.

To the coachman, James said, "Fetch Dr. Nickels and bring him here."

"Yes, Your Grace."

James led his uncle to a chair and pushed him into it, Adolphus whimpering. "Stay there," he commanded. "Don't speak."

Slipping an arm about Sophie, he led her into the foyer and then into the kitchen. He smoothed her hair, kissing her tenderly.

"Are you all right? I should have asked you that," he said, giving her a rueful smile.

"I am fine. My violin?" She shrugged. "I believe it will have to be replaced."

He laughed. "I will buy you a thousand violins to replace the one you lost."

"James, why are you even here?"

"When I left, it was the hardest thing I had ever done," he admitted. "All I wanted to do was make love to you, married or not. I had the coachman head back this way so I could stay the night with you."

"Thank goodness for that," she said.

He framed her face with his hands. "If I had lost you, I could not have gone on," he told her, his voice breaking.

"They weren't going to hurt me," she lied. "They merely wanted to hold me ransom. They had seen our engagement announcement in the newspapers and thought to use me to get money from you."

He kissed her brow reverently. "They will never touch you again. You will never see them for as long as you live."

"What will you do to them?"

"Once the doctor has removed the bow and sewn up Adolphus' eye—and put any stitches needed into Theo's scalp—my coachman and I will take them to the harbor. I have a ship departing on the early tide tomorrow, bound for the Cook Islands and other parts. I'll have them locked in the brig until the ship arrives. Then sailors will take them ashore before they sail—and leave them there. They will have the clothes on their backs and nothing else. Whatever happens to them will happen. I do know they will never make their way back to England ever again."

She threw her arms about his neck. "Thank you."

Sophie kissed him, hoping she conveyed all the love she felt for this remarkable man. A man who had undergone terrible trials from an early age, and yet he had made something of himself.

"You are going to be a wonderful duke," she told him.

James smiled down at her. "And you, love, will be an exceptional duchess."

Sophie stood still, so many women fussing over her, it was hard to keep them all straight.

It was her wedding day, the day she would pledge herself to James Strong, the Duke of Seaton. They would be leaving soon for the small chapel that stood on Shadowcrest lands. Dinah had told Sophie that it was only used for family baptisms, weddings, and funerals. The rest of the time, the family drove into Crestview, the nearest village. Dinah's estate, Crestridge, which she had received in her husband's will, was a few miles the other side of Crestview.

"Girls!" Aunt Matty shouted. "Please calm down. You are overwhelming Sophie."

She smiled gratefully at the older woman, James' aunt who already mothered Sophie. She glanced around at his sisters and nieces, all of whom she already loved. The girls were so affectionate and open, each of them quite different from one another. She couldn't wait to get to know them even better, thrilled she was now part of such a large, close family.

A knock sounded on the door, and Pippa answered it. Caleb Strong stepped into the room.

"Your coach is waiting, Sophie," he said. Glancing about the room, he added, "All you girls can walk down to the chapel now. Give poor Sophie a few minutes to herself."

"We will see you there," Mirella said, giving Sophie a hug.

She had to also receive embraces from the others, and then they filed out, laughing and chattering like magpies.

"Thank you, Caleb," she said, feeling a bit relieved at the silence.

He winked at her. "I'll see they're on their way. Take your time, Sophie. After all, there can be no wedding without the bride."

"But not too long," Dinah said. "Else James will come tearing up the drive looking for you."

Dinah slipped an additional pin into Sophie's hair, taming a stray curl which had come loose. Aunt Matty gave her the bouquet of flowers which Lyric had picked and arranged from the blooms in the greenhouse.

"You look lovely, my dear," Aunt Matty said. "And you are simply perfect for James."

"We are perfect for one another," she said. "I cannot imagine loving any man the way I do James." Turning to Caleb, she added, "Shall we?"

The four of them went to the waiting carriage, and Caleb handed up the three women, joining them.

"The chapel looks lovely," he told her. "Allegra and Georgina supervised the decorating, with flowers Lyric brought from the hothouse. Pippa and Effie placed bows at the end of each pew. Mirella is going to play the pianoforte for the ceremony. They are all so happy to make you a part of the Strong family, Sophie."

"I have never had a family like this, Caleb," she said, tears shimmering in her eyes. "No brothers or sisters. Or cousins. I only wish Mama were here to see how happy I am." She clasped Dinah's and Aunt Matty's hands. "But I know she is watching over me and shares in my joy."

The short ride to the chapel ended, and as the carriage rolled to a halt, she saw the girls entering the chapel. Caleb disembarked and handed down each of them. Aunt Matty and Dinah went inside the chapel. Caleb remained with her and would escort her to the altar.

"You and James have a bright future ahead," he said. "I am glad you will now be a part of the Strongs of Shadowcrest, Sophie." He grinned. "The next time I address you, it will be as Your Grace."

"Oh, I hope you will always call me Sophie, Caleb. Frankly, I am not certain I will ever see myself as a duchess."

"Then you will be the best kind," he told her. "Not a woman to use her title and look down upon others. You will be a duchess who leads by example." He offered his arm. "Shall we? Your groom is waiting, most likely champing at the bit."

Sophie giggled. "I'll daresay he is."

She slipped her hand through Caleb's arm, and as they entered the chapel, Mirella began to play.

As they began down the aisle, her eyes went straight to James, and in his Strong eyes, she saw so much love.

They spoke their vows, and James slipped a gold band on her finger. She was glad it wasn't fussy or ostentatious. It suited her.

He suited her.

The vicar pronounced them joined together, bound forever as husband and wife. James kissed her, and joy filled Sophie.

Breaking the kiss, he said, "I love you, Sophie Strong."

"And I love you even more, James Strong."

He kissed her again, to the cheers of his family—now their family—sounding in her ears.

Epilogue

London—May 1811—Twenty-two months later

JAMES STOOD BESIDE Sophie as they bent over their sleeping son. George was almost nine months and crawling, into everything, and delighting them each day.

"He is perfect," his wife said. "In every way."

"He is," James agreed. "Just as you are."

He brushed his lips against her temple, wanting her again as he always did. They had too much to do, however, for him to whisk her away and make sweet love to her.

Today, *Sophie* would be christened.

The ship had taken almost a full two years to build, but what a sight it was. He had switched shipyards and now had Strong vessels being built at Mr. Purdy's shipyard, with designs being provided by Mr. Fex. The two men were coming up from Greenwich today in order to see *Sophie* christened.

Besides George, other Strongs would be present. Cupid's arrow had struck several Strongs in the last two years, and James was pleased at the new additions to the family. Only love matches had been made, which he knew from experience were the best kind for a solid marriage.

The only sister missing today was Pippa, who would be returning from her honeymoon in about two months' time. He couldn't wait to hear about her travels around the world. His cousins Lyric and Allegra were both increasing and had remained in the country, where they would each give birth come July.

"I hate to wake him," Sophie fretted.

"George sleeps like the dead," James told his wife, scooping up the babe. Once upon a time, he would never have dreamed he would have a wife and child, much less be so comfortable carting about a babe. Sophie had changed everything, though. Her love and belief in him made James a better man each day.

"Our carriage is waiting," he said. "Come along, love."

George's nanny followed them from the nursery and would take the babe if he fussed during the ceremony.

James had learned all about when a ship could be christened. Even though he was a sailor, he had never been present at the inauguration of a ship. Sophie had taught him about the conventions regarding the christening of new ships, and how the ancient Greeks, Romans, and Egyptians all held ceremonies to ask their gods to protect the sailors sailing on a new vessel.

Nowadays, a christening fluid was poured against the bow of a ship, and today they would be using champagne. Sophie herself would splash the ship to christen her namesake. Maritime superstition insisted ships never be christened on a Friday, because that was the day Christ had been crucified. Even the British navy refused to launch a ship on a Friday. Shipping lines also rejected Thursdays, the day being named after Thor, god of storms. Many sailors believed a ship christened on a Thursday would invite storms and thunder, so it, too, was ruled out.

Today was a Tuesday, and they were favored with sunshine, not a cloud in the sky as they climbed into his ducal carriage. George slept in his arms the entire way to Neptune Shipping. Sophie had conceived their firstborn at Christmas, about six weeks after they wed. George had been born near the end of September last year. James was eager to give the lad a brother or sister soon, wanting to fill the nursery with their children.

They went inside the Neptune Shipping offices. James wandered about, showing off George, while Sophie handled some business with Drake. When the time came close, he collected his wife, and they walked the short distance to the docks.

At the waterfront, they saw *Sophie* in all her glory, ready for her christening. Family and friends had gathered for the ceremony, as well as employees from both Neptune and Strong Shipping.

Drake, who had accompanied them from the shipping offices, touched his sleeve and then bent to brush his lips upon George's head, asking, "How is my godson doing?"

"Crawling like mad," Sophie responded. "He will be a terror when he learns to walk." She smiled knowingly. "You'll know all about that soon yourself."

Drake beamed. "We're looking forward to the babe's birth," he agreed.

George awoke and began being fussed over by all his aunts, who passed him around, kissing his cheeks. Mr. Purdy and Mr. Fex came by to greet them, and Sophie told them how she couldn't wait to board the ship. While she had already named a captain for it, James was going to take the helm after the ceremony and sail her along the Thames a bit, the entire family joining them for a few hours of sailing.

"I suppose it is time," his wife said. "Nanny, will you claim George again?"

"Yes, Your Grace," the nurserymaid said, retrieving the little Marquess of Alinwood and standing to the side in case she needed to step away if the babe began to fuss.

Caleb handed James the opened bottle of champagne which would be used, and he and Sophie went to stand on the docks at mid-ship. A large crowd had been attracted. Besides all the Strongs present, many sailors and others who worked the docks and local businesses had turned out for the christening.

Together, James and Sophie waved to the crowd, which hushed.

James said, "Today, we come to name this ship, *Sophie*, after my wonderful wife."

The gathered crowd chuckled.

"She is to be the premier ship in the Neptune Shipping Line, and we send her to sea, asking God and the sailors of old to accept *Sophie* and watch over her. Help guide her throughout each voyage she takes and each passage she navigates—and always allow her to return to England with her crew safely aboard."

He passed the bottle of champagne to Sophie, who splashed its contents onto the ship's side, gleefully crying, "I name thee *Sophie!*"

The crowd cheered loudly, and James gathered Sophie in his arms, kissing her sweetly.

"This day was a long time in coming, but it was worth the wait," he told her.

"We have another wait to endure. This one will be a shorter time," she said mysteriously, her eyes shining at him with love.

Instantly, he knew what she meant. "Another babe? When?"

Sophie smiled. "By my calculations, he—or she—should arrive in mid-December, so that will be my Christmas gift to you, Captain."

She always called him Captain instead of Your Grace in moments of extreme tenderness. Her fingers stroked his cheek as she asked, "Are you pleased?"

"Always, love. Because I am with you."

James kissed Sophie, celebrating the new ship—and the new life which grew within her.

About the Author

Award-winning and internationally bestselling author Alexa Aston's historical romances use history as a backdrop to place her characters in extraordinary circumstances, where their intense desire for one another grows into the treasured gift of love.

She is the author of Regency and Medieval romance, including: Dukes of Distinction; Soldiers & Soulmates; The St. Clairs; The King's Cousins; and The Knights of Honor.

A native Texan, Alexa lives with her husband in a Dallas suburb, where she eats her fair share of dark chocolate and plots out stories while she walks every morning. She enjoys a good Netflix binge; travel; seafood; and can't get enough of *Survivor* or *The Crown*.